Lilly and the Stabber

Lilly and the Stabber

by

Naomi Feigelson Chase

Hamilton Stone Editions
Maplewood, New Jersey

Library of Congress Cataloging-in-Publication Data

Names: Chase, Naomi Feigelson, author.
Title: Lilly and the Stabber / by Naomi Feigelson Chase.
Description: Maaplewood, NJ : Hamilton Stone Editions, [2020]
Identifiers: LCCN 2019040549 (print) | LCCN 2019040550 (ebook)
| ISBN 9780990376767 (trade paperback) | ISBN 9780990376767
(ebook)
Classification: LCC PS3553.H3349 L55 2020   (print) | LCC
PS3553.H3349 (ebook) | DDC 813/.54--dc23
LC record available at https://lccn.loc.gov/2019040549
LC ebook record available at https://lccn.loc.gov/2019040550

Hamilton Stone Editions
P.O. Box 43
Maplewood, New Jersey 07040

Acknowledgements

First and foremost, I am grateful to Elizabeth Feigelson for her many patient readings and invaluable advice, to Rita Satz for her criticism, to Meredith Sue Willis for her unstinting work, and to Shirley Joel, Carole Rosenthal, Suzanne McConnell, NancyKay Shapiro, Joan Liebovitz, Daniel Feigelson, and especially Maury Feinsilber and Alec Neidenthal for their attention and feedback.

Table of Contents

Books by Naomi Feigelson Chase

Non-fiction

The Underground Revolution: Hippies, Yippies, and Others
A Child is Being Beaten: Child Abuse in America

Poetry

Listening for Water
Waiting for the Messiah in Somerville, Mass.
The Judge's Daughter
Stacked, Illustrated by Jon Agee
The One Blue Thread
Gittel, the Would-Be-Messiah
Anonymous Fox
The Journals of Empress Galla Placidia

There is no private life which is not part of the larger public life.

George Eliot

Lilly and the Stabber

My Dark Wood

It's six thirty a.m. on Ninety-second Street. The air is warm on my bare arms and legs, just right for running shorts and tee. The sky is undecided: oyster gray or baby blue. A clear, fresh New York morning. It's Labor Day, 1973.

Rebecca, twelve, and her brother David, nine, are at their dad's, my ex, twenty blocks south. David is probably watching some grim TV footage of the Vietnam War, which he will tell me about in excruciating detail when he and Rebecca come home Sunday night. Rebecca is probably quizzing Martin about Watergate.

Sanjay, the Indian news dealer, unbundling papers at his corner newsstand, greets me with the usual free *New York Times*. Today's headline is WHAT DID NIXON KNOW? I can't carry the paper when I'm running, so I leave it for Captain and President, the neighborhood homeless, asleep on their traffic island bench. They are friends. Rebecca and David scrounge for leftover food for them, and their father's castoff clothes.

On Broadway, delivery trucks are lined up along the street. On Central Park, empty bleachers await the crowds for today's parade.

"What's Labor Day anyway," David asked me last night, "and why is Dad taking us to a parade tomorrow?"

"Labor Day celebrates getting an eight-hour working day," I explain, "and I'm celebrating by not working. I'm going jogging."

"You work eight hours?" David asks. "That's more than school."

"I work ten hours," I say.

It's Martin's every other weekend with them. And mine free. A contrary freedom. Our too small apartment seems over large when they're not there. What's the point of all this room? The quiet echoes. No questions. No fights. But I'm free to go jogging alone. On their every-other weekends with me, they insist on joining me when I run. I never allow them to go to the park alone, so I let them come. It slows me down, even at my pace, but they're safe because they're with me.

In winter, when the park is too cold, I go to the Henry Hudson Gym. But that's for companionship as well as exercise. Today I delight in being alone. I dismiss my perpetual worries: my underpaid job at WCBC-TV writing news releases; my solitary post-divorce state; my possibly cancerous tumor. I forget my biggest worry, how to bring up my children in this corrupt culture: a criminal president, a pointless war, a dangerous city. My favorite writer, George Eliot says every private life is determined by the larger public life. How do I protect my children from this larger public life?

After four, easy cross-town blocks, I hit the hard path to the reservoir.

The *New York Times* is right, pollution is stunting the park trees. There's still luxury, a garden mid-city. Absolute privacy, dead quiet. Breathing deep, I lean against the reservoir's fence to stretch my hamstrings for my two circuits run. Starting slowly, I pick up speed. I'm a happy green thought in a green shade.

Halfway around the track, at the reservoir's northern end, hidden by shrubbery, I hear someone running behind me. I pay no attention. There are always a few joggers this early. Then a pale young man with light brown hair, not much taller than I am, comes up alongside me. He's wearing black pants, a cheap white shirt, open at the neck. His sleeves are rolled up to his elbows. A brown leather jacket is folded over one arm.

"Hi," he says, "don't I know you?"

I keep on running.

He insists. "You look familiar."

I shake my head.

"Hey, I'm talking to you," he says angrily.

Now I'm scared. "I can't talk while I'm jogging," I answer.

"That's not nice," he says. "You can talk to me." He grabs me by the wrist, exposing a knife blade under his folded jacket and tries to pull me away from the path, away from the high mesh fence enclosing the reservoir.

I was crazy to want privacy. I can't see more than a few yards ahead of me, and no one walking in the park can see me. Now I'm really frightened. I imagine myself, Lilly Jonas, lying on the ground, a knife sticking from my stomach. I back up against the fence and look at the water, wishing I could crash through the wire and jump in.

"You're making me angry," he says.

Talk, I think, remembering a *Village Voice* article, a woman who talked a man out of raping her. Try to connect with him. Say anything.

I try. I say, "Listen, what do you want to do this for? You must be scared. You must be scared as me." I, scared as I.

He pulls hard at my arm, but I won't budge. I'm determined not to let him get me off the path. I concentrate on my feet, glued to the ground. "I'm a mother," I say. "I have two children waiting for me at home. I'm much too old for you."

What if he has a thing for his mother? That's what they always say about men who commit sex crimes. "You don't want to do this, I know you don't."

Too motherly? Now I'm babbling, though my head, tongue, wits all feel frozen. He keeps tugging at my arm. I stand my ground, refuse to move, refuse to think ahead. How much time is passing?

"You better come with me." He's snarling. "Come on." He yanks my arm so hard it feels like he's pulling it right out of the socket. I'm numb, surprised I can feel the pain in my arm.

Then, just ahead, a jogger rounds the curve, a plump middle-aged man in white shorts and shirt with a fat white poodle running alongside him. Am I hallucinating? I'm afraid if I scream, my attacker will stick his knife in me. I'm sure the jogger won't stop. He'll run right over my bleeding body. Now I'm terrified. I feel a sharp stab on my arm as, incredibly, the man lets go of me.

"You're lucky," he says. "I can tell you, baby, you don't know how lucky you are." He walks quickly off the path, jacket now folded casually over the blade and disappears into the bushes.

I look down at the thin line of blood on my arm, wondering how I got that, as though my head had stopped. I step back on the path, trying to block the jogger. "Please stop," I say. "That man has a knife."

"What man?" The jogger's annoyed.

"That man." I point to nothing. "The one who just walked into the bushes."

"Just keep running," he says, slowing down, but not stopping. "Everyone in New York thinks someone's after them."

"Look," I say, running alongside, trying to thrust my arm in front of him. The cut is bleeding more. Just looking at the blood scares me.

"Keep running," he says.

I do. I run alongside him to the park exit, down Ninety-second Street. I keep running until I get home, lock my three locks, get in bed and call the police.

"Did he hit you?" the policeman asks. He sounds bored.

"He pushed me up against the fence," I answer. "He had a knife."

"Did he touch you?"

"He cut my arm. It's really deep," I say. "It's bleeding all over me."

"Lady, do you know how many guys like that are walking around New York City?" The policeman is matter of fact. "Hundreds," he says. "Thousands."

I hang up and see him everywhere.

Downward Mobility

"Hey Paul, who put that Christmas tree here?" David asks.

Struggling, our arms full of heavy SHOP-IT grocery bags, David, Rebecca and I are greeted by the hand-lettered sign **Happy End 1973** and Paul, the super, on a metal chair, straightening the tinsel star on a pitiful Christmas tree.

"Why do we have a tree?" David asks. "Everyone in this building is Jewish."

"Not everyone," Rebecca says. "Manfred isn't Jewish."

"Manfred is black," David answers.

Paul looks confused. "It's too crooked?" He steps down from the chair. "You need a fur coat for New Year?" he asks me.

Paul is Czech. He lives in the basement apartment with his wife and two children. Yesterday afternoon I caught his children zooming around the laundry room on Rebecca and David's bikes. Paul inherited the super's job last year from his brother Milo, who now sells jewelry hi-jacked from Kennedy Airport. I assume from his question that Milo has upgraded to furs.

"You need?" he asks again. "Mink? Squirrel?"

I jiggle my supermarket bags. "I'll stick with cloth for now, like Pat Nixon."

"Good, good," Paul says, rolling down his shirtsleeves. He puts on his dark green uniform jacket and stretches out his hands. "Let me carry. You think it's a bad year for the President?"

"He's a crook," David says. "He robbed some plumbers and stole everything. Let's go, Mom. The champagne must be getting warm."

"The champagne isn't for us," Rebecca corrects him.

"I hope they nail him," I tell Paul.

"Mom said we could taste it," David counters Rebecca.

"Nail?" Paul asks.

I imagine Nixon clambering down from a cross, insisting, "I am not a crook."

"Impeach," I say, and hand Paul my SHOP-IT bags. I gave him a big Christmas tip, so for another month, he'll carry my groceries the ten feet from the front door to the elevator. I'd rather he fixed the broken lock on the front door and his kids would stay off my kids' bikes. Then I feel guilty. I should be more generous. I should feel sorry for his kids, living in a crummy basement apartment. I feel sorry for my kids. The whole building is crummy. I hate to see Rebecca and

David growing up here, walking out of the elevator every morning into the lobby's stinginess. I recall the super luxurious size of their bedroom suites before my divorce, compared with David's cramped quarters now, maybe nine by five, which I built by dividing the dining room. Now the dining room is a dark hall. I feel guilty about Rebecca's bedroom window, across the street from an apartment of prostitutes. "Aren't they interesting," she says. "That woman was taking off her clothes and some naked guy was taking pictures."

"You had to get divorced," my mother accused me when she saw the new apartment. "From nine rooms to three?"

"Four," I said. I told her I believed in downward mobility.

Rebecca now tells her friends her mother got divorced to live in downward nobility, which proves Chomsky's point that language is in the genes. My mother, myself, my children, we all incline to aphorism.

"The children have a good Christmas?" Paul asks, pushing the elevator bell.

"We don't celebrate Christmas," David tells him.

"No?" he asks. "In my country, everybody celebrates."

"That's because there are no Jews left in Czechoslovakia." Why am I saying this to Paul? David is pulling on my coat. Rebecca is at the elevator, pushing the bell a second time.

"My English is not very good," Paul confesses.

"Your English is fine. My mother couldn't speak English when she came here."

I don't tell him she came at age three.

"I can leave the tree?" he asks. " Our apartment is too small. It's for my children, the tree."

"It's ok," Rebecca says.

"It's ok," David repeats.

Damn. Now I have to feel guilty because his children don't have a Christmas tree. It could be worse. I could be minding someone else's children and putting mine in Day Care.

I could be out of work and on welfare.

"Mom," David pleads. "It's almost New Year's. It's going to be over. You said we could stay up and have a little champagne."

"I did. Let's have a lot of champagne."

The elevator arrives.

I need another job. The country needs a new president. The building needs a faster elevator.

The phone is ringing as I wrestle with the three locks on my apartment door.

"Where are you? The champagne is getting warm. I'm waiting for you to get your white ass over here." It's my friend Callista on the phone. Her champagne would be several upgrades from the bottle I just bought. I forgot we had made a New Year's Eve date to drink it.

Callista, who lived one floor above us, in a nine-room apartment just like ours in our old building, is a black super star, a singer and night club performer. We met when I was canvassing for a Presidential candidate and became friends. She was impressed with my political soldiering. I was impressed with her openness and her glamour, surprised she would want to be my friend. She was always trying to glamorize me. Like the pair of false eye lashes she pasted on me. I loved them. I just couldn't get them on myself, and when I got them on, I couldn't see.

Annette. her daughter, and Rebecca, who were both twelve, had become friends, too. David disliked Annette. "She's a snob," he said. He felt left out of their girl-circle.

"Where've you been, anyway? I've been calling you for hours," Callista asked. "Have you been at Doctor West's? How's your cyst?"

"No, I haven't been at the doctor. I've been at the gym. I needed a run. I think my cyst is still lemon sized and in my uterus. I apologize. I forgot. I thought the kids were going away with Martin tonight, but they're not leaving till tomorrow. Where's Annette? And how come anybody as gorgeous as you doesn't have a New Year's date with Prince Charming?"

"A black Prince Charming is an oxymoron," she says. "Put on all your jewelry and come on over."

"You come here," I answer.

"I'm not really dressed," she says. "And I'm afraid to park my car on your street."

I never know when Callista will do the unpredictable. Get in her white Mercedes, which she bought after three cabs in a row passed her up and drive us to One hundred twenty-fifth Street for hot dogs. Then down to the Carlyle to hear Bobby Short. I love the junkets, I love her, but I feel like a plump Jewish housewife next to Queen Nefertiti. I can't handle feeling that inadequate tonight.

I explain that, besides forgetting, I started work today at six a.m. At five p.m., when I was ready to leave, my boss, Ahearne, put his four fingered hand on my shoulder, and reminded me of our slogan, WCBC-TV, The Network That's Here for You. "You have another hour to be here," he said, breathing his afternoon gin in my face.

"He's a real phrase maker," Callista says.

"He's a real ball breaker," I answer, "but I need the job. Anyway, I don't have anything to wear tonight."

"Too bad,' she interrupts. "You could have wrapped yourself in one of my fur coats, and we'd have sat around and got smashed. Come tomorrow," she says.

Why is everyone trying to get me into fur?

The Stabber

"What's wrong?" I ask.

It's David, calling from his father's apartment, and he's crying.

"What's wrong?" I repeat.

David moans.

"Are you sick?"

"It's the Stabber," he says.

I was about to leave for the gym, but this is more important. The Stabber is David's albatross. For a year now, he is on-again, off-again. We cannot get rid of him. I take off my coat and put down my gym bag.

"C'mon David. There is no Stabber. We've been over this many times."

"He's not here, but he's coming."

David always sees him coming. "Where?" I say. "Where can you see him? Out the window? On the TV? There isn't any Stabber. It's all in your head."

"That's it," he says triumphantly. "I told you. I can see him in my head."

"But David," I plead, "it's not real. He's not real. You're afraid of something and you've made up a person to go with whatever you're afraid of. He's only in your head."

"But I'm afraid of him. I'm afraid because he's got a knife and he's coming after me. If he were somewhere else, I could get rid of him but how can I get rid of something in my head?"

"Where's your father?"

"He and Rebecca went out to buy dinner."

"Why didn't you go with them?"

"I wanted to call you."

"What if I weren't here?"

"Well, I wouldn't be any worse off because you're there and I'm talking to you and he's still in my head."

"David, I think I've got the answer."

"The answer to what?"

"The answer to what you can do about the Stabber."

"Okay," he says. "What's the answer?"

"Now the Stabber's not in the apartment?"

"Right," he says.

"Or in the hall, right?"

He pauses. "Right."

"Or on Broadway?"

"Well, I don't know about that. He might be on Broadway."

"David, you told me he was in your head. Right?"

"Right."

"Well, if he's real, he can't be in two places at once, and if he's in two places at once, then he isn't real."

"Ok." David sounds skeptical.

"Now I'm going to take him out of your head and put him in mine, and then you won't have to worry about him anymore."

"Do you think that will work?"

"Well," I say,"if he's real, it will work."

"What if he's not real?"

"If he's not real, then neither of us have to worry about him." That sounds convincing to me.

"How are you going to do it? I mean, how are you going to get him from my head to yours?"

"I'll have to come over and get him. I was going to the gym, but I'll be there in half an hour, fifteen minutes if I can make it. Ok?"

"What if they're back then?"

"Who? Daddy and Rebecca? What if they are back?"

"Should we tell them what we're doing?" he asks.

"What do you think?"

"I don't think they'll believe us," he answers.

"Now look David, while I'm on my way, you have to get ready for me."

"Ok," he sounds suspicious again. "What do I do?"

"You sit down with a piece of paper and a pencil, two pieces of paper in fact. Can you do that?"

"Yeah."

"And on one of them you write down everything you know about the Stabber."

"Like what?"

"Like what he looks like and what he wears and where he lives and what he reads. Anything else you can think of. Have you got that?"

"What about the other piece of paper?"

"You draw a picture of him."

"I can't."

"Why? Don't you know what he looks like?"

"Sure, I know what he looks like." David sounds annoyed. "But I don't draw very well."

"Just draw it. And on the bottom of each picture write, This is the Stabber. He used to be my problem. Now he's yours."

"That's too long to write. Are you coming right now?"

"I'm coming right now," I say. It just might work. It's certainly worth trying.

In the hall, while I wait for the elevator, I rest my gym bag on the floor. I lock the three locks on my door. I check my watch. The elevator seems awfully long in coming. I can see by the red button it is coming down, and from the familiar grinding noise, it seems to be stopping at every floor. Some smart-ass kid like David probably got off at the top and pushed every button. Just a little anonymous harassment. Typical New York.

When the elevator stops and the door opens, I am surprised to see, standing in the corner, a large, mean-looking man in a long, dirty, blue army coat and a black vinyl snap brimmed cap.

Oh my God, I say to myself. It's the Stabber. "Going up?" I ask.

"Yeah. Going up," the man answers.

"I'm going down," I say, smiling.

The elevator door closes automatically. I can see from the red button that it was going down, just as I thought. From the stairwell, I can hear the elevator door open and close on the next floor.

I ring, holding the bell on my neighbor's apartment, and my shoulders drop with relief when Walter comes to the door. I have never been so happy to see him. "Oh Walter," I babble, "let me in. Some big creep just went down on that elevator, stopping at every floor. I'm terrified to go down alone, and I've got to get out of here fast because I promised to meet David."

"Some big what?" Walter pulls me in and shuts the door.

"Creep," I say. "Weirdo. The kind you always see in the paper with a caption that reads, The police are looking for a man that fits this description, brown eyes, blue cap, brown hair."

"Ok, Ok," Walter says. "Stay here." He walks to his kitchen and picks up the house phone. After half a minute I hear him ask the Puerto Rican hall man, "Hey, Roberto, did some big weirdo in a cap just get off the elevator? Yeah? Has he left? Okay Roberto, want to do me a favor and go send the elevator up to ten." Walter hangs up. "C'mon I'll take you down."

"I really appreciate this," I tell Walter, as the elevator door opens, showing Roberto inside, his light brown face looking tired and worried in contrast to his dark green uniform which is freshly pressed. "I see why you called" Roberto says. "I locked the front door."

"You're all so paranoid," Walter says. "Probably some actor visiting Manley upstairs."

"That guy was no actor. If I'm so paranoid, why did he tell me he was going up when he was going down?"

At the front door Walter checks outside to see if anyone is hanging around.

"Walter," I say,"It's crazy, I know, but that guy looked like the Stabber."

"Who?" asks Walter.

"The Stabber. You know, the guy David is worrying about."

"Hey, stop it," Walter says patiently. "You've told me it's just a nightmare, David's Stabber. And if that guy was the Stabber, or a Stabber, he is only one of several hundred, several thousand, stabbers, muggers, and burglars trying to make a living in the Big Apple. On the other hand, if he was not the Stabber, he's just some poor slob with too much shit in his veins to know if he's going up or down on life's elevator."

"Oh, Walter, you're such a phrase-maker."

"Sure," says Walter, as he stops a cab and helps me into it, setting my gym bag on the floor. "Listen," he says, through the window, "I'll be home tonight. So if you're worried after the gym, call me on the house phone when you get back. I'll be your escort service."

David is waiting for me. "Is that you?" he asks, from behind the locked door.

"You know it's me," I say, to the peep-hole.

He opens the door. "Didn't you tell me to always ask?"

"Always ask." I give him a hug. "Have you got those papers?"

"What took you so long?"

"I came as fast as I could."

"Did you take a taxi?"

"You are giving me the third degree."

"What's...."

"The third degree," I answer, before he can finish his sentence, "is what the police do when they sit somebody down on a chair and put a big light in their face and ask them nasty questions."

"Oh, yeah. They do it on TV. What else can they do if they want answers?"

"David, do you have the pictures?" I'm still standing in the hall.

"It's okay to come in, they're not here."

I walk in and look around as David watches me. "Do you like it?"

It's the first time I've been in Martin's apartment. "It all looks pretty familiar," I answer. It's familiar, all right. The oriental rug, the coffee table, the expensive stereo, the pictures, and the child in front of me.

"Do you feel uncomfortable being here?"

"Why are you asking me that?" I ask, though I know why. He would like Martin and me not to be divorced.

"I just wanted to know. How else can I know if I don't ask?"

"Yes, I do feel a little funny being here. In fact, I feel a lot funny and I'd like to just give you a hug and get the papers and get out."

"I just wanted to know." David sits down on the sofa.

"Well, now you know. Do you have the papers?"

David puts two folded pieces of paper down on my old coffee table. "Mom," he says,"I want to ask you something. Did you ever love Daddy?"

I stay cool. "I know you're upset about the divorce, but this is not the time."

"I'm not upset about the divorce. I just want to know if you ever loved Daddy."

"I loved him," I say firmly. "I loved him, and we are not going to talk about it now because we don't have time. We'll talk about it when you get home tomorrow. Ok? Now can you give me those papers?"

"Oh, sure." He hands them over. "Don't look at them now."

"Why not?"

"Because I'm through with them. They're out of my head. If I look at them, I'll get scared again."

I take them and stand up.

"Just one thing," David says tentatively. "I don't know what he eats."

I know it is silly and superstitious, but I do not want to look at David's papers while I am in the elevator. I read what he's written on the outside. On one, in big, red, uneven capitals, TO MOM. THE LIST, and on the other, THIS IS ALL YOURS.

What a child. What am I going to do with him? What am I going to do with myself? And then the door to the elevator opens, and there are Rebecca and Martin, arms full of bagged groceries.

"Mom," says Rebecca, looking pleased, then uncomfortable. "Is everything okay?"

My ex-husband just looks at me. There is an awkward pause. Finally, I say hello to him, and he answers.

"Oh, everything's fine," I tell Rebecca.

"What's the matter with David?" she asks.

"He had to give me something," I say casually.

Now Martin is uncomfortable. He leans against the wall with the bags. Then he puts them down on the floor. He rubs his chin. He takes out a cigar and lights it.

Walking out of the building, I feel pleased with myself. How clever I am. And what a good mother. How like Martin to have left David alone like that. And then I wonder what's in David's drawings, and whatever is there, if I have just made the two of us feel less anxious for the evening, if anything like this could really work.

In the taxi, I look at David's papers. I can just make out his list from the street lights so I turn on the overhead light in the cab and ignore the driver's protest.

I open the one titled, TO MOM. THE LIST.

This is the list

The Stabber lives in Central Park

He is TALL

He wears caps

He wears sneekers

He knows how to read but he doesn't

He doesn't like himself or anybody

He eats ____.

There is a blank after"eats."

I open the other piece of paper just as we reach the Henry Hudson gym.I can't tell if his picture looks like the man in the elevator, though his stick figure has on a long coat and cap. There is something printed across the bottom of the page and I try to read it.

In the lobby I look again at the picture. Under the figure he has written in capital letters,

THE STABBER WEARS 2 COATS

HE IS LONSUM

A Bad Idea

"Who is he?" Rebecca is sitting on my bed, watching me dress for a blind date in my old purple sweater and wraparound skirt. "I like that skirt. Can I borrow it when I get older?"

"Everything I have is yours." I look in the bathroom mirror, trying to get my eyes right. "What do you think?"

"I think you look better without eye stuff. Can I have your black glitter sweater?"

"Everything except that."

"I thought so," she says. "I want to wear it to school. It makes me look sophisticated."

"You don't need to look sophisticated. You're only twelve years old."

Twelve and a half. I'm almost having my period."

"When you get your period, I'll buy you a glitter sweater."

"Black."

"Black is too old. You want to look like Bonnie?" Bonnie, our child sitter tonight, always wears black. "You want to look as old as me? What about blue? You look so good in blue with your blue eyes."

"You do too, and you have a black sweater. Shouldn't I get to choose my own clothes?"

"Absolutely. You want to look my age I'll get you black."

"You don't look so old. What are you doing to your face? Who is this guy you're going out with?"

"He's a friend of Herb's mother."

"Didn't Herb's dad get you your job? I hope your date turns out better than your job."

"I need the job, Rebecca. Herb's dad did me a favor."

"But you hate it, right?"

Do I tell her I could be a lot worse off? Should I say there are women like me on welfare, families like us on the street? Do I tell her I'm just sidetracked, developing my real potential as a writer, though I'm not quite sure what that is. That's what she ought to be thinking about, her potential. Is this a good time to discuss why a woman needs to be independent, to do something that pays the rent?

"My job is not so bad," I hear myself say. "I could be a lot worse off. There are women like me on welfare, there are families like us on the street. When you grow up, you're going to have a job you really like."

"I'm going to be like you," she says. "Except I might be a doctor."

"Good for you. When you graduate medical school, I'll buy you a white glitter sweater."

"Black," she says. "I'm not going to wear it to work."

My date arrives, a slight, bearded man in a brown corduroy suit and horn-rimmed glasses. Rebecca shows him in. "Sylvan Lesterberg," he says, putting out his hand. She shakes it. "Sylvan Lesterberg," he says to David, who is standing at his bedroom door in his baseball pajamas.

"Never heard of him," David says. He walks into his room and shuts the door.

"My brother is kind of retarded," Rebecca tells Sylvan.

The doorbell rings and Bonnie enters with Peter, her trumpet playing boyfriend, both in black jeans ripped off at the knee and studded black leather bracelets. Rebecca introduces them.

"Hey, man," Peter says. "My name's Sylvan, too. Brothers under the skin." He slaps Sylvan's outstretched hand. "Give me five."

Sylvan looks shocked. Peter looks high.

I pull Bonnie through the small dining room into the kitchen. "What's he on?"

She's offended. "He's just showing off."

"Tell me the truth, Bonnie. I can't leave the kids with you if he's high."

"C'mere, dufus," she hollers, and Peter/Sylvan walks into the kitchen. "What's your name?" she says.

"Ok, Ok, I was acting like an asshole. The guy's such a wimp. You really going out with that meatball?" He looks me over. "You look pretty good. You could do a lot better."

"Are you high?" I ask him.

"Me?" he says. "Listen, just because I don't wear a shirt and tie, it doesn't mean I'm not a responsible human being."

Sylvan and I go to see *The Way We Were*. Barbra Streisand is a Jewish political activist. Robert Redford is a beautiful Wasp. After she meets him, she irons her hair. It's not enough. They're too different. They split up.

After the movie Sylvan and I have a drink at The West End Bar and argue about it. I like Barbra Streisand. I think it's great that women in movies can be political, not just decorative.

Sylvan is a psychologist. He thinks she was over-determined. "She's one of those heated up feminists," he says. "She's wants to break Redford's balls."

"It's just like a psychologist to get it all backwards," I say. "She doesn't want to break his balls. She wants to lick them. She wants to break his resistance to her politics."

"You sound just like her," Sylvan responds sarcastically. "Come to think of it, except for the nose, you even look a bit like her."

That gets me really mad. I'm shocked at myself, but I'm too overheated to stop. "My name is not Lilly for nothing."

"Who's Lilly?" he asks.

"Lilly for Lillith, Adam's first wife. God created her from dust, just like Adam. Not from his rib."

"Eve was a second wife?" he asks.

"Adam married Lillith because he was tired of sleeping with animals," I say. "He tried to take her in the missionary position. She cursed him and flew away."

"I never heard any of this," He looks at me suspiciously.

"Don't you know in male-dominated societies, women have to lie under the man? Don't you know Muslims say, 'Accursed be the man who makes women heaven and himself earth?'"

He doesn't know that.

"And the Catholic Church says any position other than the male superior one is sinful?"

He doesn't know that either.

At the door we agree that tonight was a bad idea.

Callista

"And I gave up all this to be single," I say, as Callista opens the door to her nine-room apartment, a duplicate of the one Martin and I lived in. I see a film of my life run backwards. Rebecca was almost three and I was eight months pregnant with David when we moved there. "Do you think it's really Ok for a three-year old to have her own bathroom? And a newborn?" I asked Martin. I was the daughter of a New Dealer. Should anyone live in an apartment with four bedrooms, five baths, two maids' rooms, and a spectacular view of the Hudson? What would our children expect in life with a start like this?

Martin was waiting to be made a partner in his law firm, so we saved money by scraping, sanding, and polishing some of the floors ourselves. I felt like we were squatting there, but I have to admit, eventually I loved it.

Callista and I have talked, but we haven't visited much since I moved. Her daughter Annette, who became best friends with Rebecca, has come for sleepovers, especially when Callista's been on the road , saloon singing, as she calls it. David dislikes Annette visiting us. He feels left out by their friendship. But Callista and I have mostly talked on the phone. Light brown skin, straight black hair, she's looking gorgeous as usual, in a sexy black jumpsuit and silver toed bare feet.

"So how is that cyst?" she asks, as soon as she opens the door. "You haven't said anything about it in weeks."

"There's nothing to say," I answer.

"Have you been to the doctor again?" she asks. "And how is David's Stabber? Is he still hanging around?"

"He's still around," I answer.

"You know if you have to have that cyst taken out, Rebecca and David can stay here. And what is that thing you're wearing? Do you dress like that at work?" she wants to know.

"I'm not on stage," I point out. "I'm an underpaid PR assistant."

"Well, I have just the thing for you to wear to my party. I even have a spare fur. Let's get a drink and go look." She holds up her champagne glass.

"Hey, wait a minute, what party?" I ask.

"I was going to tell you on New Year's Eve. I'm going to have my own TV show. Can you believe it! I'm going to be a black lady lawyer. An important TV black lady lawyer," she emphasizes. "The first TV sitcom with a black female star. So, I'm throwing a party."

"Are you a singing lawyer?"

"No singing!" she says firmly

"I have to hear about this! We have to celebrate," I say.

"We are celebrating," she points out. "Now."

I follow her down the long entrance hall into her all-white living room, MoMA crossed with MGM: white fur rugs, Noguchi coffee tables, champagne in a silver bucket. I sink into a sofa.

She settles down next to me and fills up our champagne glasses.

"You look like you were born drinking champagne," I tell her.

"Listen," she says, "I just try to keep my spirits up. I know my daddy's a garbage collector - excuse me, a "sanitation officer" - and my mamma's a nurse. I'm getting old fast. I'm probably good for a couple more years but in my business, I'm on my way to being burned out. Callista Dee, last year's burned toast."

"You're pretty expensive toast!" I tell her. "And you say I lack confidence! You just told me you have your own show."

"That doesn't impress my mamma. Or papa. They'd like me to be a nice black bourgeois lady married to a proper lawyer. Like you were. Only black. They're embarrassed that I'm divorced with a kid. And they hate Annette's French School. Mamma says the only black people there are Algerians." Callista imitates her mother, holding her nose as she says, "Algerians."

She pours us both another glass. "You know I was so jealous. I thought you two had the perfect marriage," she tells me. "When I met you, when you came to the door to get me to sign some petition. There you were, good-looking, smart, two kids, handsome lawyer husband, enough energy left over to go campaigning. I thought, boy, do I envy her."

Callista envied me? This is news. "My mother's too embarrassed by me to tell anyone I'm divorced. Or using my Ivy League degree to write TV releases. Here's to failure! Happy New Year." I lift my glass. "I'm in the spin business, my boss harasses me, I barely make enough money to live without child support."

"I'm making money," she counters. "I'm not exactly singing *Madame Butterfly*. Speaking of Butterfly, now that I'm going to be a TV star, my agent wants me to do a Broadway show. An opera. Like *Carmen Jones*."

"Not Carmen again!" I say. "Why not do something original. Besides, women always lose in opera. Or die. Why not play a woman who wins in the end?"

"Exactly," she says. She puts her hands on my shoulders. "You write it, I'll do it on Broadway."

"Do what? Write what?"

"A play. Something new. Something smart. Everything my agent has sent me is dreary. For black bimbos with no brains."

I can't believe she isn't joking. "You're crazy, I say. "I've written some short stories. I've never written a play."

"I've never sung opera. I've hardly acted in anything, but I'm going to do this TV show. It's not your experience I'm after. I've read your stories. It's your imagination."

"I can't take you seriously. What imagination? I never imagined I'd be living next to a whore house or doing public relations for TV."

"It's not a whore house," she says, "just a Love Hotel. You wouldn't have that crummy job at that crummy salary if you weren't such an idealist."

"Me? An idealist?"

"Who else would get divorced because she has an orgasm with some guy who's not her husband?"

"That's not why I got divorced," I say, taking my shoes off to put my feet up. "It wasn't just sex. It was the marriage trap. Martin charmed me, married me, and then went off to his important profession. I was supposed to stay home with the kids and entertain his rich clients. Forget writing. He said our marriage couldn't support two careers. And the worst of it," I said, getting wound up, "was that it was my fault. I wanted to be married and have children. I just didn't want it to be my whole life. I wanted to be something splendid like some Henry James heroine. Better yet, like George Sand. Like somebody I just hadn't imagined yet. But there was no room for that in our marriage. No novels where the heroine gets married in the prologue." I stop, amazed at myself.

Callista's amazed, too. "What can I say?" she says.

"What about you?"

"You don't know?" she asks me.

"Don't know what?" I answer.

"That I got divorced because I met Daniel Cameron. He was going to get divorced and move in here. We were going to get married. But now, here I am, jilted. He's English. He's not getting divorced. And he's not moving in."

I put down my glass. "You're kidding! Cameron, that TV reporter who's always interviewing heads of state?"

She stands up, taking her glass and a champagne bottle. "No sad stories of the death of kings," she says. "Let's go get that dress for you. And the furs."

"The show, Callista, tell me more about the show. And Broadway."

"Later," she says. "First the dress."

We walk down the hall, passing Annette's room with the white wicker swing, the four-poster bed draped with dotted Swiss. And the small make-up table. Rebecca wants one of those.

"You don't wear make-up," David told her. "What do you need a make-up table for?"

Callista's room has a four-poster bed, too, but with a mirrored ceiling. She says it turns her on to see herself screwing, and when she's not, she loves to watch people look at it and gasp. Now she walks into her dressing room and comes back with a black dress and two fur coats, gives me the dress and the beaver coat, puts on the silver fox.

"You don't think I'm mink?" I ask her.

"If you'd stayed married to the lawyer. Now, definitely not."

"Martin once offered to buy me a mink."

"See, I was right." She lies down in the coat, looking up at her reflection. "I want to be a silver fox." She closes her eyes. "Why do I have such lousy luck with men? You want to hear about Daniel?" She starts to cry, and the mascara runs down her cheeks.

I do want to hear about Daniel. I lie down next to her in beaver.

Politics

Politics was the spoon I was fed with. Callista, too. It was one of our bonds. My dad was a lawyer; hers was a sanitation worker. Both went to Washington, D.C. on the first bonus march. Our families were old fashioned liberals and in our respective social circles, we were equally middle class.

Callista's mother was a nurse and an early Feminist. My mother was a lawyer's wife. She had a Bachelor and Master's Degree from Cincinnati University. Her only job, both while she was in High School and College, was as a clerk at the local Five and Ten in the ribbon department. In her generation, women worked if they had no husbands, like my mother's chemist friend Doris, or because their husbands couldn't make enough money to support them, like Callista's mother and my father's secretary. Callista's mother worked her way up to Head of Nursing on the Surgery Ward at Presbyterian Hospital.

My mother was an indifferent cook. She served iceberg lettuce with A &P salad dressing every night. For vegetables we ate string beans or cauliflower with bread crumbs fried in butter, and as a main course, steak or fish, broiled. Her specialties were jello mold, meaning jello speckled with canned fruit cocktail, and chocolate chip cookies.

Callista's mother sang in her church's choir and cooked as little as possible. Her dad was a superior cook. As a child, Callista sat down to a much fancier dinner than I did. Her father's specialties were sweet potato pie and southern fried chicken.

Our house was clean, though my mother hated to clean it, a trait which I have inherited from her along with her ferocious love of music and books. Once a week, she'd get down on her knees to wash the kitchen floor, then spread newspaper over it till it dried. I never understood why the ink from the newspaper didn't spot the clean floor, why the soapy water she dipped her brush in didn't ruin the bright red polish on the fingernails someone came to our house to manicure. Why she wore flowered housedresses and lace up black shoes with socks, when my friends' mothers wore fancy dresses and silk stockings with high heels. Later, I saw pictures of her when she was first married and realized that she was beautiful. It was a revelation. It didn't jibe with the kitchen floor.

As my father's practice and income grew, we had more household help, *schwarzes*, my mother called them. It shocked me even then to hear black people referred to that way. My mother could not understand how Callista, my best friend, and later, a lover, were both black. When I was growing up, black was neither beautiful nor ugly. It was colored.

My parents met at the Cleveland YMHA. Callista's met at a church supper. My father did a couple years in Washington as a New Deal administrator, and then, as he never tired of pointing out, my mother induced him to come back to Cleveland and practice law. She thought settling down to a busy law practice would keep him from running around. It did, in a way, He took up with his secretary. My mother ignored it and kept on being Mrs. Bestor and Partners.

My father read the newspaper every day and listened to the news in the car and at breakfast, lunch, and dinner. I took up being well informed as a defense.

I grew up wanting to have my cake and eat it, too. My piano teacher, whom I thought of as my music mother, claimed I was her most rebellious student. A maverick wanting to be wanted, I pledged the local high school sorority and quit after I was initiated. I went to the country club and read *War and Peace* by the pool.

Callista grew up wanting to sing, act, and have straight hair. She stayed out of the sun because it made her skin look ashy. She went to Music and Art High School, one of New York's most competitive, though she could have gone to Bronx High School of Science, which also took only the best and the brightest. Her first big break was winning a talent show sponsored by a local TV station. She met her first husband, a white talent agent there. He took her on as a client, promised to make her a big star, and married her. By eighteen, she was acting professionally. At twenty-one, she became a mother. Her parents were delighted with her success and their granddaughter, Annette. They were not so happy with her white husband.

Insisting he'd be on the Supreme Court if he'd gone to Harvard, my father, who had gone to law school at night, encouraged me to go to Wellesley, where I met Martin. Martin was headed for Harvard Law School and ridiculously handsome. David looks just like him. Martin was from a poor Jewish family living in an unfashionable part of Brooklyn. His grandfather had been an anarchist in Russia. His father was a Legal Aid attorney, his mother, a school teacher.

Martin was the youngest of six children. "God knows why we had six," his mother always said. Bertha, the oldest girl, always claimed, "If we didn't have the rest of them, especially baby Martin, we'd be rich." But they did have the rest of them and they were poor. Martin was bound and determined to be rich and if fame came with it, that was Ok. My father wanted to be famous. Being rich was less important.

I thought Martin was an idealist. That is, I thought he wanted to make the world better for everybody, as his father and grandfather did. I fooled myself at that.

Callista and I both illustrated Gloria Steinem's new axiom: you're either a feminist or a masochist. We were feminists until it came to men. Then we were masochists.

I Go to the Gym

"Hi" he says,"don't I know you?"

I'm on the bus, reading *The New York Times* on my way to the gym, when the man behind me taps me on the shoulder. I turn around.

"You look familiar," he says.

I am breathing too fast. He does look familiar. He looks like the man in Central Park with the knife. His face is the same pale color. He's wearing a brown leather jacket, a blue wool cap pulled over his ears. I feel the reservoir fence at my back, the sharpness of the knife blade on my arm.

I shake my head. My mouth is dry. I turn back to my paper. The bus stops. I say, "Excuse me," grab my gym bag and walk fast to the rear exit, the bag slowing me down as it catches on all the aisle seats. "Getting off, getting off," I yell to the driver, terrified he'll start before I can get down the bus steps. I jump in the first taxi I see and lock the doors.

"What's the rush?" the driver asks.

"Somebody's following me," I say, though I think that may not have been the man in the park at all. "Hurry up. Take me to the Henry Hudson Gym."

"Everyone in New York thinks someone's after them," he says.

Why did I say excuse me to my maybe-would-be rapist? I am getting paranoid. The driver is right. It can't be the same guy. New York is full of men in leather jackets who ask, "Don't I know you?" I remind myself New York is also full of would-be rapists. I shudder at the would-be. How many women has he slashed since I got away?

The driver complains the next twenty blocks. No one is going to the airport, business is lousy, Nixon is being framed by the Jews.

"What Jews?" I look out the rear window to see if anyone is following.

"Haldeman and Erlichman."

I tell him they're not Jews.

"They sound Jewish to me." He stops at every traffic light, though there's hardly any traffic. He knows it's not the real Nixon in The White House. Nixon has been drugged and flown out of the country like that Dominican they kidnapped up at Columbia two years ago. "What's 'is name?" he turns and asks me angrily.

"Galindez."

"Right. Another Jew."

"He wasn't Jewish."

"They're all Jewish," he says.

At the hotel, I pay him the exact amount on the meter and get out fast. He rolls down his window. "Cunt," he screams. "Whore. Kike."

The entrance to Purgatory must be brighter than the lobby of the Henry Hudson Hotel. There are twenty-watt bulbs in the sconces. In the midst of this gloom, the lobby newsstand is lit up, outlined by naked bulbs, like Callista's make-up table.

The Hotel, like its Columbus Circle neighborhood, once knew better days. I'm sure the upper floors are tenanted by cheap private eyes with live-in offices and merchants who deal in hi-jacked toaster ovens and furs. Our super Paul's brother lives here.

What would Dante have made of this scene? He would be a perfect patron poet for twentieth century New York. His Florentines also made their way through garbage-filled streets, worried they'd be mugged, knifed, murdered and left to rot. They suffered class war, political corruption. Like me, he woke in the middle of his life in a wood of doubt and darkness. But he didn't have to worry how to raise his children.

The usual OUT OF ORDER sign is taped to the lobby elevator. I walk down one flight to the gym, holding my nose to shut out the smell of chlorine from the pool.

In the Gym Club Lounge, Hal, the wall-eyed manager looks up from his cantaloupe and cottage cheese, the latest diet fad. I point to the wall of autographed glossies behind him: Elizabeth Taylor, Muhammad Ali, Henry Kissinger. "Tell the truth, Hal. Have they ever been here?"

"Lilly," he says. "You're a trouble-maker."

Hal and I have our differences: whether Nixon knew; if the men's gym is better than the women's, if you can eat too much fruit.He says no, I say yes to all three. We argue over chlorine in the pool. I say, too much. He says, not enough. I ask why the only black people here are the visiting Wednesday-night telephone-operators. I tell him the balcony we run on is too damp. He tells me I should worry more about foreign policy. You'd think we were married.

Passing the entrance to the men's gym, I see the orange-carpeted exercise room, the shiny, well-oiled machines, the rows of exercise bikes and rowers. Twice as many and all newer than what we have in the women's gym. I've suggested Hal put up a sign: The Facilities Here Are Separate and Unequal.

Today the carpet in the women's gym looks more than ever like faded turf, the mirrors in the exercise room look dirtier, the yellow lockers more blistered. Bridget, the tired locker attendant who guards the entrance, is giving out towels, one to a customer, fifty cents for two. Hal insists they're bath towels, 'though they're barely big enough to wrap around your head. I resolve, as usual, to bring my own, and put the fifty cents toward an answering machine.

But why buy one? No one calls when I'm not at home. Just Callista. Or Rebecca and David, when they're at Martin's for the weekend. And they always call back. It's painful to realize that since I'm divorced and working, since I've moved on from my fancy life and fancy apartment, many of my old friends have moved on, too. Maybe they were really Martin's friends. As one of those how-to-divorce manuals puts it, it's not who gets the china that counts, it's who gets Miriam and Howie for dinner Friday night. It's no coincidence that my best friends now are single: Callista, who was never part of my married social scene, and Angie, my co-worker at WCBC-TV.

The gym is a bigger part of my new life than it used to be. My habits are changing. I make up new ones as I go along. Like learning how to jog, it takes one foot before the other. It takes endurance, training.

I read on the exercise bicycle. I try to read in the sauna. I listen and observe as though I'm watching a play. Maybe this is the play I could write for Callista. She could be an actress who works out here. She could be one of the black telephone-operators who comes on Wednesday. Instead of working in a cigarette factory like Carmen, she'd work for Ma Bell. I won't know until I punch up my confidence and try writing it.

Today, on the bike, I'm planning to read *Cleopatra*. I'm trying to keep up with Rebecca, who's studying Egypt in school.

"Hey, I'm in love with her. Are you reading that?" It's Sally, the airline stewardess on her way to the pool in her minute orange bikini, pointing to my book on the counter.

"I just bought it to read on the bike," I say. "My daughter's reading it in school."

"Cleopatra's why I became an airline stewardess," Sally tells me. "When we studied Egypt in school, I was fascinated. I had to go there," she says, unexpectedly sitting down next to me. "Do you know the Nile flows backwards, from south to north?"

I did know that. "When were you there?" I ask her.

"I haven't been there yet," she says. "When I signed up with the airline, they promised me in two years. But it's a pretty good job," she says. "I've been to lots of boring places. But I've also been to London and Paris. And Rome is next."

I learn that Sally is from Plainfield, New Jersey. "Just like it sounds," she says. "Plain and boring. No Temples of Dendur. No gold buildings. Definitely no pyramids."

I tell her you could pretty much say the same thing about Cleveland, where I'm from.

She's the middle of three girls, and if she were going to be a queen, she says, she'd pick Cleopatra. Queen Elizabeth had a lot of power, she points out, but not much fun. Mary Queen of Scots was in jail half her life and then lost her head.

I've never thought about which queen I'd like to be, but I agree with her about Cleopatra.

Lorraine, an aspiring actress, and Sallie's room-mate, who earns her living as a stripper, is walking around naked, a shower cap perched on her curly black hair. She stops before the mirror to examine herself: long waist, full breasts and hips, dark red lipstick, bright black eyes. She is telling Myra, the school teacher, about last week's audition, when she read for the part of a Scottish nurse. "I floured my hair and did a great burr. The director asked me to take off my clothes. I asked him, 'Since when do nurses go around naked?'" She picks up a roll of Saran Wrap and winds it around her legs. "You should try this. It really sweats your thighs."

"So, what did he say?" Myra asks.

"He said, 'Aren't you a stripper? I thought that's your job, going around naked.' I told him that's what I do at the Pussy Cat Lounge. Not in the theater."

"And?" asks Myra.

"And I didn't get the part."

Myra clucks sympathetically. "It's such a drag not having a job." She takes off her carpet bag coat, steps out of her jeans, pulls off her maroon turtle neck sweater. "It's worse than not having a man. I've been looking since Christmas."

"You got fired before Christmas?"

"That's when they told me. The principal said they had to let me go right after the holidays. No more dance classes. No more extra-curricular stuff. Nothing personal. Budget cuts all over the city."

Since then, her Yoga is more intense. She stands on her head a little longer, her thin body upside down, toes pointed, hair a flat brown halo on the floor. It doesn't seem to help her equanimity.

Myra dresses like a teenager, or a student at Music and Art. Today, for gym, she's wearing a leopard leotard with black lace tights. Sometimes she wears tie-dyed rajah pants with a matching bra. When she's not on her head, she's wrapped in towels, one around her torso, another turban style around her long hair, exchanging woes with her friend Shoshona.

Myra reminds me of a Cleveland neighbor's daughter, always in trouble with men, jobs. Her name was Myra, too. Except her parents always took her in. This Myra seems to be without background, without relatives.

"The last time I had no job and no man I put on fifteen pounds," Myra says.

"That's one good thing about being an airline hostess," Sally says. "The Union protects us. But I know about gaining weight. I was five foot four and one hundred fifty pounds in high school, and I hated myself until I went to Weight Watchers."

"But you're so thin," Shoshona says, looking at Sally in her bikini. "How do you do it?"

"I weigh everything I eat,"Sally says. "Otherwise I'd eat everything put in front of me."

"You carry a scale?" Myra is astonished.

"Oh, no. Now I just do it mentally. I taught myself how to meditate so I could control myself."

"You're lucky you don't have kids," Shoshona says. "At least you don't have my kids. I taught myself to meditate to keep them from driving me crazy, but it didn't work." About to start a gym class, she tugs at the crotch of her crocheted lavender leotard, pulls at her white tights. "I brought them up wrong. They're ashamed of me."

"That's disgusting," Myra says. "After all you do for them."

"They don't mind what I do for them. They mind how I get the money. They tell their friends I'm 'in retail.'" Shoshona looks at me and laughs. "They know I'm a belly dancer. And frankly, at forty-four, I'm pushing it."

"I should look as good as you at forty-four," Myra says.

"Yeah, to you at twenty-seven, forty-four is a hundred."

I agree with Myra. An attractive, freckle-faced, good-natured red-head, Shoshona wears mid-thigh skirts, high heels, and no stockings, even in winter. Stockings are too expensive, the way she runs them. She's saving the money for graduate school. Hers, not her kids. "When I have enough money, I'm taking off," she tells Myra. "You don't believe me? My kids are adults. Let them go out and work. Let them come home every day and make themselves a hot meal."

Like me, the birdlike old lady at the counter listens. No one knows her name or age. She could be seventy. She comes to the gym several times a week, takes off an always elegant black dress and pearls and changes to black tunic and tights. She twists her thinning gray hair on top of her head. In the exercise room, she hops around for an hour, practicing some extinct form of ballet. Then she goes back to the locker room and chain smokes for fifteen minutes.

I wonder if she wants to talk, tell someone her troubles. Or just what she had for breakfast. Maybe to Shoshona, who seems the most sympathetic, or to Myra, who seems as fragile as I feel under all her brashness.

I'm on the bicycle, ready to go six miles in forty-five minutes. I settle down with *Cleopatra*. I can't jog today, can't face the ninety-nine laps it takes to make three miles on the balcony running track. Or the ninety-nine cheers from the ping pong players as I come around each bend. I can't listen to the thin, long-haired lifeguard at the pool below, sitting cross legged on a small towel, practicing his flute, pretending he's in India. The last couple months, I've tried reading *The Inferno*, but pedaling is rough on meter, so I reread *Pride and Prejudice*. Where is Mr. Darcy? The bike is no good for heavy stuff. Magazines are better. *Vogue*, *The Nation*. Sometimes, I give in to sloth and read *The New York Post*.

As I pedal away, I watch Myra on her head, Shoshona at the pulleys. Genevieve, an astonishing blonde mother of eight, in a ruby leotard and matching tights, stands still inside a thin circle of vibrating black leather which exercises her ass. Sally, the airline stewardess, who rooms with Lorraine, passes through in her minute orange bikini. The bird lady is dressing now, adjusting her pearls.

Myra finishes the headstand, stretches out to relax, then jumps up. "We need to talk," she says to Shoshona. "I need to meet someone. Maybe Harry knows somebody."

"Harry? My husband Harry? You don't want to meet any of his friends." Shoshona pulls on her short skirt, her nylon peds, her purple suede high heels.

"I want to meet anybody."

"Become a stewardess," says Sally, on her way back from the shower. "You'll have men all over you."

"You're just lonesome," Shoshona tells Myra. "Frankly, I'd rather be by myself."

"I hate being alone," Myra answers.

"You want to be like me?" Shoshona settles her huge carryall on her shoulder. "Off to make dinner for a complaining husband and complaining kids?"

"At least you have your kids," Myra says.

"You want my kids I'll give them to you. You are better off on your head."

I'm Management

"Thanks for coming in today. I'm thrilled to see you." It's my second week at WCBC-TV News. My new boss, Tom Ahearne, puts out his four-fingered hand to shake.

"My pleasure." I smile.

There are various obscene office stories of how he lost his middle finger.

Ahearne's face is redder than usual. His gray curls look ironed. He is very hung-over.

The phone is ringing in my office cubby. It's Janice, Dick Garrin's secretary. Garrin produces The HELLO Show, seven to nine a.m. everywhere in America. HELLO is WCBC TV's cash cow and though I'm its chief publicity person, I report to Ahearne, head of WCBC TV News.

I'd like to work for Garrin. He rescued HELLO two years ago when its ratings plummeted. As *Variety* wrote, "The new boss, Dick Garrin, is a novelty in TV. He thinks many TV watchers have IQs above one hundred. Maybe that's why kings and queens and presidents are once again waking up to HELLO."

It's rumored that Garrin reads ten books a week. They're piled around the office couch he sleeps on weeknights. The fifteen-minute segments he produces on everything from hemlines and fashion to the new drugs and the new politics have won TV's most coveted awards, and its most lucrative advertisers. Sunny Matthews and McDermott Hughes, HELLO's co-anchors, are household words to millions of Americans.

Garrin's secretary is returning my call, a plea for an appointment. "How about May?" she says. "I think I could squeeze you in then."

"Give me a break, Janice. I might not be alive in May."

"Who would be," she says, "working for Ahearne?"

She offers March. I beg. She'll try for February.

I was foisted on Ahearne by Don Clyde, my old neighbor and father of Herb, my son David's best friend. Don had read my *Village Voice* stories. He offered help when he heard I was getting divorced and needed a job. I'd never done publicity, but Don saw that as an advantage. "Don't act too smart and don't discuss writing. This is public relations."

"I'll act very stupid for a paycheck," I told him.

"You can't be too stupid for Tom Ahearne. You'll earn every penny," Clyde said.

As if having to hire me weren't enough, Ahearne dislikes me because I refuse to be obsequious. We disagreed at our first interview, sitting in his cramped office, surrounded by yellowing stacks of newspaper. He offered me a choice: the Munter News Report, or HELLO. I could have either one, plus the WCBC Children's Theater, Special Reports, and general Public Relations. "For HELLO, you show up at six a.m. For Munter, you leave after eight p.m.

I chose HELLO, telling him I had to leave at four forty-five to be home for dinner with my kids.

"You leave at five," he said.

I pointed out that six a.m. to five p.m. is eleven hours.

"You leave at five," he repeated. "You're management. You don't work by the hour."

After three days, Ahearne called me into his office. "I understand you've been talking to Angie Novella. We don't discuss our salaries here."

I had told Angie that my salary was eighteen thousand dollars. That was before she told me hers was seventeen thousand dollars. After five years.

I guessed that Clyde had told Ahearne what to pay me. The men in our department were definitely making more.

"I hired you because Clyde asked me to, but I can always fire you for insubordination. So, watch it," Ahearne said

Angie's office cubby is next to mine. The only other woman in WCBC TV News, Angie is a short, sweet, thirty-year old ex-reporter, and the sole support of her parents who live in Queens. She looks like those plain Janes in the movies who, given the right chance or a little attention and a new hairdo, take off their glasses and become a star. Or marry the boss.

I am trying to bolster her self-confidence. It's another way of bolstering my own. It's easy to know what's good for someone else.

Angie's my best friend at WCBC. Actually, she's my only friend here. When she thinks I'm heading for trouble, as she does this morning, she repeats what she told me my first day of work. "One, Ahearne can fire you. Two, Ahearne favors men, so we have to work twice as hard and be twice as good as the guys here."

"Forget it," I say, offering her half of my buttered bagel. "I've heard that too often about Jews. You and I already work longer hours than any man here.And we write better. Though that's not much of a compliment. They're all lousy."

49

"It's easy for you to talk like that," Angie tells me. "You get child support."

What can I answer? I do.

Mom's Meatloaf

"Add one-third pound veal," Rebecca reads to me from the recipe. "Isn't veal from babies?"

"I'm making meatloaf for dinner. Meatloaf is from animals," I tell her.

"But babies, Mom, I don't want to eat babies."

" I'll take that part out," I assure her.

"Can you find the veal in all that?" she asks skeptically, eyeing the molded loaf.

"Of course not, I'll throw it all away," I say, nonchalantly, trying to calculate how much in dollars and cents I will be putting in the garbage.

"You could cook it, and David and I could give it to those homeless guys, you know, Captain and President. They always look hungry."

David comes to the kitchen to tell us somebody else has just been kidnapped on TV. "Like that Hearst girl."

"What about a cheese omelet?" I ask, hoping if Rebecca becomes a vegetarian, she'll be an ova-vegetarian. "Or a tuna fish casserole?"

"I thought we were having meatloaf," David says.

"Who was kidnapped?" I ask David.

"Some rich lady. They buried her for eighty-three hours."

I wait for David to ask me how she could still be alive.

He tells me how. "They had a tube in the coffin so she could breathe. Like this." He puts a straw in his mouth and lies down on the floor, half of him in the kitchen, half in the dining room. "This is creepy," he says

If we all became vegetarians, I wouldn't have to put my hand in the chicken's cavity, the one I was making for tomorrow, to clean it out. Can chickens get ovarian cysts, like the one I've had for a year. I'm waiting for it to shrink from a lemon to a blueberry.

Suppose it's malignant and big as a grapefruit. Maybe I should make a will. But I have nothing to leave. Rebecca wants my black glitter sweater. Can I make a will for that? And what could I leave David that he'd want?

Enter Rebecca, wearing her best very torn jeans and favorite very faded Indian shirt. "Do you think I could wear this to school tomorrow?"

I wish she would stay this age forever.

"Mom," David hollers from the living room, "Mom, Rebecca, come here and look at this. Nixon still has those tapes and he lied on his taxes."

"David," I holler back, "set the table."

"You have to see this first."

"I'll see it second. Set the table."

"He's going to get impeached." David comes into the kitchen for knives and forks. "Don't you think so?"

"Not for lying on his taxes," Rebecca says. "Everybody does that."

"Everybody does not lie on their taxes," I say sternly,

"Dad says it's just stretching the truth," David says. He sets the table and goes back to the news.

I need to get this straight. "Is that what your father says about Nixon, or about everybody?"

"I hate it when you and Dad fight," Rebecca says.

"We're not fighting. How can I fight with him if he's not here?"

Rebecca shrugs her shoulders.

"What does it feel like when they cut your ear off?" David asks, walking into the dining room and sitting down at the table.

"You mean like Van Gogh?" Rebecca asks.

"Who's that?"

"That artist who cut his ear off so he could give it to a friend."

"I don't think that's funny."

"I'm not trying to be funny, stupid," Rebecca is indignant. "I'm trying to be accurate."

"It's some boy whose grandfather is a millionaire. Someone kidnapped him and cut off his ear." David pauses for emphasis. "His whole ear and mailed it to a newspaper. Like a ransom note. I just saw it on TV."

"They showed his ear on TV?" Rebecca asks.

I set the tuna casserole down on the table.

"I thought we were having meatloaf. I'm not going to be a vegetarian like Rebecca. I want to be like Dad," he says. "I want to be normal."

"We're normal," I say.

"Then why are we divorced?" he asks.

LSD

A trumpet blast of *White Rabbit* from the rock band across the street shakes our apartment. The trumpet player's girlfriend lives in our building and comes to child sit. She was here a couple weeks ago. This morning, before they go off to their Dad's, Rebecca tells me how nice the trumpet player is. "He smokes pot instead of cigarettes," she says. "It's healthier."

"That's stupid, it's a drug," David hollers from his room.

"So is tobacco," Rebecca hollers back.

"Neither of them are good for you." I say.

"Especially tobacco," Rebecca insists. "Did you see that TV ad where they show what it does to your lungs? Smoking is disgusting."

"LSD makes you crazy." David joins us in the living room.

"You can take a little bit and just have visions," Rebecca says.

"Like that kid in your school who had visions and jumped off his roof?" David asks.

I look up from my paper. "What do you know about LSD?"

"I know about Aldous Huxley," Rebecca answers. "He started LSD and he wasn't crazy. He was brilliant. Even Mrs. Harris says so."

"He started it at your school?" David asks.

"He's a writer. He's dead, stupid."

"I bet he died from LSD. I'm never going to take drugs or smoke. That's a stupid way to die."

"I think Huxley died a natural death." I offer.

"What's a natural death?" David asks. "Like if Patty Hearst had died in that trunk from not breathing? Or that other guy that got kidnapped?"

"That's an unnatural death. Most people don't die in car trunks," I say. David thinks I know everything.

I Worry About the Class System

On Wednesday nights I go to the gym. Pansy comes to clean, make dinner, and child sit. Born in Jamaica, she emigrated to England with her husband ten years ago. He is still there with their two children. She came to New York last year to earn enough money to start a restaurant in London.

Rebecca worries about Pansy's children. David worries about Pansy's husband. I worry about the class system. I see it as a bucket brigade where the women at the top put their children in a bucket and hand them to the women below for caretaking while they go off to work, or maybe just to have their hair and nails done. The women below take those children out of the bucket, put their own children in, and pass it on to women below them. At night time, or once a week, everyone gets their own children back.

I don't think it's a good system for anyone, though my friend Callista says that Marxists would claim it's good for the bucket makers. She says class and color are more complicated than economics. Or buckets.

I tell her, "Nothing is more complicated than economics except being a woman and a single mother."

"Except being a black single mother," she says.

On my way to the bus, I pass President and Captain on their traffic island, handing out flyers for draft counseling. "Where did you get those?" I ask

"It's for him." President says. "He's a draft dodger."

"They'll never find me in this." Captain points to his camouflage suit.

"You don't have to worry," I say. "You're too old to be drafted."

"I'm AWOL," he answers. "Any spare change?"

I give him all my change.

At the gym, I start to change into my running clothes and call home from the phone booth in the hall.

"Mom, it says on TV that Patty Hearst girl is still in the trunk," David tells me.

"I haven't seen any TV all day."

"But how can she breathe in the trunk? Won't she die?"

"Let's talk about it when I get home."

"What if the Stabber comes before you get here?" David asks.

"There is no Stabber," I say firmly from the gym phone booth.

"Mom, he's not after you."

"He's not after anybody. He doesn't exist."

"I'll wait up for you," David promises. "Just in case."

Rebecca gets on to tell me that "Jay Lieberman told Mrs. Harris to drop dead and she started to cry."

"Poor Mrs. Harris. She's scared," I say.

"She's a dope," Rebecca answers. "Why would anyone be scared of Jay Lieberman? He just has a big mouth."

"I have to get off the phone," I tell her. "There's a naked lady in pink plastic curlers banging on the phone booth door. I have to hang up."

Rebecca is too upset to let it go. "You know our class. She screamed at us and the twins threw spitballs at her."

I take off my shirt, open the phone booth door and tell the lady in curlers, "My daughter has a hundred and six temperature. I'm talking to the doctor." I shut the door and turn my back.

The woman in curlers raps the glass several times with her newspaper.

"I didn't do anything," Rebecca's voice is shaky.

The lady pounds on the glass again. I open the door. "The ambulance just arrived," I say.

"I need to call my husband," she tells me. "He's having a heart attack."

"Hey, Rebecca, can we talk about this later. The lady standing outside is waiting for me to get out. She says she has to call her husband because he's having a heart attack. I just need to get a run. I'll be home early," I promise, and hang up.

"Sorry," I say to the lady in curlers. "You know how children are."

"You know how husbands are," she snorts. "He's probably dead."

The sharp, smell of chlorine, the dampness, the pock-pock of balls assail me as I enter the track, a balcony for ping-pong and running which overhangs the pool. Thirty-three circuits to a mile. One of the ping-pong players, a man in his sixties, always in tight green satin trunks, stops as I run past the table and bows. When I round the track at fifteen, he waves. "Nice form," he says.

At thirty laps, almost a mile, my mind wanders off.

"Aren't you overdoing it, a young woman like you?" he says, as I come around for, I think, the forty-ninth time. At sixty laps, he offers dinner. He has a nice place in mind.

I ignore him and mentally register my second mile. I have to keep going if I'm serious about losing ten pounds. Will smaller hips change my life?

Sixty-nine. Thirty-one to go. I'm flagging. Finish what you start, I argue. Where's your will power? This is faulty logic. If I finished everything I started, I'd still be with Martin. But maybe, seventy-three, divorcing was the finish. So, the logic is right. Or maybe this is masochism, not will power.

Why should I be thin? The Venus of Willendorf was hefty. Catherine the Great didn't worry about her weight. Of course - seventy-five - she didn't have to. An Empress can weigh what she wants. She just orders men to bed her. Relationships are not the point. Or horses, if the story is right.

Who would want to screw a horse besides a mare? History is full of people who don't know what to do with power. Catherine the Great. Richard Nixon. Eighty. I'm in overdrive. If I can make three miles on this track, I can do anything.

Your Mouth is Too Big, Big, Big, Big

"Guess what! That girl Patty was just arrested for armed robbery." David greets me as I walk in the door. "Didn't they do that before?"

"They indicted her," Rebecca says. "They can't arrest her. They don't know where she is."

"I'm going to ask Dad. Lawyers know that stuff."

"I'm going to have a glass of wine," I say.

"Why?" David asks. "You never drink."

"I'm not drinking, I'm having a glass of wine."

"Isn't that drinking?" he says.

"I'm just trying to relax before dinner. I've had a bad day. I'm not planning to become an alcoholic."

"Susie's mother drinks all the time," Rebecca says.

"Dad does, too," David says.

"He just drinks at dinner," Rebecca insists.

"And after."

"Hey, would you two cut it out! I'm just having a glass of wine. And I want to talk to you about this summer." I tell them the "Y" Day camp starts in June and goes through July.

"Yuck," David says.

"Double yuck," Rebecca offers.

Maybe I'll start drinking after dinner, too. I wonder what Patty Hearst's parents are drinking right now.

"Why can't we go to camp in Maine? Like that camp Herb goes to," David asks

"Jay Lieberman goes there, too," Rebecca says.

"It's too expensive. And I don't want to send you away for the whole summer. Let's make the broccoli. I'm starving."

"Dad could pay for it."

"I don't think so."

"I'll ask him when I ask about Patty Hearst."

"Please, David, don't ask your father to pay for camp."

"Why not?"

"You know, it's about the divorce," Rebecca says.

"It's not for Mom, it's for us."

"I hate arguments," Rebecca says

"So, let's not argue," I say. "How was school?"

"Mrs. Harris says not eating meat helps save the planet."

"Teacher's pet. All wet. I don't want vegetables for dinner," David announces as I start steaming broccoli. "I'm getting sick of them. I think Rebecca should be a vegetarian by herself. Or she could go live with Mrs. Harris."

I give him a piece of cold cooked chicken.

"Can I have two?"

"Your muscles are going to be too big," Rebecca says. "You'll have big, big, big big shoulders and big, big, big, big arms and then you'll be all scrunched in at the hips and you'll just look stupid."

"Nobody's going to marry you," David says. "Your mouth is too big, big, big, big."

"He's disgusting. You and Dad should have got divorced before he was born."

"You're disgusting. I hate you. I'm going to tell Dad you said that. I'm leaving the table." David stands up. He's flushed and near tears.

"Stop it, stop it, stop it," I yell. "That's enough." I am just about to say, "I've had a really tough day at work, and I can't stand coming home to this," when I think how much it sounds like a cartoon of marriage. Should I tell them to go to their rooms?

"I've had a really tough day and I can't stand coming home to this," I say. "Go to your rooms. Go on, go."

They look at me, astonished. David sits down on the edge of his chair. "We haven't had dinner."

"I think we should apologize," Rebecca suggests.

"You have to take back what you said about them getting divorced before I was born," David says angrily.

"You have to take back what you said about no one ever marrying me," Rebecca says.

They apologize to each other. They apologize to me. We have cold chicken and broccoli for dinner.

Peacock Blue

"That dress would look good on you. It matches your eyes," Sunny says, when I accidentally sit on it in her HELLO office. I'm there to talk about publicity, and maybe a trip to California. As co-host of HELLO, Sunny may be the best-known woman in America. She has a reputation for arrogance and a contract which guarantees her the highest salary of any woman on TV. Brains and looks got her there. The network plays up her looks. She gets a new on-air honey-colored hairdo every day, along with a new designer outfit. She looks good on camera, but airbrushed. I like the real lines around her eyes.

"What a klutz," I say. "Sorry." I pull the dress out from under me and hold it up. Maybe I could wear it to Callista's party. "Anything would look better on me than what I've got," I say, looking down at my green turtleneck sweater and brown skirt. "I'm still wearing my clothes from graduate school."

"You went to graduate school!" Sunny says admiringly. "Why are you doing publicity for WCBC?"

"I'm grateful to have a job. What's my degree good for? You think WCBC TV would like a sitcom on Beowulf ?A monster series?"

She likes the joke. When I met her, she had just interviewed Kissinger, snagging his first TV comment on the Vietnam Peace Accords. A real coup for HELLO and WCBC. It would definitely make the front page of *The New York Times*, above the fold. I told her the interview was great. She'd said, "You're the new person doing our publicity? How did I look this morning? What did you think of my hairdo?"

"Your questions were very sharp. You never let him past you," I tell her.

"But what about my hair? My dress?"

I swallowed. She looked like a Barbie Doll. "I think the ponytail is too cute."

"And?" she said.

"And the skirt is a little...uh...short. Could we talk about this in your office?"

"I want these clowns to hear it." She pointed to her staff. The show had just gone off the air and everyone was still on the set, standing around, holding their collective breath.

I let mine go. "If your questions weren't so good, it might have undercut you."

"You see!" She jumped on it. "I told you," she said to the assembled crew. Later, I heard, she raised hell with the wardrobe department, the make-up guy, and the hairstylist. She was always nice to me.

Now she's saying, "You really ought to talk to Garrin about writing for me. I'll back you up. And take the dress if you could use it. It's one of my designer freebies. And the skirt's too short for the ladylike on-air me."

Rebecca and David both think the dress looks great for Callista's party. I'm thinking of having Ceil, from the gym, do my makeup. Ceil does make up for TV sitcoms, Broadway choruses, Off-Broadway shows. She claims henna is what got Cleopatra Antony. Since I'm self-conscious about my weight and dowdiness next to Callista, makeup could be literally a blessing in disguise. I'm already feeling naked at the thought of appearing my usual self in borrowed finery.

Probably Not

I hate this. The whole routine. Sitting in Doctor West's crowded waiting room, trying to figure out which of the other people waiting here might have what kind of cancer. I hate taking off my clothes, putting on those awful paper tunics, lying with my feet in the stirrups, trying not to contract my vagina when Dr. West puts that metal thing in. At least when he comes in the room, he doesn't ask me how I'm feeling.

"It's bigger than a lemon," he says. "We can wait a couple months but we'll have to take it out."

That's the diagnosis I've been dreading for a year now. I can't tell if I feel nothing, or if I'm terrified. Can you be both? Why is it bigger than a lemon? Why not a lime? Why not a kumquat?

I ask him what that means, bigger than a lemon?

"What it means?" he answers, emphasizing the word "means." He says he can't tell if it's malignant till he takes it out and biopsies it.

"And then what?" I ask. I can't say the word "cancer."

"Do you want to have more children?" he asks.

"God, no," I say.

"Then you probably don't have to worry."

I persist. "Don't have to worry about what?"

"If we get it all out, and it's not malignant, you're probably Ok."

I have to ask, "So I won't die?"

He hesitates. "Well you know I can't promise, but probably not. We just have to watch it."

I have a lot more questions. I ask him how I can watch something that's in my uterus? And what's with the fruit analogy? Because Eve ate fruit? Why not a vegetable? A Brussel sprout? And what if it's probably something, instead of probably nothing?

"It's probably nothing," he says. "It's not a Brussel sprout."

Callista Throws a Party

"Hi, Morty." I 'm waving to Morty Oxford, the once fat comedian who's been dieting since I last saw him at Callista's. He walks right past me. I'm just another white face.

Callista is celebrating. A black woman lawyer in a first ever all black series. A first black woman star on TV. It's definitely worth a big party.

The Ritz Ballroom is dense with sequins and feathers. I put on a happy face. Who's going to notice me, circling the perimeter, an extra in an opera crowd, expecting the tuxedoed waves to part, and my prince to surface on a pedestal. Maybe singing.

There must be a better way to meet men. Sally Sanders, the airline hostess at the gym, says her job is ideal for that. No worry about what to wear or how to start a conversation.

"Frozen out?"

I turn around to see a handsome black man in a white suit He has short curly hair and a confident smile.

"Are you laughing at me?" I ask.

"Now don't be defensive. I'm laughing at Morty on his thin high horse."

"Maybe he doesn't recognize me since he's lost so much weight. Do you think Morty goes to Weight Watchers?" I ask.

"I'm sure Morty's got his own personal weight watcher and she's white and blonde."

"That sounds blondist to me. Not to mention racist and sexist."

"Morty?" he asks.

"You."

"I don't recognize you, either, but you sure don't have trouble saying what you think." He flashes that wonderful smile again.

I put out my hand. "I'm an old neighbor of Callista's. We have long talks about class consciousness while someone is doing her make-up."

He takes my hand, turns it over, and studies my palm. "My Indian ancestors say the palm is the seat of insight."

"You're Indian?"

"An eighth. Around the nose, maybe."

I search his face for the Indian eighth while he scrutinizes my hand for insight. "The hand of the Magic Goddess. This," he puts his finger and thumb around my index finger, "is the magic mother finger. And this," taking my middle finger, "is the phallic father. The thumb is the child."

I'm relieved he moved off the phallic father. Is this bullshit? Or am I an easy mark? No man has held my hand in months. It unsettles me. His voice sounds familiar, but he's too attractive to forget. I'd remember if I'd ever met him at Callista's.

"I don't recognize you," I say, "but it's a pleasure to meet someone as pedantic as I am."

"I just use whatever comes to hand. You know how black people make do. And I've been to many of Callista's makeup sessions. That's two things we have in common. How about a drink? My name is Larry Brill."

"Larry Brill, really? The folk-singer? I love his—uh-- your records but I always thought he was big and fat."

"Really."

"I'm a fan." Am I sounding sappy? "I guess I've never seen a picture of you. That's why I thought you were older and fatter, sort of a black Burl Ives."

"Some fan," he says.

"I'm such a fan, when I got divorced, I insisted that I get all your records."

"Now that's loyalty. I owe you a drink at least." He takes my elbow and guides me through the dancers, towards the bar. "So, you didn't know what I look like. I guess I'm not a household word."

"I'm not a household word, either."

"You don't have to be. You're not in show business. Or are you? You're pretty enough," he says, getting us both wine at the bar.

"How can you tell? I could be the voice of Bambi. Or Snow White," I insist.

"You think of yourself as Snow White?"

"Doesn't every girl?"

He doesn't know what every girl thinks. But he knows the voice of Snow White. And he's been watching me standing at the door, taking in the crowd. "Show business people jump right in with their hands out and a big smile on their face."

"You don't?"

"You didn't even know what I look like," he says.

"Does that bother you?"

"I'd rather be right in the spotlight. But I've come to terms with it." He pauses. "That's a lie. I am trying to come to terms with it. Hell, maybe someday I will come to terms with it. What are you coming to terms with? Do you know where you are?"

"You're asking me two minutes after meeting me where I am? In life?"

"What else is important?" he asks.

"I was afraid that's what you meant. Well, let's see, where am I?"

"I'm waiting," he says.

"It's going to be a long wait. I'm in a wood of doubt and darkness."

"A wood of doubt and darkness. Pretty good. You make that up?"

"I like to think I would have, if Dante hadn't done it first," I say.

"You are as pedantic as I am. Let's dance." He puts our empty wine glasses on the bar. "We're made for each other."

He's got both arms around me, holding me close as he asks, "Well, Snow White, can you see me in your future? Do you think it's possible?"

I feel giddy. I close my eyes and think of Emma Bovary when she's Jennifer Jones in the movie, waltzing with the Count. A bad comparison. He jilts her. She kills herself. The music gets wilder.

"Everything is possible. It's a free country, isn't it?"

Larry loosens his arms, pulling back enough to look at me. "Where did you get that idea?"

Later, he takes my hand as we walk across Fifty Seventh Street and warns me, "I'm not a free man."

I ask if that's a bad joke about slavery, or does it mean he's married?

Neither. It means he has two children and he's a ridiculously devoted father. Which might be a kind of slavery. His great grandmother was a slave, a kitchen slave. Upper Class.

"You made that up? Upper Class Slave?"

"I don't make anything up," he says, as we turn onto Broadway. "I go where history takes me. And biology."

I'm out of quick comebacks.

"Take biology. Darwin knew how important size is. I've always wanted to sing opera, but for opera, you've got to have a big voice. For movies, you've got to be a big black stud."

I don't point out that size killed the dinosaurs, because, actually, I'm not sure it did.

At my door, he says he's off to California next week to do a concert. Maybe we can have lunch before he leaves.

I tell myself not to hold my breath.

Rebecca and Susie Are Lost

I'm at my desk when Mrs. Harris, Rebecca's teacher, calls from New Trent, to ask why Rebecca hasn't come to school.

Don't panic, she's Ok, I tell myself, and panic immediately.

"She's at school," I say. "Her father picked her up this morning and drove her to school with Susie."

"She hasn't been in class," Mrs. Harris says.

"What about Susie?"

"She hasn't been here either."

I know Rebecca left for school today with Susie, who lives two blocks away. Susie comes over every morning at seven fifteen and follows Rebecca around while she brushes her teeth, takes a shower and gets dressed. "Does she sit there while you pee?" I once asked.

"Oh, mother," was all Rebecca said, leaving me to guess whether she thinks I'm vulgar or just hopelessly old fashioned about bathroom etiquette.

Mrs. Harris switches me to the principal's office. On hold, I picture New Trent. It's at the north end of Central Park, the one refurbished structure on a street of boarded-up apartment buildings, many filled with out-of-work men and shooting galleries. I think of the man who stopped me in the park. I think of all the lurid TV stories David reports of kidnappings, especially Patty Hearst.

Mrs. Reese, New Trent's principal, has not seen either Susie or Rebecca. She promises to check every room in the school. I call home but no one answers. I call Susie's mother, Rena, who has just got to her office. She hasn't seen Susie since she left for our apartment this morning. Now she's alarmed. She'll call home and call me back.

Rebecca is so conscientious, I can't imagine her just leaving school. What if she has come home sick and is just not answering the phone? Maybe I should go home. Maybe she's not so conscientious. Rena calls back. Susie is not at home.

I call Martin. Maybe he didn't take Rebecca to school. But he did. He dropped her and Susie at the park corner. We decide that I will go home and if Rebecca isn't there, I'll call the police. Martin will go up to the school.

I catch a taxi and try to read *The New York Times*. I read that Patty Hearst is spending her twentieth birthday in captivity. To celebrate, she broadcasts a message to her parents, "I feel pretty sure I'm going to get out of here."

"Pretty sure" sounds ominous. It's too scary to be reading this. I turn to an article about singles, "the newest lifestyle phenomenon," some forty-nine million people like me: divorced, formerly married, never married, widowed. Our biggest problem, the *Times* says, is loneliness. Maybe the *Times* doesn't know that it's second to paying the rent, finding a job, and taking care of the children.

I feel sick. I'd like to get out of this cab and take another because we're stuck in traffic at Columbus Circle. I read carefully through the Index. I look at something about Kareem Jabbar. I have no idea what I'm reading.

Martin has been to the school, but neither Rebecca nor Susie has showed up. I call the local precinct station. The police captain promises to send a detective. "It would help to have a picture of them when he gets there," the Captain says. "And a description."

There are boxes of pictures on the bookcase. I've never managed to arrange them in albums. Rebecca and me in the hospital right after she was born. Rebecca, Martin, David and me, mugging. A strip of Rebecca and Susie last year in a photo booth at their school fair. I feel a shooting pain in my stomach. I should write a description of Rebecca "last seen wearing." How can Katherine Hearst stand it? What did Susie wear?

I go into the bathroom and throw up, brush my teeth, look for an old bottle of Listerine. Rebecca is not the hooky playing type. Or is she? She always seems so reliable. I'm overdoing it. She's Ok. I know she's Ok. Would I be this worried if New Trent were anywhere but Harlem? Or New York? Are children kidnapped in Iowa? California's different. That's ridiculous. She wasn't kidnapped. She wasn't in Central Park. I have to stop this. I mustn't panic. How do parents stand it while posses search the woods with dogs?

Both detectives look much too young. They speak in low tones, to mark the seriousness of the event, but I can't talk. I can still taste the vomit in my mouth. As I hand the older looking one Rebecca and Susie's picture, I start to cry.

He's embarrassed. "How old did you say? This is just their faces."

I find a picture of Susie, Rebecca and David ice-skating in Central Park. "Mine is twelve," I say. "Blue eyes. Brown hair. Her father said she was wearing blue jeans and a green sweater with patches. He dropped them across from the school at the park."

"Her father says?" He's thinking, I'm her mother and I don't know what she's wearing? *Cherchez* the mother. Don't police always suspect the parents?

The front door guard has reported they were standing just outside of school before classes started. He didn't speak to them, though Rebecca always asks about his family. He has no idea where they went. Rena calls. I ask her what Susie was wearing. Blue jeans, heavy denim jacket.

"Well, ma'am," the policeman says, "we'll file a Missing Person Report, but you know, we don't do anything for forty-eight hours."

"Forty-eight hours!" I yell. "By then they could be dead. Or a million miles away." Don't yell at him, I tell myself. It isn't his fault.

"That's the rule, ma'am. You know in New York, it happens all the time."

"What happens all the time?"

"Kids play hooky. They run away. Parents get scared. We're just too busy to follow up every report."

"How many are still missing after forty-eight hours?"

"I really can't say, ma'am."

'It is twelve thirty when the police leave, two and a half hours since Mrs. Harris first called. I call Martin. His line is busy. I hang up, count to thirty and dial again. Still busy. I count to forty, then sixty. I am still dialing, counting, hanging up when the doorbell rings.

Rebecca is standing there, with the picture I gave the detectives. "Everybody's very mad at me," she says. "Are you mad?"

"I'm fucking furious. Where the hell have you been?"

She hands me the picture. I pull her in as though someone is waiting to grab her from me. "Where's Susie?"I ask.

"I saw the policemen outside. One of them shook his finger at me. The other one said, 'Next time, tell your mother where you're going, kid. You just scared the hell out of her.'"

"Where's Susie? Where were you?"

"Susie's at home," she says. "Right after we got out of Dad's car, Susie threw up. She threw up on her shoes and she smelled awful. I told her I'd go home with her."

"You're Florence Nightingale? But I called you at Susie's. So did your father. He went to her apartment."

"I know. Dad told me. But we didn't hear. On the way home we bought some candy bars and went into her room and put on the Rolling Stones. We turned the volume all the way up."

"You got candy? What kind of candy? I thought you said Susie was sick."

"She was. She felt better after she ate it."

"Really Rebecca. Your father and I had an absolutely horrible morning. So did Rena. I can't begin to tell you what I thought. Promise me you'll never ever do that again."

"I promise. Dad is so mad. He yelled. In fact, he screamed. When I opened Susie's door, he said, 'God dammit, I ought to beat the shit out of you.' He never talks like that."

I hug her as hard as I can.

"I'm sorry, mom. I feel really stupid. Can I keep the picture?"

She goes in her room, tapes her picture on the wall over the gerbil cage. I go in the living room and call Rena. I call New Trent. When I sit down and shut my eyes, I hear the man in Central Park, telling me to stop. I see Patty Hearst being thrown in a car trunk. Maybe Rebecca isn't so conscientious. I stab the man in Central Park.

Happy Valentine's Day

I attach a string to the plan of the Minotaur's Lair on Rebecca's Valentine, and write, "I'd follow you anywhere." Rebecca's class is studying Greek Mythology and she's obsessed with Ariadne's thread. Why did Ariadne give the thread to the wrong guy?Did it turn out for the best that Theseus left her, and she ended up with Dionysus, who after all was a God? Is marriage to a God a plus if he drinks as much as Dionysus?What kind of role model is Ariadne?

What kind of role model am I, for that matter? I don't want to push this on Rebecca as a myth about divorce.

For David's Valentine I paste a photo of his face on a picture of his idol, Joe Namath, and sign it, "You're my VIP."

"Dad has a girlfriend," David says at breakfast.

Rebecca gives him a dirty look.

He dirty-looks her back. "We aren't supposed to know it, but she's with him this weekend on his business trip."

"You're a jerk," Rebecca says.

"He's going to take her on our boat trip this summer unless there's still a gas shortage."

"She's not his girlfriend," Rebecca says. "He just likes her."

"She is," David says.

"She is not, and I don't want to talk about it." Rebecca bites into a chocolate heart.

"Yes, she is," David insists. "You're just jealous."

"How did the Minotaur get into the lair?" Rebecca asks.

"He sleeps with her," David says.

"Really David, you're so young, A lot of men sleep with women who aren't their girlfriends. Susie says her father sleeps with every woman he knows and none of them are his girlfriend. Susie says he doesn't even like them."

"He sleeps with them overnight?"

"Of course, stupid."

"Why would you sleep with someone you don't like? Then you have to have breakfast with them."

"Susie's father is a sexist pig. Men are pigs," Rebecca says.

"Rebecca!" I'm alarmed at this reverse misogyny.

She corrects herself. "Many men."

We discuss our plans for the day. David is going to his friend Herb's and maybe Herb's father will take them bowling. Rebecca has to buy more gerbil food and finish a book report.

After they leave, Rena, Susie's mother calls to tell me the parents at New Trent are forming an escort committee to take the children to school. There's been trouble at the subway stop. Kids with knives. She knows Martin drives Rebecca and Susie three days a week, but Rena is worried about the other two days. She can't take them to school because she has to leave for work too early. I tell her we can't put our kids in armored cars. They'll be fine on the subway.

Phantom Limb

I'm reading a HELLO show script about phantom limbs and trying to think of a lead for a release.

"Pain in the phantom limb is the scariest of all sensations. It usually starts soon after amputation, though the onset may be weeks or years later. The common sensation is that they are still part of oneself."

What I think about is divorce, how much it is like amputation, the pain, the scars, how, in fact, the sensation that something is missing and still part of you can actually start before surgery, the fact that it's never over if children are involved.

Martin said divorce was not part of his picture. He loved me. He needed me. I could tell he needed me. After seven years of marriage, he couldn't make dinner or bathe the kids. We argued about whether or not we loved each other for half a year, both of us feeling progressively worse: sad, angry, depressed. I told him I could never make him happy, but I think the real truth was that I couldn't make myself happy. I didn't know who I was. I didn't know what I wanted.

Then I had to ask myself why I married him, which I did, repeatedly, daily, astounded that I couldn't really answer. Not in a way that made sense, As the script on phantom limbs noted, "The phenomenon is clearly more complex than any of the current scientific explanations might suggest."

He was handsome. He was smart. I was ready to get married. I wanted to have children. We had a common background. We celebrated the same religious holidays. He was going to be a lawyer like my father. When I thought about it, I was appalled. Not about Martin, but about myself. How could I spend so many years going to school, getting so-called educated, and not know anything?

My lawyer thought it foolish, I thought it principled not to take alimony, just child support. He asked me what I felt guilty about. The answer was, everything. Especially the children. Rebecca was eight. David was five.

We called them into the large living room, then huddled together on the sofa, Rebecca on Martin's lap, David on mine. I looked at my old piano and wished I was Rebecca's age, sitting at the keyboard, practicing scales. Maybe we should just forget the divorce. Stay together till the children are in college. I could sleep in the maid's room. I looked at Martin, surprised at how handsome he was, a handsome stranger.

The children had known for months that something was wrong. David told Herb that his father never came home at night. Strictly speaking, that wasn't true. His father just left for the office very early and stayed very late. He was getting ahead. I was getting breakfast, dinner, baths, and bedtime stories. When they were younger, I took them to the park. When I started to write magazine pieces, I scheduled my interviews around their school hours and wrote at night when they were in bed. Martin was on the fast track while I had barely left the stable. We might still be married if Martin considered my work as important as his. But how could I blame that all on him? I went along with it. Was that Martin's fault? Clearly not. We were both stuck in the attitudes we'd been brought up to have. I hate to think how much it was like needing to be asked into the sorority, then quitting. I was warped.

"Your mother and I just can't, well, we can't," Martin said. Rebecca started to cry. She came over to my lap and David went to Martin's. It was so painful, I wanted all of us to just disappear. David didn't understand when Martin said that not much would change, he wouldn't be sleeping at home, but he'd see him every weekend. David only saw him on weekends, anyway.

I'd thought I'd feel relieved when Martin moved out, but everything pained me. I thought I'd love sleeping alone, and had trouble sleeping. On the street, I'd see couples holding hands, kissing, and I'd cry. Martin and I fought more than ever, mostly on the phone. He accused me of not moving in order to get alimony. I screamed back: rent was too high, even with alimony. The *Village Voice* paid twenty-five dollars for an article. Proofreading paid three dollars an hour. Editing paid three dollars fifty cents. But all the divorce books advised against sudden changes, especially with children. I stayed in our big apartment longer than I could afford to.

It made me angry just being there. It infuriated me when Martin came to the door to pick up the kids on Friday night. I couldn't stand the sight of him at school on parents' night, at David's first post-divorce birthday party. I'd think, God, I'm still not rid of him. It was heartbreaking to see how stilted the four of us all were together.

I moved in four months. Our new apartment was too small. When Martin came to the door, I could hear his voice in every room. I was angry at myself for ever getting married, for having understood myself so poorly.

I don't hate him anymore. I still hate myself. He's a decent man. He loves the children, he takes them every other weekend, as he said he would. He never lets them down. His checks for child support are never late. I wonder what he feels now about me.

Of course, we'll never be finished with each other. He's Rebecca and David's Dad. He'll be there at birthdays, graduations, weddings. We'll stand together outside the nursery window, looking at our newborn grandchildren. We'll have strained discussions about who has the first *Seder*, the Thursday Thanksgiving. I'm sure if I die first, he'll come to the funeral to make the kids feel good. I'm sure I won't marry again, and he will.

Blini with Caviar

It's not just David, who's obsessed with Patty Hearst's kidnapping and her kidnappers, who call themselves the Symbionese Liberation Army. At the gym, where I go to run before lunch with Larry, she has become the main topic of conversation, eclipsing the price of gas and Watergate. Everyone has a theory:

1 Patty is a cooperative victim.

2 After being locked in a closet, Patty has been brainwashed, maybe with drugs. That's why she helped the SLA hold up a bank.

3 The men in the group, especially Cinque, the black leader, have raped her repeatedly, subduing her through sexual terror.

I wonder if the man in Central Park has ever kidnapped anyone. I think Patty's a poor little rich girl who finds herself in a terrifying real-life psychodrama. I'm on her side, whatever that means. Rebecca has not yet offered an opinion. I'm curious to hear what Larry thinks.

"That Cinque, he's just a nigger gone crazy," Larry says, when I bring up the subject. We're at the Gotham, a favorite of tourists and New York show people. The walls, like those in the gym lounge, are decorated with smiling, autographed pictures of celebrities. Our waiter, in a Russian tunic and Cossack boots, is pouring us champagne, compliments of the management.

The management is Zabel Fishman, an old friend of Larry's. He arrives at our table right after the champagne, short and balding, in a Shepherd plaid suit with black shirt and white tie.

"The suit's business," Larry explains. "The rest is art."

Zabel kisses my hand and pulls up a chair. "It warms my heart, a famous *schvartze* and a nice Jewish girl. We're related. You know the blacks are The Lost Tribe of Israel."

"Lost is right," Larry says, laughing.

"She'll have the blini," Zabel tells the waiter.

I ask for a half-order. Zabel looks hurt. Larry explains that I'm worried about my figure.

"With her figure, why should she worry? Bring her the whole thing. I'll eat the rest."

"What do you think about Patty Hearst?" I ask him.

"Why should a Fishman worry about a Hearst? If she were Jewish, I'd worry."

"If she were black?" Larry asks.

"If she were black, they wouldn't kidnap her."

"It's all ridiculous," Larry says. "That girl that calls herself Mizmoon and those white lesbians, they're playing Revolution. They've never read Marx. They've never read anything. If she's not a victim, no one is."

"Some victim," Zabel interrupts. "From Auschwitz we have victims. From California we have spoiled brats. We need something to drink. How about a bottle of Muscadet? On the house."

Our food arrives with the Muscadet.

Zabel stands up and blows me a kiss. "I get the message. A nice girl," he winks at Larry. "Maybe a little radical."

"Jews are supposed to be radical," I say.

"Since when?" he says. "Jews should mind their own business." He bows and leaves the table.

"You are wound up," Larry says. "I was figuring on a romantic lunch. I'll split the blini with you. Right now, I'd much rather eat and look at you."

"You can look and still talk."

"Why ruin our lunch?" He smears the blini with sour cream and caviar, rolls it up, cuts it, gives me half. "Let's stick to food," he says. "Just like mother used to make." He pours the wine.

"Not my mother. She was a lousy cook, except for her peanut butter cookies."

"I'm a great cook. I have a couple of shows in Chicago next week. When I get back, I'm going to make dinner for you." He leans over and kisses me on the cheek.

I like it, though I feel self-conscious. Are people looking at us? It's noisy and everyone is eating or staring at people they think are stars. Some of them obviously recognize Larry. He looks terrific in gray pants and navy blazer. When I wonder out loud whether what he wears is business or art, he asks if I think he looks too white. I think he looks great. But very proper.

"I am very proper. And you? I don't see you in love beads and tie dyes."

"I'm not in California," I say, wondering how Patty Hearst dressed before the SLA forced her into khaki. I ask him what he thinks it's like to be kidnapped? Or have a child kidnapped?

Larry's face tightens. "I've had a child kidnapped," he says. "Only she was brainwashed first. A son arrested, a daughter kidnapped." He refuses to say more.

Outside the restaurant, he puts his arms around me and gives me a long hug. "I'll call you Friday night from Chicago," he says. "We'll have dinner as soon as I get back."

Spud, the Big Boss

"Hey, the Big Boss wants you in his office. Now." It's Ahearne, sticking his head around my half wall to tell me I am in trouble again for protesting my long work hours. Spud Milstein, the head of WCBC TV News and Ahearne's boss wants to see me.

"Milstein is into fame," Don Clyde warned me before my first job interview. "Everyone in Spud's family is famous. His father is a famous painter; his wife's father is a famous millionaire; his aunt is a famous dead movie star. If you understand that, you'll get along with Spud."

I got along with him. Our first meeting went this way. "I see from your resume we're both Ivy League. I'm Princeton, myself. Ever dated any Princeton guys? Clyde tells me you're a pal of Callista Dee's. Boy, is she some looker."

I agreed.

"I'm sure Clyde told you we're into celebrities."

"Oh, yes," I said.

"They make for high ratings and high ratings make for big ad budgets. That's what we like here at WCBC."

I agreed.

"Your job is to make sure we're in the news. Quoted. Front page of *The New York Times*. Above the fold."

I agreed. He hired me.

I'm sure Ahearne has told Milstein that we've argued over hours. It's bad enough I complain about eleven hours a day and argue about staying after five o'clock. When I asked for a personal day for Rebecca's school fair, Ahearne accused me of wanting special privileges.

"It's not a special privilege. Everybody's entitled to personal days. It's in the Personnel Manual."

"You haven't worked here long enough."

"I've worked here as long as Phil and he got two days."

"He needed to help his wife move."

"Why is it what's policy for men is special privilege for women?"

"That women's lib bit again! You just want an excuse to take a day off."

When I threatened to go to the City's Human Rights Commission, I got the day. But Ahearne has made it clear: this is a man's army and we are at war.

The plaque on Spud's door reads, Sterling Milstein, Vice President for News and Entertainment. Which means Public Relations and

Publicity. Spud is sitting in his big corner office with three TV sets, one on top of the other, all turned on so he can monitor our competition at any hour of the day. As soon as I walk in, he puts his boots up on his big, executive table, bare except for a silver lighter, a large silver ashtray, and a burled walnut humidor.

"Great boots," I say, hating myself for saying it.

"Two hundred bucks a foot. Ralph Lauren. I've got three pair in different colors."

"I guess they're the primary colors," I say.

He likes the joke. Asks what I think of his shirt. Yves St. Laurent. And the suit.

I think he's torn between wanting to look like an expensive Princeton graduate and looking hip. I tell him, "The shirt is gorgeous. I love those Big Andy Warhol flowers. I'd like a shirt like that myself, but I'd need a raise."

"Oh, you girls. You always want what the guys got."

"You mean a raise? Or being on top?" I ask.

"So, how's your pal Callista Dee? I hear she's opening at the Ritz next week. Throwing one tremendous party."

I tell him I hope it's tremendous because I'm going to be there. Maybe that will impress him. Tired of standing at attention, I sit down facing him.

He re-crosses his feet, blocking my view of his face. "I hear you've raised some questions about your hours."

I tell him I'm against eleven-hour days for eight-hour wages.

He tells me I'm management, not labor.

I giggle involuntarily. "Management? At eighteen thousand dollars a year?"

From behind his boots, Spud points out that I'm paid by the year, not the hour. That makes me management, a decision maker. He leans over his humidor, takes out a cigar, cuts the end off, and lights it. A puff of white smoke goes up, the kind that signals the choice of a Pope from the College of Cardinals. He swings his feet around and puts his cigar in the large silver ashtray. "You know what I think? I think you're a troublemaker. I bet you were against the Vietnam War."

The switch throws me off. "Are we talking politics?" I ask, trying to regain the advantage.

"No, we are not talking politics. We are talking labor-management. And if you want to stay part of WCBC TV management, you work when Ahearne tells you to. I hired you as a favor to Don, but I don't have to keep you if you're insubordinate."

He stands up, a signal for me to kowtow out of the office.

I stand up. "What about giving me a chance as a writer. Garrin says he'd love to have me. I'd work my ass off."

"I'm sure Garrin would love to have you. You may have noticed that we don't have many women writers around here because they always have to run home to their children. And if I hear any more about you going to the Human Rights Commission on that one, you can figure on pleading your case from the unemployment lines." He walks around the desk and opens the office door. "See you around."

A Murder

"Guess what? I just saw a murder." Rebecca is back from her errands, her arms loaded with sawdust and gerbil food.

"Rebecca, please."

"I did, Mom. On Broadway." She's patient, as though I'm the child and she must explain carefully. "You know that bank on the corner of Ninety-first and Broadway. Some guy came bursting out of there with a big bag, just like in the movies, and he ran up to Ninety-second and all these police cars drove up with sirens and lights going and four policemen jumped out and shot him dead. I saw it. I was standing right there. I saw them kill him."

I put my arms around her.

"It was scary," she says. "People on the street were screaming and running."

I put her gerbil food on the floor and sit down with her on the sofa. "It was awful," Rebecca says. "He was twitching, his legs were twitching. There was blood all over everywhere and they kept on shooting him in the face. Why do they have to shoot people in the face? Why do they need four policemen to shoot one robber? And there was a whole crowd of people across the street and they were cheering. Can you believe it, cheering! At a man getting killed."

'People aren't sane in crowds," I say. "And he did rob a bank."

"Mom," she says, "they were killing him for robbing a bank."

Why did she have to see it? Should I lock her up in the apartment? Should I lock us all up?

"I don't know, Rebecca. They're scared. They're angry. And they're trying to protect us."

" I don't want to be protected that way," she says. "Isn't that an extreme way to be protected!"

"Let's talk about it while we clean out your gerbil cage," I offer.

But Rebecca can't stop. "They could have told him to stop or put down the bag or they'd shoot. They could have shot him without killing him, couldn't they?"

"Yes, but police shoot to kill."

"But they shouldn't," she says. "That's wrong. Don't you think it's wrong?'

"Absolutely," I say. "It's absolutely wrong."

"Well, someone should do something about it," she says. " At least the gerbil is safe in her cage."

Flowers

The doorbell rings twice. By the time I get from the bedroom to the door, it rings again. I'm not expecting anyone. It's Saturday afternoon and the children are at Martin's. The downstairs buzzer didn't ring. "Ask," I always tell David.

"Who is it?"I ask.

"Apartment 10 A? I have some flowers for you."

I look through the small glass peep hole. Through the dirty glass, it looks like the man on the bus, the man who stopped me in the park. Or does it? He's wearing what appears to be a leather jacket and carrying what looks like flowers. He rings again.

"Stop ringing," I say. "Who are they from?"

"Really, ma'am, I have no idea. I just deliver."

"Leave them at the door."

"Listen, lady, this is 10 A. isn't it? I can't leave flowers at the door. I'd lose my job. You have to sign for them."

"How did you get in?" I ask, glad I have three locks.

"Hey, is this a game, lady? I'm trying to deliver some fuckin' flowers. I walked through the front door, that's how I got in. How do you get in?"

He doesn't sound like the man in the park, but I'm not sure I'd remember what the man in the park sounds like. I sit down on the floor next to the door. Who would be sending me flowers? "You can leave them with the doorman downstairs," I repeat. "He'll sign for them."

"There isn't any fuckin' doorman downstairs. Are you going to open up or what?" He bangs on the door. The metal police rod shakes on its track.

"Give me the name of the florist. Give me the phone number. I'll just call and check."

"They're not from a florist. They're from the fuckin' flower market. Listen, lady, I've had it. You don't want your fuckin' flowers, I'm takin' them back."

"Go right ahead. And tell them to get a delivery person who can get through a sentence without saying 'fuck.'"

"Fuck, fuck, fuck," he says. "You're nuts lady. Must be some fuckin' asshole sending you flowers." He bangs a couple more times on the door. The pole rattles. "Fuck, fuck, fuck," he says.

I hear the elevator door open and close. I can't see anyone through the peephole. I buzz down for Paul, but no one answers. I'm due at the gym for a class. I call Walter and ask him if he'll take me down in the elevator in fifteen minutes.

Of course, I wonder if the delivery man was the man from the park and the man on the bus and he's after me. Or if I'm just obsessing, like David about the Stabber.

Waiting

Larry doesn't call from Chicago Friday, as he said he would. Or Saturday.

Friday night, at six p.m. Rebecca and David go downstairs to wait for Martin. It's strange, watching them go off with their suitcases. For the first few months, they would tell me about Martin's new furniture, his freezer full of steaks, his two doormen, and eventually, his girlfriends. They emphasized that Daddy didn't make them go to bed early or wear sweaters. Daddy didn't make them clean up.

"Great," I'd say. "All experience is broadening."

Gradually they stopped reporting, and I wondered if I hadn't liked it better when they had. Their blanked-out weekends left large gaps in my picture of their life, as I was sure their weekdays did with Martin.

After they leave, I pay my bills, read the Friday *Times*. Larry must be in the middle of a show. Then why had he promised to call Friday?

Forget "promise." Why had he said he would call at all?

Forget Larry.

On Saturday at eight p.m., feeling fragile, I pick myself up gingerly and go to the Thalia Movie House where I sit through Buster Keaton in *The General* one and a half times. When I can't concentrate on the screen, I listen to the live music. Why should I get upset about this? I hardly know him. Men! White, black, neutral. It's pointless to get excited about them.

On Sunday at nine a.m. the phone wakes me.

"Hey, sweet lady, it's Larry Brill from the windy city."

Don't sweet lady me, I think. I say, "You're a couple days late." I'm angry at myself as soon as I say it.

"Late?"

"I thought you said you'd call on Friday."

"Baby, I have two shows every night. Just couldn't do it. C'mon now, don't get hung up on time. I'm not on Daylight Saving."

"No?"

"No," he laughs. "I'm on colored people's time."

"I guess I'm on Daylight Saving."

"C'mon now. I called, didn't I? I'm coming home this afternoon. How about dinner tonight?"

I explain that Sunday nights are always tense. The kids come home upset and I have to be here. What about next weekend? We negotiate and settle for Wednesday when I'll have Pansy to child sit.

"You come to my place," he says, "and I'll make dinner."

I decide to take a fast walk up and down Broadway, maybe call Callista later. The elevator door opens on the sharp-nosed blonde twins who live on the fourteenth floor. They're wearing the same outfit in different colors, as they have ever since I've lived here. They're always startled. "You never know who'll be getting on. The building has changed so," they whisper together.

On the ground floor, the hospital gray walls look grimier than ever. Will Rebecca and David remember the smell and color of this lobby? Does it depress them every morning when they leave for school, comparing it with the marble floors and flowers in Martin's lobby? Or do they compare it with the fancy lobby in our old nine room apartment building? Will they hate me for it?

Outside the sun is warming the windows of the transient hotel on the corner where people put their butter on the ledges in winter. Captain and President are on their traffic island bench, drinking from bottles in paper bags. Captain is wearing khaki sweat pants and several layers of black tee shirts. President's brown shoes have no laces.

"Did you hear about that soldier tried to kidnap President?" Captain asks me.

"Today?" I answer. "I haven't read the papers yet.".

President corrects him. "He didn't try to kidnap me. The one in The White House."

That night I see on TV that some soldier stole an Army helicopter and landed it on the White House Lawn. No one knows what he was after or why he did it. The rumors are he might be a Russian spy or a crazy would-be assassin. Someone who wanted to make a point, though no one knows yet what the point is.

Give Me Your Watch

"I just nearly got killed," David says, walking into the living room and dropping his jacket on the floor.

"David, please, that's a dreadful joke," I tell him.

"It's not a joke. Herb and I were playing catch near the monument and these two big black kids came up and said they wanted to play catch with us. We didn't want to, but they were really big, so Herb threw one of them the ball. Then the bigger kid said, 'Give me your watch, white boy.' 'I can't,' Herb said. 'It was a birthday present from my father.'

'So, the big kid pulls out a knife and says, 'What a coincidence. Today's my birthday.' And he points the knife at Herb.

"So, Herb gives him the watch and this kid says, 'Thanks. I'll keep the ball, too.'"

"And then the other kid says, 'How about singing, Happy Birthday, white boy?'

"You know how stubborn Herb is. He says, 'I don't know the words.'

"But the big kid says, 'What if I cut your finger off? Would that help your memory?'

"So, Herb starts to sing, 'Happy birthday to you, Happy birthday to you. Happy birthday, dear white boy.'

"And the black boy says, 'Are you some dumb motherfucker?'

"And then," David pauses dramatically, "this police car comes driving up Riverside Drive. I guess something looked fishy because they stopped and one of the cops yelled out, 'Are you kids ok?'

"And I yelled back, 'Could you wait a minute, officer. I'm lost and I need directions how to get home.' And Herb and me just walked up to the car. The kids took off and the cops drove us home."

"David, come and sit on my lap. I need to hug you.," I said.

"I'm too old for that," David answers, walking over, to sit down on my lap.

Myra Blames Nixon

Myra can't find a job and blames Nixon. It's his fault the economy is at a stalemate. Everyone's worried about gas rationing and electricity bills. Thousands have been laid off. Who needs a dance teacher? The panic is with her all the time. Then, through a friend of a friend, she gets an interview at a girl's school in Westchester and reports the details to us later.

It's lovely weather, she's feeling hopeful as she sets out in her rented Datsun. On the way, she stops for gas. Shoshona had told her to wear a dress, but of the three she owns, a sari, a slinky shift, a granny dress, none seemed appropriate. She's wearing jeans, a handmade belt with a silver buckle, and an Indian blouse. She looks groovy. That's what the guy filling up at the next gas pump tells her. He invites her up the road for a picnic.

Myra likes his beard, his mustache, the silver tips on his black boots, but there's not much time before her interview. Why not picnic right there? She gets in his car and they drive to the nearest Hot Shoppe for two burgers with everything and two enormous chocolate sundaes. After a dynamite joint, they dance by the side of the road to his portable radio. When Myra gets to the school, she's half an hour late and an hour and a half high.

The school is picture-postcard ivy-covered buildings, well-kept grass, girls of all sizes in blue jumpers. The uniforms make her uneasy.

Myra's sure that Mrs. Muller, head of the school's dance department, never danced in her life. Not with that pincushion hairdo, a big bun stuck with tortoise shell combs. Not in that white, high necked blouse with the little gold circle pin, the straight blue skirt, the low blue pumps. So prissy. She's surprised that Muller wears pink nail polish and smokes, holding her cigarette between her thumb and forefinger.

Myra sits down and shifts around in her chair. Maybe she shouldn't have worn blue jeans. She closes her eyes. It was so nice outside, dancing with that guy.

"Is something wrong?"

"Oh, no." Myra opens her eyes and sees Muller blowing smoke all over the place. Sit up straight, she tells herself. You're acting stoned. "Everything is groovy," she says.

Muller frowns. "We are very careful about language at Westchester Prep."

"Oh, me, too. Absolutely careful. I'm very careful about language. I mean, isn't dance the body's language?" Myra hopes she sounds serious. With a high crowned hat on her pincushion head, Muller would look like a pilgrim. "Are you from an old Mayflower family?" she asks.

Muller squashes her cigarette in a little ashtray full of broken stubs. "My background is not the point here."

"You're absolutely right." Myra sits up straighter.

"I'd like to know why you think you'd be suitable for this job. At Westchester Prep, we believe dance is discipline."

The job. Myra tries to line up her thoughts. "I'm a very disciplined teacher," she says. "I believe dance is grounded in the physical. And discipline. For trying to express various emotions, there's your body." She gives Muller a big smile. "There's your body right in front of you. Take my right arm, for instance." She extends her arm. "Now, what do I want that arm to do, and how does that affect the rest of me?" Has she said enough about discipline?

Mrs. Muller stands up. "I doubt you'd fit in with our philosophy."

Myra is indignant. "You can't tell how someone teaches from a conversation. I mean, I'm quite good in the classroom. I'm very," Myra hesitates, "I'm very focused and disciplined." There, that was a good thing to say. "It's hard to demonstrate in these clothes. Maybe I could just rest up? I'm pretty foggy from the driving."

"Foggy? I'd say you're drunk, Miss Berman. I don't believe your background is what we're looking for."

"Drunk? I am not drunk." The old bag! Who does she think she is, Miss Mayflower Pilgrim! "I have a great background," Myra says.

"Your recommendations looked impressive, but I'm afraid with your character, teaching here is out of the question. We expect our teachers to look and act like ladies."

"I am a lady," Myra says, standing up too fast. She feels dizzy and sits down. "What makes you think I'm not a lady?"

"Putting down my character, would you believe it," Myra says the next day to Shoshona.

"I don't get you, Myra," Shoshona says. "That was so self-destructive. I can understand why you don't want to teach in a school like that. So, don't apply for the job. Don't go for the interview. But if you're going to go, don't stop and smoke pot on the way. Don't go dancing by the road with Mr. Silver Tip."

"That was the only fun I had all day."

"I thought you were looking for a job," Shoshona points out.

"I am," Myra insists.

"Well how come you're not old enough to know jobs aren't the same thing as fun?" Shoshona scolds.

"Ok, Ok, you're right. Next time, I won't get stoned. I'll wear a dress."

"That could be progress," Shoshona says

Myra tells us she gets seventy-two dollars a week from unemployment. Her rent is one hundred sixty-five dollars a month for three rooms in a rent-controlled building. That leaves sixty-four dollars a month for food, dope, movies, gym and emergencies. She eats fruit and peanut butter sandwiches. The peanut butter makes her gain weight. The fruit gives her diarrhea, so she switches to yogurt and vegetables. Once a week she eats dinner at Shoshona's. Shoshona has not yet acted on her plan to change her life, move out of her apartment, and go to college. She is still belly dancing at night and bellyaching at home, as she puts it.

Myra's fine, translucent skin has been looking white and pallid. Once a week I bring her Pansy's fried chicken or a tuna fish casserole. Ceil gives her free makeup. Sally brings packets of airline coffee, tea and sugar, packaged rolls. "The food is too awful to steal," she says. Genevieve comes to the gym with a shopping bag of smoked oysters, English biscuits, and a stack of tights and leotards she claims clash with her complexion. " Help me out," she begs Myra. "They're unreturnable."

At first Myra declines.

"Don't be a dope," Shoshona says. "She's being nice to you. What's wrong with smoked oysters?"

"I'm not a private charity," Myra says.

"You're on unemployment, aren't you?" Shoshona asks.

"That's not charity. This is America. You're supposed to be entitled if you've worked," Myra answers.

"I wish they had it for homemakers. I'd have quit already."

"They have it for homemakers. It's called alimony," Myra says.

Shoshona points out that alimony is private. Like the smoked oysters and English biscuits. "If you don't like that stuff, I'll be glad to relieve you of it. Bring it when you come to dinner."

"How can I take anything from that uptight, square, capitalist snob? Bitching about blacks and welfare on her way to the analyst. Her husband makes his millions on the sweat of the South American poor so she can sit around all day on her perfect ass. And I should sit in her leotards?"

"You're receiving welfare in the name of the poor," Shoshona lectures. "Myra Berman, you are inheriting the earth."

"Some inheritance!" Myra says. "Leopard print leotards!"

Myra and Shoshona have what they call a service and commodity exchange. After her weekly dinner, when Shoshona's family is in the living room watching TV, Myra brings out a joint. Shoshona cleans up the kitchen, and Myra does Shoshona's ironing. At first Myra refuses to iron anything that doesn't belong personally to Shoshona. "How can you let them get away with it?" Myra asks. "You're always lecturing me about being self-destructive."

"If I send out the ironing, I pay for it," Shoshona says.

"Ever hear of wash and wear?" Myra says.

"Yeah. I wash and they wear."

"Very funny." Myra tries to joke.

"I'm not trying to be funny. I'm trying to be realistic."

Myra says she can't make it on seventy-five dollars a week unless she stops smoking dope, her only real pleasure, aside from movies and Yoga. Thank God she paid her gym membership in advance when she was employed. In April, just as her unemployment is running out, and she wonders how she'd be at porn flicks, she gets a call to come for an interview at a boarding school in Connecticut. "I'm going to get this job," she tells us. She buys a pink print dress at a secondhand store on Madison Avenue. I tell her it looks great with her hair and probably belonged to Jackie Onassis.

Shoshona tells her, "Don't wear your Dr. Scholl clogs, don't get stoned, and try to keep your mouth shut."

The department head who meets her train is a great improvement on Muller. He drives her through exquisite countryside and the iron gates of a school that looks a lot like Westchester Prep. The school has just gone coed, and she's the most interesting candidate he's seen, he tells her, looking at her breasts.

At the faculty living quarters, he suggests she change to her leotard and do a couple steps. Myra doesn't mind screwing him, but the room is too small to dance in. "Tell me first," she says, "do I get the job?"

It's twelve thousand dollars plus room and board, a fortune for nine months, if she can last that long, she tells Shoshona and me. The students wear uniforms: ties, jackets, loafers and chino skirts or pants. "What'll I do about my spirits? What'll I do about my wardrobe? I'll be a freak."

"You are a freak," Shoshona tells her.

David Can't Sleep

David can't sleep because the boys in the park are after him. Rebecca has nightmares about people getting shot on the street and wants me to go out and march. Or write letters. Or do something. I lie awake asking myself how a mere parent can deal with all this.

If you tell your kids to stay out of the park, where can they play? If you tell them not to wear their watches, how will they know when to come home? My would-be rapist is running around outside while I stay in with a pole and three locks on my door. Richard Nixon robs the country and is still in the White House.

My college course, The History of the Novel, taught us that novels tell you how to live with right and wrong, how to navigate the moral world. This morning I feel like Oblomov, the hero of the novel, who doesn't know how to live so he never gets out of bed.

I am not prepared for this. In an Austen novel my job would be to find a husband. Then the story would be over, and my universe would be secure.

Martin calls. He's back from his trip earlier than expected and wants Rebecca and David to come over. Does this mean the new girlfriend didn't pan out?

I say fine. I tell him the kids are a little on edge. Rebecca just saw a man get killed on Broadway and David was attacked in the park. What can we do to protect them?

"What do you have in mind?" He thinks I'm blaming him.

"I'm just worried about it."

"What's 'it'?"

I'm on the witness stand. Does this remind me of my father? I try for a calm, rational answer.

"The world, the war, Patty Hearst."

"What can I do about the war. And why are you worried about Patty Hearst?"

"I'm not worried about her. But David is obsessed with all this kidnapping. It's like an epidemic."

Why go into this with Martin? I am worried about Patty Hearst. I feel sorry for her. It's not her fault her father is a millionaire.

"You're getting paranoid. Remember the Cuban Missile Crisis?"

He's referring to my leaving the city in panic while the world waited to see if THE BOMB would drop. I was pregnant with David. The papers were predicting that if a nuclear bomb landed at Fourteenth Street, and you were at Eighty-sixth, your bones would melt.

"Everyone was worried. It's not fair to call it paranoia."

"You wanted to go to Australia. You have to admit, you're inclined to over-react," Martin says.

"No one could accuse you of that," I answer. This is stupid, I think. The SLA is replaying the Sixties and Martin and I are replaying our marriage. "It's not over-reacting when a twelve-year old sees a murder on Broadway and it scares the hell out of her."

"Ok, I'll talk to her."

"And could you talk to David? Could you do something about the Stabber?"

"I thought you tried that."

I give up. What do I think I've accomplished? I remember the first time I went out with Martin. We went dancing. I wore a powder blue dress. Was there really such a color? He said it matched my eyes. I used to love him.

Black and Blue

"Is this another one of those blind dates?" Rebecca is sitting on my bed while I dress for dinner with Larry.

"He's not blind," I answer.

"Very funny. Where did you get that underwear? Could I borrow that sometime?" Rebecca asks.

"Sure," I say, "when you're sixteen. Make that eighteen. Could I have some privacy?"

"Who is he?" she wants to know.

"Who is who?"

"Mom," she says, in that don't-be-coy-with-me tone.

"You don't need to know everything I do. I'm your mother."

"That's why I need to know," she says. "Can I meet him?"

"Maybe. If I ever go out with him again."

"Why wouldn't you?"

"You can borrow this," I tell her, zipping up my pink wool above-the-knees *Courreges* knockoff.

She looks dubious. "Pink really isn't my color," she says.

Why am I wearing all this black lace underwear? I ask myself on route to Larry's on the subway, trying to block the picture of me in the lingerie with him in white boxer shorts. I'm way ahead of myself.

I'm a dinosaur. I'm remembering the first time I slept with a man, my college boyfriend. When I walked down the street with him the next day, I thought everyone could tell I wasn't a virgin anymore. I feel like a virgin now.

Larry's building is a brick box. He hugs me at the door, takes my coat, tells me how pretty I look in pink.

Like a baby, I think. Is this me blushing?

His living room is a collection of familiar objects out of context. In the entrance, a toothy cranberry thresher on the wall, like sculpture. In the living room, a hanging garden on glass shelves. His prize possession is an old brass camp bed he found on the sidewalk and covered with maroon velvet. It's beautiful, but uncomfortable. I take off my boots and sit on it cross-legged.

He puts on a record of his from *The City of Mahagonny* and hands me the cover. The liner notes describe "Brill's always rich voice, his range from delicate to electric."

"I had a small role," he says.

I'm jarred by the gap between his obvious talents and his self-deprecation. I tell him he's any maiden's dream. 'You sing, you cook, you're even a homemaker."

"Wait till you taste my *bouillabaisse*." He ties a white chef's apron around his jeans and blue denim shirt, sits me down at a blue tiled table. "We'll have time to kill a few," he says, opening a couple bottles of wine to breathe while he makes the soup base, chopping onions like a chef, peeling tomatoes, rinsing clams, deveining shrimp. I can't believe this attractive man is going to so much trouble making me dinner. Martin couldn't make tea.

Larry stirs and pours the wine. I drink. He cooks and describes his last ten years. A small name in the late fifties when folk music was the rage. He's had to change with the times.

We are on the second bottle of wine, the soup is bubbling, and I'm getting more than a buzz. I jump when Larry brings his fist down hard on the table. "I hate this life. What I want to sing is John Henry, C. C. Ryder. That's me. I can sing that other White Rabbit stuff. But what does that have to do with me?" He grins, leans over, and unexpectedly, kisses me. "I'm not 'in' anymore."

"You look pretty good to me."

"On the screen, you have to be a big black stud. I'm not perfect off screen, either. My wife left me. For playing around. She was a tight-assed, straight up, black lady lawyer. We lived in Stony Brook. Bringing home the bacon weekdays, antiquing weekends, barbecuing outdoors in the summer. How long do you think you would have lasted there?" He spoons a couple ladles of soup into big, white soup dishes. "I'm done. Black men make great chefs."

"Do you ever forget you're black?" I ask.

"How can I? Society doesn't let me forget. Being black has ruled my life. My great grandmother was a slave. When my father was seven, a white mob tried to burn down our house. I'm followed by house detectives in department stores," he answers.

How could I have asked that question? I don't know what to say. I finish my soup, wondering why I'm here.

Dessert is Russian cake with vodka, made from a recipe he got on his Russian tour. I ask about the tour, hoping it will lighten the mood.

"Being a hit in Russia was the biggest thrill of my life. The Russians treated my whole family like stars. After that, it was all downhill."

"Why exactly am I here?" I ask. "What does that have to do with you and me? Why can't we just be ourselves?"

"You mean step outside history? Make up some imaginary selves?" He sits down next to me, takes my hand and kisses it. "Should we run away together, go someplace we don't exist?" He turns my hand and kisses the palm. "Where would you like to go? Italy? France? They're not as crazy about black Americans as they used to be. I see a black cloud on your horizon. It looks like me."

I can't tell if I'm excited or just scared as he reaches for my other hand. "Wait a minute," I say, pulling back. "If it's all black with you, how do you feel about white? How do you feel about me?"

"You're asking if there's any gray?"

" If you want, call it gray."

He's cleaning up the dishes and pouring us both more wine. If this is a seduction, it's the strangest one I've ever been party to. Is what's going on with us just about color? Does it make each of us more exotic to the other?

I ask him just how militant he is.

"I don't know who I really am. Where I stand. My children are always asking me that, always pushing me to face myself. I used to think I was a real fighter. But then, for me, the fight wasn't in the streets. It was in the theater." He picks up his glass. "You're safe with me. I'm only a revolutionary in my heart.

"My children, now, that's different. They're into being militant. They like all that Black Panther shit, all that paramilitary stuff, all those guns. I'm not about to pick up a gun. And I've already been *bourgeois*. I had that feeling about you when I saw you standing on the edge of the crowd at Callista's party. I don't fit anywhere. You certainly didn't belong in that ballroom. We're on the outer edge in this society. I'm not into shooting guns, I'm not into shooting heroin."

"I thought I looked pretty good in that ballroom. You came on to me just because I looked out of place?" I ask him.

"You looked too good," he says. Holding a finger to his lips, he gets a pen and writes on a paper napkin, "This place is bugged."

I wonder for a moment if he's crazy. Then I think it could be bugged.

He pours another drink. "I wanted to save my kids from all that tough black talk, raise them differently. But where could I go? What about you? I've been talking about myself all night. You should have stopped me."

"What about me? You don't know anything about me. You're so into yourself. I'd say you were unstoppable." I look at my watch. "It's awfully late. I ought to be going."

"We'll make the next time about you. I won't say a word about myself."

I laugh despite my qualms. "I really need to know who you are when you're not being black. I have to go," I say.

"Where are you going? My cooking is just the beginning."

"Of what?" I ask, knowing the end, as he pulls me to my feet, puts his arms around me, kisses my eyes, my ears, my neck, unbuttons the top button of my dress. It's been so long since anyone touched me, it feels wonderful.

"So, was he dumb and blind?" Rebecca asks me the next day.

"No, he was black and blue."

"You mean like the song?"

"How do you know that song?"

"Mom, you have the record," she says. "You play it all the time."

Pregnant in Jail

"How could she not know she was pregnant? When did you know you were? How could they put a pregnant woman in jail?" Rebecca asks as soon as she and David walk in the door on Sunday night. At first, I think she means Martin's girl-friend, but the jail bit throws me off, and then I am temporarily distracted by their haircuts. Rebecca's once long ponytail is now in short curls around her ears and there are small emerald-like studs in her earlobes. David has one of those preppy dos with bangs. He looks like Prince Valiant in my childhood comics.

"Dad took me to J Press for a suit and some guy wrote all over me with chalk and then she got a dress and we both got haircuts."

"And I got pierced ears," Rebecca says. "Dad said he was sure it would be Ok with you." From there she launches right into Roxanne Alard of the Black Liberation Army, accused of killing a policeman in the East Village last fall and now in jail, pregnant.

Sunny Matthews had interviewed Alard on Friday after Alard's lawyer announced that the prisoner was expecting a baby. The lawyer wanted Roxanne moved and a delay in the trial. It was all over the Sunday TV News.

I decide not to react to the haircuts. "Maybe the police didn't know Alard was pregnant when she was arrested. Maybe she didn't know."

"How could you not know? How long did it take you to find out?" Rebecca asks.

"Maybe a month," I say. "Maybe two. But then I wasn't distracted by being in jail."

"What does it feel like?" Rebecca puts her hand tentatively on my stomach to see if she can read its past like braille.

"You mean physically?" I ask. I've decided I don't like the haircuts but I'm not saying anything.

"Yes. Were you sick? How fat did you get? How did you feel about me?" Rebecca asks.

"One question at a time, please," I say. "I was excited." I don't tell Rebecca I was depressed to be pregnant and worried about my marriage.

"But how did you feel about me?" she insists.

"And me?" David says.

"I didn't know it was you, either of you, of course, but I felt good. I felt I had two hearts, yours and mine."

"Wow, that's four hearts," David says.

"I like that," Rebeca says. "That's how I want to feel."

I think about Rebecca's having babies. I can't imagine it.

"How did Dad feel?" David asks.

"Men don't feel anything," Rebecca says. "They just give out cigars after the baby and then they go back to work."

"Your dad was very excited," I tell them.

"See, I told you. Who's stupid now?" David gives her the finger and we have a few words on that subject. "Both of you get ready for bed," I say. "We'll talk about babies tomorrow and I don't want any smartass sign language from you, David."

He mutters something I'm sure I don't want to hear as he goes into his room, slamming the door after him.

"But physically, how did you feel? Were you sick?" Rebecca asks.

"I wanted to lie down all the time," I tell her. "Which is just how I feel right now." I lie down on the living room sofa. "Please, get ready for bed."

"Exactly." Rebecca pounces on it. "That's the problem. Where do you lie down in prison?" She sits down on the sofa and starts taking off her shoes and socks. "Where do you think that woman lies down?"

"Rebecca," I say. "What about taking off your coat.

"No fair," yells David. "She's not getting ready."

"She lies down in her cell," I say. "Where else can she lie down?"

"Yuck. It must be so ugly. Do they clean it?" Rebecca asks.

"Don't be silly," David comes out of his room in his pajamas. "Jail isn't supposed to be happy. It's not supposed to be like a hotel. And I just looked in the mirror. I think my hair is too short."

"I'm not talking about being happy. I'm talking about being clean," Rebecca points out. "Not about having chocolates on your pillow."

"What do you know about chocolates on pillows?" I ask her.

"I hope I never go to jail," David says, on the way to the bathroom with his toothbrush. "Speaking of chocolates, could I have a snack first?"

"Well just don't shoot any policemen," Rebecca warns.

"Dad always gets chocolates in hotels."

"You can go to jail for lots of things, it doesn't have to be for policemen," David says.

"And don't get poor," Rebecca adds. "Nixon's not in jail."

"He's the president," David says. " How many presidents do you know in jail? Dad says if he were Nixon's lawyer, he'd make him resign so he couldn't get impeached."

"He should go to jail," Rebecca says. "They should take that woman out and put Nixon in."

"You think she should just be allowed to shoot people?" David asks.

"What do you think?" Rebecca asks me.

"They should move her, and you should get undressed."

"Those policemen I saw kill that bank robber, are they in jail?"

"There has to be a hearing first. You can't just send people to jail," I say.

"Then what?" David says.

"A trial, I guess. Rebecca, go brush your teeth."

She goes to brush her teeth and comes back. "I think you should write a letter about it," she says.

"Why me?" I want to know. "Do I have to defend the rights of all the accused?"

"Mom, don't you care?"

"Of course, I care, Rebecca. I just don't know what to do about it. Poverty. Injustice. Pregnant women in jail. Everything. I'm just your mother. I've had it. I'm going to bed," I say. "You two can stay up all night and discuss the Fourteenth Amendment."

I start for my room, but Rebecca won't let me off the hook. "Well, who should do something about all that? Isn't this a democracy?" she asks.

Ceil on a Diet

"Go home and take care of your children." That's what the men in the Baltimore bakeries used to say to my Polish grandmother, when she picketed them for not paying decent wages. I think her genes passed through me to Rebecca. My mother was a reverse role model for me. I didn't want to be like her, staying home with the children. Maybe I didn't want to be married like her, since I was told throughout my childhood by relatives who thought I ought to know that my mother often contemplated divorcing my father. Did I act out her frustrations? Does it make any difference? Am I likely to be as unthinking about men – or about myself – as I was with Martin? Like the story the psychiatrist tells, you're afraid of wolves and you go to the forest and yell "Wolf" and the very wolf you're afraid of appears.

"Wolf," I yell, like throwing salt over my shoulder. "Wolf," as I start around the gym track. What kind of role model am I for a daughter who wants me to do something about four policemen killing a black man? What does my life say to David? A boy has got to be upset by a mother who rejects his father. What kind of woman will he marry?

I've always taken them to vote, I answer myself. Isn't that good? I always took Rebecca on marches protesting the war. I've taught them to be against nuclear power and for civil rights and regaled them with stories of my father's involvement with New Deal legislation. I take them to ballet, as my mother took me. I once took them to see Margot Fonteyn and Nureyev in *Romeo and Juliet*. Martin was working. Rebecca loved Fonteyn and David was thrilled by the curtain going back and forth by itself. He was only three. "Wolf," I yell. "I'm doing the best I can."

The sound of a flute drifts up from the pool below. A woman in a gray sweat suit joins me. "Ceil," I pant, "is this really you?"

"Huh, huh, huh," she answers, waving a stop watch. "Later."

What is Ceil doing here? She's made such a point of not exercising, telling her plump self in the mirror, "Barry likes you fat."

Barry, her husband, exercises. But only at home, Ceil says. The minute they get back to Rye, he jumps into their pool and does thirty laps. Then twenty pushups. Every day, she says. I've seen Barry in the lounge waiting for Ceil. With his trim figure, his thick black hair and handlebar mustache, he looks as elegant in jeans and flowered shirts as if he were strolling down a European boulevard, coat jacket over his shoulders. Barry wants Ceil to stay just as she is. When she asks him if he thinks there's a little too much of her, he tells her if he liked skinny, he would have married Twiggy. So why is she jogging now?

When I finish my laps and go back to the locker room, Ceil is toweling off, looking triumphantly at the scale. "I did it, I did it," she hollers. "Five pounds down. Twenty more to go."

It has nothing to do with Barry, she explains, sitting at the counter, spooning diet cottage cheese from a container. It's her ex-husband Charlie and Bettina, his new wife.

"You're losing weight for your ex-husband?" Shoshona asks.

"It's like this," Ceil says. Linda, her daughter with Charlie, is getting married in three months. At Charlie's country club. Charlie called Ceil last week to ask what color she's wearing. Bettina, his wife, needs to know so they won't go clashing down the aisle. Bettina's got to wear something very subtle because she's so diminutive. Size four. "Diminutive," Ceil snorts. "What he was really saying is she's going to make me look like a pig." The minute she hung up, Ceil knew she had to go on a diet.

Barry thinks she's crazy. Let Charlie sleep with a bag of bones. But she has to lose it. She's not going to let that *meiskeit* show her up in public. Barry will love her, whatever she weighs. And after the wedding, she'll gain it all back.

Sally has convinced Ceil to join Weight Watchers. Sally is size four. She has to stay that way in her stewardess's job. She's told us how she weighs everything mentally so she can eat a bit of almost everything.

Sally suggested Ceil go out and buy a sexy dress three sizes too small. And she did. Saturday, Ceil went to the same Madison Avenue store that Jackie Onassis shopped at and bought an exquisite gown. Ceil wraps herself in a towel and disappears into the locker room, returning with a heavy plastic garment bag. Sally told her to hang it in the front of her closet and look at the dress every day. Ceil unzips the bag and pulls out a jade green silk dress with heavily pearled shoulders. "Barry says I'm going to look like a Botticelli with clothes." She takes the dress back to the locker and goes for her second exercise class.

We wonder if she'll make it. Quietly, we take bets.

Most People Don't Get Kidnapped

"The SLA did it just to get attention," Rebecca says.

"I thought they did it to get her father's money," David answers.

"They wanted her father's money to feed poor people. First, they had to get everyone's attention. Most people don't get kidnapped."

"What if they want to feed everyone in New York?" David asks.

"People just get murdered in New York," Rebecca says.

"You said he was holding up a bank and the police shot him."

"That's murder," she tells him.

"What's the difference? Weren't the police right? Some policemen are Ok. What about the ones that saved me in the park?"

"You're a bleeding-heart liberal,' Rebecca says. "You're a knee jerk reactor."

"That's what you are. I hate you," David says. "I hate you, I hate you, I hate you." He goes into his room and slams the door. A minute later he comes out. "Why should I go in my room because you're ignorant about policemen?"

Whoever heard of normal children arguing about policemen? Maybe I should move us upstate and they could grow up ordinary. Maybe Martin and I should have waited. Now their world is divided into two apartments, and they live part-time in each, discovering that parents have genitals and dates, lovers, other lives. We all find out eventually. Divorce speeds up the process.

Bags, Baguettes, Bagatelles

Shoshona is telling Myra and me how she invented her new art medium, Bags. She was about to throw away some old garment bags, the heavy nylon kind, with a zipper from bottom left to top right. She looks at one and sees a Picasso face. She looks at it again and imagines the Grand Canyon, with layers of earth and time on either side. She takes the bag into the kitchen and puts it on the table.

She doesn't have oils, they're too expensive, so she tries acrylic.

Maybe a Byzantine-like portrait. She first paints gold mixed with red on one side of the bag, red and silver on the other. Then looking in the bathroom mirror, she does a fast sketch of her face and pastes it on the bottom left corner of the bag.

She paints it blue. It's Eve. She adds a large tree with several apples on it. Now she needs snakes. She takes the ties from her sneakers and dips them in the red and gold on her palette, winds them through the tree.

In a box of old snapshots, she finds photos of herself, Harry and the children at the beach, crawling on the sand, making a castle. She cuts out the figures and pastes them on the other side of the zipper. Then she colors the figures, and paints in the background like a Byzantine painting. Of course. It's Eve, Before and After. There she is at left, in Paradise, unknowingly about to seal her fate.

What should she call it? Some kind of bag. She takes the dictionary from its living room stand and looks up "Bags." "Baggage." "Baguette." "Bagatelle." The first definition of Bagatelle is "little property." That's it. And she likes the sound of it. "Bagatelle."

When she shows slides of it to Myra and me, Myra asks what it's about. Shoshona says it was cruel of God to make Eve leave the garden. Giving birth in pain is more than punishment enough. Once you have children, you're out of Eden. Maybe that's the meaning of the myth. If Adam and Eve had separate beds, they might still be there among the trees, running naked, eating fruit.

She's so pleased with this bag, she's going to paint the Grand Canyon. And she knows just how she's going to start it.

Rebecca Goes on a Double Date

"I can't go to Dad's this weekend. I have a date," Rebecca announces at dinner.

"Great," David says. "Then Dad and I can go bowling."

"A date?" I ask.

"I have a double date."

"You're going out with two boys?" David asks.

"Susie and I with Harris and Geoffrey. We're going bowling."

"Really," I say, "since when?"

"I guess I forgot to tell you," she says breezily.

"You hate bowling," David says. "And you can't bowl."

"Didn't I tell you?" she says to me. "I meant to ask you. I'm sure I asked you."

I'm calm. "No, you didn't ask me. And I have to discuss it with your father."

"I'm getting sick of this divorce," David says.

"What does the divorce have to do with my date?" Rebecca asks.

"It has to do with everything," David says. "Aren't they twins? You'll probably get them confused."

"You say the dumbest things."

"Well, nobody can tell them apart."

"I can't wait till you grow up," Rebecca says.

"I can't wait till you grow up," he answers.

"Over my dead body," Martin says, when I call him.

"It's a double date," I say. "With Susie and the Berger twins. They're going bowling."

"Bowling?" he says. "She hates bowling. And she can't bowl."

"I guess she plans to learn," I say.

"That's just what I said." David has been listening in on his phone. "This is the stupidest conversation I've ever heard of."

Martin and David reported to me later. Martin didn't want to leave David home alone, so he and David walked Rebecca and Susie to Who's Bowling. Rebecca wore torn blue jeans and a sweater. Martin didn't remember what Susie wore but Harris and Geoffrey, dressed in identical khaki pants, blue striped shirts, and blue blazers, were waiting outside. Martin claimed he couldn't tell them apart, but Susie and Rebecca seemed to.

As they had agreed, after bowling, the four of them went to Artie's Pizza, which was next door to the bowling alley and had pizza and cokes.

Jerry, Susie's father, picked up Susie and Rebecca and walked them to his apartment where Susie was spending the weekend.

Martin and David went to see a movie called *Whelk Two*.

Martin said it was marginally better than *Whelk One*. David said *Whelk One* was better. After the movie Martin and David had hamburgers, cokes, and chocolate chip cookies, then took a cab to Susie's Dad's apartment, where they picked up Rebecca and went home to Martin's.

David reported that he thought dates were stupid and that Susie's Dad's apartment was a lot nicer than Susie's mother's place.

"Who would go on a date with you?" Rebecca says.

"How was it?" I ask.

"The pizza was great," she says. "Susie acted really stupid. She was just flirting like crazy and she kept taking Geoffrey's hand. He was supposed to be my date. Sometimes she took Harris's hand. She's never going to be my friend again."

"What do you think about dates?" I asked.

"I'm never going on a double one again."

Which is just what Susie told her mother, when I asked Rena what Susie thought about it.

What I worry about is the day Rebecca will be going on single dates.

Shoshona Is Going Back to School

Shoshona sees it on the gym Bulletin Board. Sarah Lawrence is offering two-year Fellowships to women who want to go back to school in the Arts and Sciences. The program offers free student housing and meals, or a stipend for rent and meals, a studio, and a Master Degree. Master's graduates must teach for at least two years in New York City Public Schools or in City or State Colleges.

That settles it for Shoshana She's going. She's also thinking of leaving her husband. "I can't decide which to do first," she tells Myra, me, and Sally. "If I leave, I have to find a room I can afford."

Myra has a better idea. Why not throw Harry out? Why should Shoshona leave?

"Because I'm thinking of leaving the children with him. If Harry leaves, I'll be stuck with them."

Here she is, the least educated member of her family, and she comes up with a third of the family earnings, plus she does all the domestic jobs. Hunter College has cheaper tuition if she had to pay, but this Sarah Lawrence deal sounds really possible. It's free. And she'd be unique. She doubts many belly dancers are applying. The only problem is transportation. She'll need a car.

Myra suggests she take out a loan.

"A loan? Someone will loan money for a car to a belly dancer who wants to go to college?"

"Why not try to write something about it?" I suggest.

"Me? Write what?" Shoshona asks. "I've never written anything. Including letters."

"You've never been up for a Master's Degree, either," I tell her. "Besides you'll learn how to write. You'll have to take Freshman English."

Myra loves the idea. For her Freshman theme, Shoshona can write about life as an exotic dancer.

"Belly dancer," Shoshona says. "I'm not going to be a Freshman. I'm going to be a Fellow. And I'm going to apply in Art. I've got my Bagatelles to show and I've got Kivas."

"What's a Kiva?" Sally asks.

"It's an Indian pit house. Some of the Southwest Indians use them to live in or for special rituals."

"You're making houses?" Myra asks.

"No, I'm making boxes."

"Boxes?"

"Yes. Like shoe boxes. Joseph Cornell's boxes got me started. I didn't want to imitate him, but I thought of turning boxes into small scenes. Domestic scenes. I loved the cycloramas I saw at Mesa Verde, women making baskets and pots, men setting off for the hunt with netting and spears. I thought of the kids in front of the TV, or Debbie on her bed reading."

"I'm totally confused," Myra says. "Scenes in shoe boxes?"

"Well I just took Playdoh and I made small figures and furniture and I put them in shoe boxes."

"Well, I want to see them," Myra says. "I guess you're really an artist."

"Maybe you could try miniature pyramids," Sally says.

Why Larry Can't Take Me to The Tony's

"I don't think I'm going to get it," Larry says, for the third time this evening, as he sets a plate of pasta and sausage on the dinner table.

The past month, when he's in town, we have Wednesday dinner at his place. It suits us both. He loves to cook. I love to eat and be cooked for. David and Rebecca like Larry, and he likes them, but I'm reluctant to involve them too much. The best advice for divorced mothers is keep your children separate from your lovers.

I guess I'd refer to Larry as my lover. Besides, week-ends when the children are at Martin's, we spend our week-ends together. We enjoy each other's company, never run out of conversation, and like to make love. But there's something that hasn't happened between us. I don't know if it's something I don't feel or won't let myself feel, and if so, why. I can't tell which of us is holding back, or if both of us are.

"I think Juan will get it," Larry says. "He's Latino. Emmeline is going to get the best supporting female role, and one Tony a year is enough for blacks."

The Tony awards for the best Broadway musicals will be announced two months before I go to the hospital. Larry has been nominated for his supporting role last year in a Broadway musical. The ceremonies are always a big event, New York's equivalent of the Oscars.

"Aren't you pleased you were nominated? I ask him. "It's an honor, isn't it?"

"I'd rather win," he says. "Honor's invisible."

"Does everyone get all dolled up, like the Oscars?"

"I'm sure Emmeline will. She'll probably come in feathers. God knows what Callista will wear."

"I don't have any spare feathers. What should I wear?"

Larry concentrates on winding his pasta around his fork. I repeat my question.

"What should you wear?" he asks.

"Yes. Aren't you taking me? What should I wear?"

"I better check the dessert." He gets up and pours more liqueur on the fruit that's marinating in the refrigerator. When he comes back and sits down, I can see he's uncomfortable. "I'm sorry if I let you think that," he says, his fork fooling around with what's left of his pasta."

"If you let me think what?"

"That I was taking you."

Now I can't finish my dinner. I can't tell how angry I am, but it feels like I'm going to find out. "You've been talking about it for weeks, so I assumed you were taking me. Why aren't you? What's the matter with me? Am I unpresentable?"

He gets up to clear the table. "Of course you're presentable," he says, removing my plate.

"Would you sit down, Larry, and finish this conversation. What's the 'but?'"

"The 'but' is that you're not black."

"I'm not black."

"Right."

"You mean you didn't know I wasn't black when you introduced yourself at Callista's party? You saw me and you said, 'Gee, she sure looks black to me.'"

"You know what I mean," he answers.

"No, I don't. It doesn't keep you from going out with me. Or sleeping with me. Or involving me in your life. But you're not going to be seen at a public ceremony with me because I'm not black?"

"You're being unreasonable. I've been seen in public with you. It's not because it's public. It's the kind of event it is. I'm identified as a black performer. If I take someone, she ought to be black."

"So, it's Ok to go with you when you give a concert at some college because that's just for college kids. There's no TV, so it's personal?" I ask.

"Right," he says. "But.."

"But this is for public relations. This is big time. Your bigtime public won't think you're black enough. Is that it? You're trying to be a role model? What would you do if I couldn't take you somewhere because you're not white enough? How would you like that? I always thought you were white."

"You're making a ridiculous fuss about this," he says spooning himself some dessert.

"You're damn right I'm making a fuss. Who are you taking? Who's the lucky lady that's black enough?"

"I don't know. Probably no one."

"But you're not sure. Because if you go alone, then maybe your public won't think you're sexy enough. Or they might think you're gay."

"Actually, that's an irony." Larry laughs.

"You think that's funny?"

"Yes. That's funny. The irony is they probably would think I'm gay. Honestly, Lilly, I'm surprised at you. Are you living in some fantasy universe? Do you believe there's no difference between what you think and what the public thinks about white and black couples?"

I realize he's got me. Maybe I have been living in some fantasy world. Rebecca and David haven't said anything about his being black. But they're definitely not the public.

"What do your friends say about you going out with a black man?" he asks.

"I don't know. They don't say anything." My friends haven't said anything. No one at the gym has said anything. But I realize I haven't said anything, either. No one but Callista and my children know about Larry. What would my friends say? I've just lost my appetite.

"I don't think I want any dessert," I say. I push away the small glass bowl Larry gave me when he put the dish of fruit and coconut on the table.

"Think about it," Larry says. "You're missing a good dessert."

What Color Is Cuban?

"What do you think about Larry not taking me to the Tony Awards because I'm not black?" I ask Callista.

"You're not black?" she says. "Well, I'll be damned. How come he's going out with you if you're not black?"

"I figured you'd say something like that."

"Well, isn't that why you asked me?"

"You're my friend, not my analyst. I thought you'd be sympathetic. Who else can I talk to about this?"

"I am sympathetic. If I were your analyst, I'd ask you how you feel about it. But I know how you feel."

"You're going to tell me you warned me."

"What kind of friend would do that? Actually, I take that back. What kind of friend wouldn't warn you. I did, didn't I?"

"Thanks for the warning."

"What if he weren't black? How would you feel about him?"

"He wouldn't be the same person."

"Would he be less interesting? What is it about that black Larry that you like?"

"I like his imagination. I like being with him. I like his feeling about his kids." I hesitate.

"You can get back to me on that. I have a new guy. He's half Cuban."

"What color is Cuban?" I ask.

"I'm not worried about his color. I'm worried that he's a new producer, and I'm more successful than he is."

I suggest she forget about being a star.

"I'd like to," she says.

"I'm sick of this whole conversation." I tell her.

"Come on over tonight and bring the kids. We can talk about all of us going out to Fire Island. I'm renting a house there. And we'll have a fancy dinner."

"You're going to cook a fancy dinner?"

"No, I'm going to order expensive Chinese"

"That's my favorite kind of Chinese," I say.

Myra Gets A Job

We are laying bets on whether Nixon will keep the tapes and/or be impeached when Myra bursts into the Gym dressing room, waving her bag around her head like a lariat. "I've got real news," she says. She's turned down the Connecticut job because she found one in the city. After Easter, she starts at New Trent teaching Movement, Yoga, and Dance. The pay is sixteen thousand dollars with an extra thousand for coaching dramatics. She likes the school atmosphere, it's so progressive. I tell her Rebecca goes to school there.

"Your daughter must love it," she says. "The kids there are really loose."

"They are loose," I say, thinking of poor Mrs. Harris.

"The guys all have pony-tails, teachers, too." That makes Myra feel better about teaching at a private school. If the kids are rich, you would never know it from their clothes. They dress worse than she does. "Don't you think I'll fit right in?" she asks.

"I do," I tell her. Rebecca will love Myra's carpet bag coat, her long red hair, her enthusiasm. All the kids will.

"And it's full of dope smokers," Myra says approvingly. "You can tell by their manners."

This alarms me.

What worries her is the location, right on the border of Harlem. They have a guard at the front door to make sure anyone who leaves after three can get walked to the subway.

That's not all that bothers me, I tell Myra. Harlem is neither more nor less safe than the streets, the buses, the subways. Students are routinely relieved of their small change on the way to school. They've learned to keep their subway passes in their shoes. There are lots of black students at New Trent, but their color is no help, especially if they go home with white friends. They're attacked impartially by kiddy gangs of both colors.

"New York City is worse than Montevideo. At least the Tupamaros don't bother children," says Genevieve. "What are we coming to when children get robbed?" she cries, suddenly all mother. "My Peter and two friends were bike riding in Central Park last week when a gang of kids knocked them off and took their bikes. Then two days ago, in Riverside Park, some Puerto Rican kids pulled knives on Marco and Tony and took their rackets."

Myra has got down from her headstand and is sitting rigid on her towel. I have stopped pedaling.

"Somebody's following me," Sally says. "I think it's that black guy in the pool ."

"Because he's black?" I ask.

"Because he bothers me."

"Guys are always bothering her," her roommate Lorraine says.

Sally goes to the gym to swim and relax, not to worry about other people, black or white. That's what she does as an airline hostess. Do they want a drink? A pillow? Orange-juice diluted with water for their baby? The mothers want her to hold their kids while they spend fifteen minutes in the bathroom. The men want to date her. One actually tried to fuck her in the Ladies room on an international flight.

"See what I mean. Everyone's after Sally," Lorraine sighs. "Passengers, pilots, strange men in swimming pools. How come they're after Sally and not me? It must be that sweet face, that pale blonde hair, that skinny body." Here's Lorraine all round and *zoftig* and who makes passes at her?

"I'm not skinny. Just permanently insecure." Sally, who weighs one hundred six, always thinks of her pre-Weight Watcher's shape. "And what's so great about guys making passes? That black guy is really driving me crazy. Tonight, he followed me up and down the pool. Last week he asked me where I got my terrific stroke. When I told Hal those black guys are too much, he says, 'You're an airline stewardess and you never had anyone try to pick you up before?'"

"Are you sure that's the guy following you?" Shoshona asks.

"I don't know. The other day I got back from Rome, exhausted after a six-hour delay. I thought maybe my mind was playing tricks, but I know some guy in Gristede's was giving me the once-over. And today, I had that feeling of somebody behind me."

"You've got to be careful," Myra tells her.

Sally wants to know what being careful means. Should she wear a whistle, get a gun? Should she learn Jiu Jitsu? Hire a bodyguard? It's dreadful when you can't walk down the street without thinking someone's after you.

"You are getting paranoid," Lorraine says. "I should know. I live with you."

"How can you be too paranoid?" Genevieve asks. "Every other black man in this town is a thief."

"Hey, wait a minute. That's pretty exaggerated," I say. "There are plenty of white thieves. And most of the people who get robbed in New York are black. The guy with a knife who stopped me in Central Park was white."

"That's an exception. Everyone knows American blacks have the highest crime rate," Genevieve says.

"No kidding, honey. What kind of crime rate you whites got?"

We turn around to face three black women, telephone operators from the six o'clock class.

"Everybody knows whites got a big crime rate," one of them says. "Number one lynchers, number one bombers of little black school girls"

"Worst is those whites don't work," says another. "Vice President? Gets driven around in a Cadillac, gets one hundred thousand dollars welfare and takes a bribe in his office."

"And what color trash killed Martin Luther King?" asks a third.

Now everyone's talking or shouting or trying to get the rest of us to calm down.

"The President's the biggest criminal," someone hollers "The whole country knows that."

You're Going Out with Whom?

"This guy talks about racism, but he's quite a sexist," I tell Larry at dinner. I am reading my way through Larry's Race Library, as he calls it, with special attention to his favorite, Fritz Fanon's *Black Skin, White Masks*. I place the open book in front of Larry's Pasta Alfredo. "Look what he writes: 'The European, who 'created' the black, made 'the white man' the symbol of reason and 'the black man' the symbol of the primitive and biological.'"

"Isn't it true?" Larry says.

"What about women? He never mentions women unless they're objects. White women, that is. Black women don't even exist for him."

"I guess we do unto others," Larry hands me back the book. "If you want to read about black women, I'll give you *The Street*. Aren't you going to eat your dinner? It took me two hours to make this pasta."

"What about this? He says, 'A black man who goes to bed with a white woman has a lust for revenge and a wish to be white.'"

Larry goes for more wine, pausing to kiss me. "All black people have a lust for revenge. And most people who are honest about it prefer to be white. Would you prefer to be black?"

"No. But I'm Jewish, and I don't prefer to be Christian."

"Because no one is persecuting you right now." He pours my wine, sits down, and gives it to me full blast. "No one is opening the door to the oven with the foot ready to kick you in. No one has burst into your house and smashed your furniture and loaded you and your children into a cattle car to take you off to the death camps. No one has turned you into a living skeleton or bayoneted your babies in front of you or made you dig a grave for your bunkmate."

I'm alarmed by how fast he has worked himself up. "Under those circumstances, I think I would just prefer to be dead," I tell him.

"Under those circumstances, you don't have a choice. My great grandmother didn't have a choice about being a slave." Larry pours wine into my full glass, splashing it over the rim. "Neither did your Polish relatives."

I look at the spilled wine. "Everybody's blood is the same color."

"White people don't look at our blood."

"What about you and me? Are you sleeping with me for revenge? Am I me, or a racial representative?"

"You're both." Larry clears the table and refuses to look at me. "How can black men separate them?"

"I'm asking about you, not black men."

"I've slept with other white women."

"For them or for revenge?"

"My wife was black."

"Would you marry a white woman?"

"Black or white, I'm never getting married again." He concentrates on wiping up the spilled wine. "What about you?" he asks.

What about me? Would I marry a black man? I've said I'm never getting married again. But suppose I do? Does Larry's being black allow me to postpone the answer? That's the attitude my friends take when they find out whom I'm going out with. It shows I can't be serious, doesn't it?

"There's nothing wrong with it, but why are you doing it?" Herb's mother, Stephanie Clyde asks. We're sitting in her apartment in the building I used to live in. The building Callista lives in. I don't like my attitude. I also don't like to be snotty with her. After all, her husband got me the WCBC job. She fixed me up with Sylvan Lesterburg. Why in the world did she think we would hit it off?

"Doing what?" Perversity insists I make her spell it out.

"Going out with a black man." She goes to the kitchen for soda.

"I like him," I shout after her. "Isn't that a good enough reason?"

"But you're not serious, are you?" She hands me a TAB.

"Look, Stephanie, if there's nothing wrong with it, then why ask why I'm doing it?"

My friends prove Fanon right in one thing. Because Larry is black, they assume he must be a fantastic lover, that his genitals must be big, and the tie between us must be sex.

Even Angie, whose usual reticence about the body makes me wonder if at thirty-odd, she has ever necked. "You're joking, aren't you?" she asks, when I tell her I am going out with Larry Brill. She's wearing the same hairdo and I guess the same clothes she wore in college. I want to take her shopping, jazz her up a little till I realize this is probably how Callista looks at me. "Why should I be joking?"

"The singer, the one who got a Tony nomination for that all-black musical?"

"That's the one."

"Then he's black?" she says, still unbelieving.

Several days later, she walks into my office, sits down, and comes to the point. "Lilly, I just have to ask you..." She fools around with her hair and shifts in her chair. Very un-Angie-like.

I wait.

"I hope you don't mind."

"I don't mind, yet."

She looks down at her lap. "Is he.... I mean does he...?"

"Does he what?"

"Does he have a big, well, you know...."

"Brain?"

"A big...I'm embarrassed," she says.

"A big prick?"

"Well, yes." She drops her shoulders with relief. "I mean, I'm not prejudiced about anybody's color. But they are supposed to be...well. aren't they...?"

"Have you ever seen Larry?"

"I can't remember. I think I must have seen him on HELLO."

"Then you know he's just average height. He's not a big black stud."

"I know," she says, "but aren't they all supposed to have really big...well...."

"Pricks. Cocks. Members," I say.

The next day I bring in Fanon's book and, ignoring Ahearne, who is standing, listening to us at his office door, I read out loud to Angie:

"The average length of the penis among black African men rarely exceeds 120 millimeters (4.6244 inches) (also) the European. But these. facts persuade no one. The white man (believes) the Negro is a beast; if it is not the length of his penis, then it is the sexual potency that impresses him. Face to face with this man who is 'different' he needs to defend himself."

"I get the point," Angie lowers her voice, "But is he a better...?"

"A better fuck?"

"Well, is he?"

"I wouldn't want to ruin his reputation, but he's just your standard, considerate, satisfying fuck. If that's standard."

"What's this conversation that seems to be taking so much of your valuable time?" Ahearne asks, walking into my office and taking the book out of my hand.

"I just told Angie that Franz Fanon says white men think black men are better fucks. It's that paragraph I marked, right there."

The blotches on Ahearne's face get redder. He slams the book down on my desk. "That's disgusting, that's crap, talking like that."

Everyone in the office looks up

"I'd like to see you in my office, immediately. Right now," Ahearne says.

I follow him silently into his office. He slams the door.

"I've had just about enough of your lip."

"Maybe the New York Commission on Civil Rights would like to hear about this." I turn around to go out.

"You're not going anywhere. The next time you're insubordinate, I'm firing you, and don't give me any of that Commission shit."

Afraid I'll ask him to define "insubordinate," and be fired on the spot, I walk out on automatic pilot, past Angie, the other writers and the two receptionists. How can any self-respecting person take this? Heading for the Ladies Room, I know I better take it until I have the operation I've been putting off since my divorce. I need the network to pay my health insurance.

How Shoshona Became an Artist

Shoshona is reciting her Fellowship benefits, when Myra interrupts her. "Hey, Shoshona," she says, "how does a belly dancer become a painter? Was someone in your family an artist?"

"No," Shoshona says, "but in a way, I became an artist because of my belly dancing. It's a long story if you want to hear it."

"Absolutely," Myra says, settling into a seated Yoga position.

I'm on a bike. I stop reading to listen.

"When the stock market plummeted, my father's very small savings from his pushcart business went with it. He wanted to jump out the window, but he said with his luck, he'd just be paralyzed. He was a broken man. He'd say, 'I used to come home with dresses for you.' Now he sat from breakfast to bedtime with the newspapers in one hand and a glass of tea in the other. He didn't live very long after that.

"My mother went to work in a shirt factory. After high school, I'd work at Lenny's Luncheonette, wiping off counters, waiting tables. But I stayed away from Lenny. He was always trying to corner me, brushing against me, squeezing past me behind the counter. 'Not much room here,' he'd whisper in my ear. Or he'd say, 'Your apron is crooked,' and he'd pull the bow out and retie it, running his hands up and down my butt. I'd push him away, but I was afraid if I pushed too hard, I'd lose my job, and we needed the money. Then my brothers, who were in the fur business, brought Harry over. He was their lawyer. He was tall with dark wavy hair. He wore a suit and tie, took me to dinner and the movies, and he always brought me flowers. 'People always need lawyers,' my mother said.

"I liked him, but I didn't want to depend on a man. Look what happened to my mother. I'd have a better life if I went to City College -- it was free – and depended on myself. Gina, my friend in Freshman English, had a job belly dancing in night clubs for more than I made in the luncheonette. I started lessons with her teacher, who danced professionally as Theodora. She named herself after the Empress who started out in a circus and ended up ruling the Roman Empire."

"But what about your drawing?" Myra asked.

"I'm getting there," Shoshona said. " Theodora gave me a book with pictures of the Empress's church, which had these brilliant colored mosaics of real animals in fantastic gardens. I tried to draw them, but my colors didn't sparkle. I started hoarding pieces from my mother's sewing: ribbons, buttons, or a piece of glass I found on the street. At night in my bedroom, I'd paste them on canvas and make my own mosaics.

"Then my mother's mind went blank while she was sewing at the factory and she caught her hand under the needle. She came home, unable to talk, barely able to move. I left school to take care of her. I thought I'd never finish college. I'd never know what life I wanted, but I loved my mother, who never had her own life, either. I thought I might be at my mother's side for years while my own life turned into cobwebs. I still worked at the luncheonette and my brothers gave us money. One day, watching her sleep, I noticed how the strands of her hair arranged themselves on the pillow-case, how her hands disappeared in the folds of her blanket. I started to draw her, sleeping, sitting in a chair, at the table. Then I drew everything in the house, lamps, the furniture. I looked in the mirror and drew myself.

"The day after New Year in 1951, I married Harry. He was a lawyer for the City of New York, with a very small salary. I went back to school and back to belly dancing. My mother moved in with my brother Steven and his wife. I just kept on drawing."

Children

It happens because of Genevieve's twin girls. We're startled when she walks into the gym with one in each hand, little blonde replicas of her. We don't want children at the gym. We don't want Genevieve's because they are eight- year-old girls, not women. Sitting in the locker room, they stare at our naked bodies, pointing, giggling, babbling to each other in French. In their school in Montevideo, the nuns had counseled modesty. It is not a virtue here.

Nakedness takes getting used to. It did for me. I wasn't accustomed to walking around without clothes. But once I did, I found it easier. It's more natural and more sensual to sit in the sauna naked than in a bathing suit. If some of the women look better than I do, there are always others who look worse. Why be self-conscious about bulges on my thighs when two of mine would make one of the Swedish sisters? Why worry about wrinkles on my face when the bird lady has them all over? Shoshona has ripples on her belly, Sally is flat-chested, Genevieve has love apples. No one is perfect. We can all take our clothes off and relax.

But not with those little girls here. The twins find us hilarious. They'll never have hair between their legs. They'll never have bumps on their chests.

I am in the sauna trying to read a wet magazine. Myra is to my right, her hair in a towel. Shoshona is lying naked on her back, Lorraine next to her in a shower cap. The Swedish sisters are reclining in their flesh.

The sauna door is pulled wide open and held while the heat drops. The twins enter in pink fluorescent bathing suits. They put one towel carefully on the upper bench, climb up, sit down next to each other and stare. First, at the Swedish sisters. They stand up to get a better look, pretending to rearrange their towels, and sit down again. They complain in French about the heat. They look carefully at everyone's breasts.

Suddenly there is a lot of talking. Lorraine describes a potential acting role. Shoshona talks about her graduate school classes. The Swedish sisters speak to each other in Swedish.

Myra is the most uncomfortable. "I can't stand those fucking children," she mutters to Shoshona. "Just think, Genevieve's got six more like that pair."

"I don't know," Lorraine says. "Sometimes I'm sorry I don't have any. I wouldn't be so absorbed in my non-existent career. Don't you get tired of thinking about yourself?"

"Don't kid yourself, it's no holiday living with children," Myra says. She's very tense.

Shoshona says she could live much cheaper if she only had to pay for herself.

"That was my problem," Myra says.

"What was your problem?"

"I couldn't afford him. I didn't have a job. I didn't even have a place to live. Would you fucking kids get out of here?" Myra hollers, as the twins scramble down from the top bench and hold the sauna door open to let in some cooler air.

"Hi sweethearts." Genevieve walks in, sits down next to Myra. She stands up to pat her girls' heads.

Shoshona sits up. "What are you talking about? Who couldn't you afford?"

"Phillip," Myra says.

"Phillip? Who's Phillip?"

"Phillip is my son."

"You're serious? You have a child? Where is he?"

"Well, I wanted...." Myra starts and stops. "I wanted to keep him."

"Of course, you did," Shoshona says.

"I did. I wanted to. But my husband wouldn't give me a nickel. He said, 'How do I know it's my kid?'"

We all listen to the steam hiss.

"It was his all right," Myra continues. "He knew it. But he didn't want the baby if I left him and then, I couldn't keep him. Phillip, I mean." The sweat is pouring off Myra. She starts to cry. Her whole body seems covered with tears.

Shoshona takes the towel from Myra's head and wraps it around her shoulders, hugging her. "Why didn't you ever tell us?"

Myra is crying too much to answer.

"You must have felt so awful having to give him up."

"She should feel awful," Genevieve says. "How can you give up your own child? It's immoral."

"No one knows what it's like for anyone else," I say to Genevieve. "It's hard to bring up children by yourself. Especially if you have to work."

"Money is no reason to give up a child. Look at all the black mothers on welfare."

"You're such a revolting bigot," Myra hisses, while I'm saying, "Really Genevieve, most mothers on welfare are white. And what does that have to do with Myra?"

"I still think it's immoral," Genevieve says primly.

"Have you ever been on welfare?" Myra asks. "You get shit a month and by the time you pay your rent, there's nothing left for food. You can't have a phone. Or a boyfriend. Or a baby-sitter, so you take your baby to the movies. If he's sick, you wait half a day in some lousy Emergency Room. Have you ever done that, Genevieve? Have you?"

Genevieve hugs her children tighter. "I am happy to say I have never had to go on welfare."

"You bet your ass you haven't," Myra says angrily. "You have your own private welfare. You've got a rich old husband buys you smoked oysters and fur coats and haircuts at Kenneth's. And best of all he buys you breakfast, lunch and dinner."

"He's not old. And at least I have a husband," Genevieve yells back.

That puts Myra in a rage. "You're the one who's immoral. At least I work for my dinner. I don't see you standing on your feet all day selling handbags. Selling anything. Not you. Your work is lying on your back doing leg lifts. You're on your old man's welfare. You have some nerve looking down on me."

"You bitch," screams Genevieve.

At that, the twins, who've been swiveling their heads from Myra to their mother like tennis watchers, run out of the sauna. The Swedish sisters sit bolt upright, the sweat pouring down their breasts, their stomachs, and say something to each other in Swedish.

Myra shrieks. She stands up, leans over Genevieve and shakes her by the shoulders. "How dare you call me a bitch. You're just a spoiled whore."

Genevieve slides around on the wet bench as Myra shakes her.

"Hey, Myra, take it easy," Shoshona says. "Help me," she says to me, "they'll get hurt. Stop it," she yells at Myra.

Myra can't stop. She's shaking Genevieve like a big, wet, naked doll. Lorraine tries to free Genevieve while Shoshona tries to pull Myra off. I've got my hands on Shoshona's back so she won't fall. It's a rope pull. Everyone is so slippery, it's hard to get a good grasp.

The door opens and Ceil sticks her head in. "What's going on in here? It looks like mud wrestling. Has anyone seen Sally?"

"Don't ever bring those stupid children back," Myra yells, Shoshona still in back of her and me in back of Shoshona.

"You're hurting me. Let go," Genevieve shouts back.

"You take back what you said about me."

"Shoshona," I say, "maybe you should just order her."

"Let go of her, Myra," Shoshona orders. "You can't go around slapping people."

"I'm not slapping her," Myra says, shocked. But she lets go of Genevieve and sits down on the bench. Shoshona and I steady ourselves. I sit down fast.

"This is ridiculous, women fighting like this. Aren't we all in the same boat?" We are all seated. Shoshona is standing, a naked Caesar addressing a fractious Senate. "I mean, Myra's sick because she couldn't keep her kid and I'm going nuts because I didn't bring mine up right, and Genevieve comes here all the time to escape hers."

"That's not true. I never said that," Genevieve says.

"You don't have to," Shoshona answers. She turns to me. "And what about you?"

"Me? That's easy. I feel guilty for getting divorced and ruining my children's lives."

"God, I wish I had." Shoshona says. "Gotten divorced I mean. I ruined my life instead."

Genevieve sits up straight. I have to admire her perfect posture while condensed steam drips down to her toes. I can see her composing herself, looking around, thinking of her six-bedroom triplex, her bank account. She gives a big sigh. "You're right, Myra. I have no idea what it's like not to have money. It was stupid of me. Really, I'm sorry."

Myra is sitting with her head in her hands, elbows on her knees. She studies the sauna floor and shakes her head.

"I'm sorry," Genevieve repeats.

"It's Ok. I've been pretty stupid myself. I've been stupid the last six years. I've been stupid my whole life."

"Why didn't you tell us you had a child?" Shoshona asks. "We could have talked about it."

"I couldn't. I wanted to forget. It made me feel so dreadful. But now I'm glad it's out because I know I have to do something about it."

"We've all made mistakes," Genevieve says.

"Mine are whoppers. I'm so confused, I don't know what to do."

"It's Ok," Shoshona says, as though she's comforting a sick child. "We'll talk about it. We'll try to figure it out."

"Let's talk about it now, " Myra answers.

Angie and Kevin Want to Get Married

Angie Novella and Kevin Donaldson have decided not to wait any longer. They want to get married now and they want to get married in our apartment. Why our apartment? Angie explains that they can't get married in a church because neither Irish nor Italian churches want what they consider a mixed marriage. "We can't afford a fancy hotel," Angie says, "and your apartment is really homey. We want to get married among friends."

Rebecca suggests we make the living room larger by putting some of the furniture in her room. David says the guests' coats could go in his. "Or we could borrow that rack Dad puts in the hall for parties, if someone in this building wouldn't steal them. Dad has a real doorman."

"We have a real doorman," Rebecca says.

Angie says not to worry. "There won't be that many people. Just Kevin's parents and Morrie, the best man, and the three of you. I've invited my parents, but I don't think they will come."

Angie met Kevin Donaldson in High School. She followed him to *The Daily Tribune*, where she worked as an entertainment reporter before she came to WCBC-TV. He covers sports as well as the violence beat: murders, kidnappings, perverts. Sometimes he tells Angie the worst stories: dead bodies in car trunks, cut up bodies in city parks, children living in basements. I try to keep her from repeating them to me. Just living here is violent enough.

Angie's parents won't give their blessing to her marrying him. He's not Italian. He's Irish and he's not a real Catholic. Her parents don't want to lose her to a world of unbelievers.

Morrie, Kevin's friend, will be best man. I'm to be matron of honor. Rebecca, the flower girl will hold Angie's bouquet when she's saying her vows. David, the ring bearer will hand the rings to Morrie who'll hand them to Kevin.

"What if I drop them?" David asks. "I'm nervous."

"Why? You're not getting married?" Rebecca says.

"The whole idea makes me nervous. Weddings, marriage." He hesitates.

"Divorce," Rebecca says.

"I didn't say that. What are you, a mind reader?"

"I'm reading my own mind," she says.

Myra and Stuart

Of course, we wanted to hear about Myra's child. At dinner she told Shoshona and me what she called an abbreviated story. Stuart was her brother Ronnie's Harvard Medical School classmate. He visited over their first Christmas and fell in love with her. She liked him but she didn't really want to marry him when he asked her. She was a dancer, she wanted to dance, but her parents persuaded her she could dance when she was married. She'd be more comfortable. He'd be a rich doctor.

They married as he was starting his internship. He was on call every other night. They lived three blocks from the hospital in an apartment Myra hated, a fifth-floor walkup that looked out on an airshaft. Every morning she took three trains to the lower East side where she taught dance and fourth grade. The huge subway elevator at one hundred Sixty-eighth Street was an old rusty vault that dropped below ground. She was always afraid it would stop halfway down, or the doors wouldn't open when they reached bottom. Except for teaching, which she liked, it was a prison like her life.

She often met Stuart for dinner in the hospital dining room. The food all tasted like fried fish, but she didn't have to lug groceries up five flights every day and cook dinner.

No matter how tired Stuart was they made love every night. When he was on duty, he insisted she sleep in his room at the hospital. After three weeks, she grumbled. Stuart said it was the best thing in his day.

Myra closed her eyes and thought of the victim in *The Rites of Spring.* Bearing it was her penance for marrying him. But she was afraid to leave him. One night when she refused to sleep with him, he took her by the shoulders and shook her till her head hit the wall. She was terrified. He accused her of sleeping with someone else, one of the male teachers at her school.

She swore she wasn't sleeping with anyone. "I can't stand screwing every night. I hate this apartment and the five flights up. I hate the meals at the hospital. I hate this life and I'm leaving you." She was astonished at her courage and frightened at his anger when he threatened to throw her out or kill her.

They went to bed exhausted, Stuart swearing he would change. The next day she experienced such nausea she couldn't teach. Her breasts were swollen.

When the doctor told her she was pregnant, she cried. That Saturday she cried on the bus to the Cloisters, where she looked at paintings of the Madonna and child and felt worse. She looked at the tapestry of the unicorn trapped in a bright red enclosure and wondered if animals thought of suicide. She was sure Ophelia was pregnant when she drowned herself and Juliet when she took poison.

She had never considered that the gynecologist, who knew Stuart, would tell him she was pregnant. Stuart was thrilled. He came home that night with flowers. What they needed was a family. He was ashamed he had threatened to kill her. He refused to discuss an abortion.

"I'd rather die," she told him.

She was afraid of the baby when he was born, afraid of dropping him, frightened by thoughts of putting a pillow over his head.

When she couldn't think of a name, Stuart decided on Phillip, after his grandfather.

The only Phillips she knew were kings. Phillip the Bad, Phillip of King Phillip's war. If he grew up to be a king, she might like him better. He might rescue her.

What I Didn't Have

I wish I could say that Larry and I had a happy, uncomplicated, give and take relationship, the kind Angie and Kevin have, the kind Callista and I, in our endless discussions, insist we want.

"Some dude to give me arms and legs at night," says Callista, opting for the minimum.

"And intelligent conversation, like Dante and Beatrice."

"Lamb," she says, "you are educationally impaired and stuck in history. Dante and Beatrice are not real life. Screwing, earning a living, paying your bills is real life. Come on over and we'll talk about it."

"I'm always going to your place. You come here and pretend you're slumming."

"Give me ten minutes," she says.

An hour later, she slides down on my fading Danish sofa in a leather outfit that costs more than my furniture. How equal can we be?

"What's with Larry?" she asks, pulling two glasses and two champagne bottles, one corked, from her large leather bag. "I hear you two are a real item."

I omit telling her that I do have glasses, refrigerate the bottle that is unopened, and settle down beside her on the sofa. "I hear something you're not saying," I tell her.

"You met him at my party, didn't you?"

"You don't have to feel responsible. I'm a big girl. And isn't he your friend?"

"I've always liked him as a friend," Callista says. "He's a good friend. But I don't think I'd want him for a lover. Since his divorce, he's been into this thing with white women."

"What do you mean 'he's into this thing with white women?'" I ask, pretty sure I know what she means. "What the hell does that mean?" I'm talking to her back.

She's on her way to the kitchen for "nibbles" to go with the drinks, rummages around in my kitchen, returns with a jar of olives, a box of Ritz crackers, another bottle and several dish cloths. "Thank you, God," she says as the cork pops and champagne fizzes down her legs. "It's washable. Who ever thought my mamma's little girl would be wetting herself with this. Lilly, you have to get out of this shithole. I turned on the light in the kitchen, and I was run over by roaches."

"You know I'm downwardly mobile. Divorce is not a moneymaker," I tell her.

"I'm divorced. You could still be in that apartment if you wanted to be."

"You are making thousands of dollars a year."

"Hundreds of thousands."

"Maybe this place suits me. I never liked the idea of my children having their own bathroom when there are all those homeless people with nowhere to shit or wash their face. The best thing about that apartment was meeting you there. As for who I go out with, didn't you keep inviting me to your parties, telling me I'd find Mr. Wonderful?"

"Well, lamb, I always invite plenty of white people."

"Are you saying I shouldn't go out with Larry because he's black?"

"As my mamma would say," Callista puts her hands on her hips, purses her lips and becomes her mamma, "Girl, I just don't think that nigger's right for you." She returns to her own voice. "It's hard to explain."

"Try. You're awfully vague for you."

"I don't think he's up front with the ladies. Any color ladies. I have to admit, it always pisses me off to see black guys sporting a white mamma, but I wouldn't mind you being the mamma if I thought he was heavier. I mean Larry's never made it big. That's cool with me to be small-time. Some of my best friends are has-beens and failures. And who knows, next year I might be down in the dirt with them. But I'll go down busting my ass and beating my brains out. He can't turn himself around. I think he's not working at it. Or have I said that?"

"You've said that. Isn't there something called being true to yourself. And your best friends are not has-beens and failures. I've never met one at your apartment."

"Shit, you're back on that Dante and Beatrice stuff." She offers me what's left of her drink. "Take mine. I've got more to say."

"What's left to say? Did he beat his wife? Does he go after little boys?"

She turns to face me. "Now I don't want you to take this wrong because you and I are friends. A lot of black guys like a nice tumble in the hay with a white lady, but when it comes to getting down to it, they're going to take black. You said it sarcastically about LeRoi. You told me, 'LeRoi's got a white wife. The authentic sign of a black leader.'"

"That's what Fanon says."

"You can quote Fanon. I'm just quoting you and me. When it got to be 'inauthentic,' as the critics like to say, LeRoi dumped her. Don't nobody never send me no white man, because I know what I am. I'm a black lady and I'm going to boogie with black. Now that's nothing against you or any other white person who is really my friend." She kisses me on both cheeks. "I don't know many mixed couples that made it."

"What about your ex-husband? What about Emmeline?"

"Lamb, I said 'made it.' Emmeline's husband wears her for dress and makes out with guys. She gets off on spending his money. A lot of it on other women. As for me, I think Sherman married me because I was black. I look coffee colored, but I'm black. He has lots of black friends. He has lots of black clients. He gets off on it. I got off on being molded. I was too young to think of getting married. When I say couples that made it, I mean people who really get along, I mean they really like each other."

"How many married people do you know who really like each other?" I ask her.

"That's just the point. If you don't really like each other, why mess with all that color shit?"

"Don't you think it's possible people could just fall in love?"

"Anything is possible. I don't think you're in love with him. Are you?" she wants to know.

"I don't know," I say.

"Didn't your pal Beatrice know? If you were in love with him, you'd know it."

I thought about what Callista said and I told her she was prejudiced. "Your first husband was white. But he was a big promoter, who could, who did make you a star. His color didn't matter. And David Cameron is white, and you'd have married him. Jack is Cuban. That is not black. And I'm your only real friend who's small time. And white."

"You're different. You are busting your ass. And I'm right on principle," she says.

David gets right to the basics. "If you marry Larry and have children, will they be half black and half white?"

"I'm not getting married and if I do, I'm not going to have more children."

"But if you do," he insists, "will they be split down the middle?" He draws an imaginary line, starting at the top of his head and running through the middle of his nose and lips to the middle of his chest. "Would half their face be white and half their neck and half their penis?"

"Only if they were boys," Rebecca says

"They'd be light brown, like Emmeline's kids," I say, "but I'm not having any."

"I hate Emmeline's kids," David tells us.

"It's like mixing things when you make a cake. You put them in separately, but they all get blended," Rebecca says.

"When you're having a baby, where do they get blended?"

"I think you need sex education," Rebecca suggests.

Myra's Mrs. Downey

"Sometimes I'm afraid I'm going to kill him," Myra told Mrs. Downey, her baby-sitter.

Mrs. Downey was everything Myra wanted to be. She was warm and loving with Phillip, gurgling at him when he kicked his legs in the crib, cuddling him when she carried him around the apartment. It made Myra feel less guilty for teaching part time, for taking long, solitary walks, thinking about leaving Stuart.

"Babies are very sturdy, dear. You don't need to be afraid of them." Mrs. Downey said.

"It's myself I'm afraid of."

Sometimes instead of going out, when Stuart was at the hospital, she'd sit and talk with Mrs. Downey. "Who do I baby-sit today?" Downey would ask. They'd sit in the park with Phillip, while Myra described her angry fantasies, how much she needed to escape.

Downey said a lot of new mothers felt the way Myra did. She thought Myra should see a psychiatrist. Stuart agreed. They should go together. He wanted to work it out. She wanted to leave him. They hadn't made love since Phillip was born. "I'm not having any more babies," she said. He asked her who she was fucking this time. When she decided to fuck him, he'd pay for a psychiatrist.

The next day, Myra put Phillip in the new, expensive carriage from Stuart's parents and walked over to the park. The sun was shining, her tightest jeans finally fit. Why not enjoy the weather. The park was full of mothers and children. She could make some friends.

A pretty woman with a blonde ponytail sat down on the bench next to Myra and wiped the sand off her little boy's hands. Going back to the sandbox, he tripped on the edge and fell in, kicking his feet and crying. The blonde woman opened a book and started to read. The child cried louder. Myra looked hard at her, but she refused to look up. The boy was working himself into a tantrum, hitting his arms against his hips, screaming.

"I think that's your child," Myra said.

The woman glared at her, threw her book on the bench, and walked over to the sandbox. She pulled the screaming child to his feet by one arm and shook him hard. "You did that on purpose. You're just like your father."

Myra looked at Phillip asleep in the carriage. He was a sweet baby. She loved him. She tucked the blanket carefully around him. Someone needed to protect this child. But she couldn't protect herself from Stuart.

When Stuart came home that evening, Myra was holding Phillip and a packed diaper bag.

"What a picture." He leaned over to kiss her.

She pushed him against the door. "We're leaving. I want a divorce."

"Myra, that's crazy!"

"If you touch either of us, I'll call the police."

"You can't leave. I won't let you." He walked towards her.

"I'm warning you, stay away."

"I'll ask my folks for money for your psychiatrist."

"It's too late. I want a divorce."

"Women are always depressed after they give birth. It's natural. Just let nature take its course."

"I let it take its course and look what happened."

"Put Phillip down. Let's talk about this rationally."

"I was rational when I wanted an abortion, but you wouldn't listen. After Phillip was born, I thought I was going crazy and when I needed help, you offered to fuck me. That's all you care about, fucking. I'm being rational now. I'm leaving. Just get that through your rational doctor's head. And if you lift a hand to me or Phillip, I'll sue you. I'll broadcast it all over town that you beat me."

"I think you're having an affair," Stuart said. "Get out. Get out before I lose my temper." He moved toward her with his fist raised. "I wanted to work it out, but you don't love me. I don't think you ever did. I think you were going at it with some guy in New York. I don't think Phillip is my child."

Plato

I don't know what to do with Callista's advice about Larry, if that's what it was, so I do nothing. But the next time Larry and I are in bed, I try blending David and Plato. I ask Larry if he knows what Plato says about lovers and eggs.

"Tell me," he says, his lips, moving up the inside of my arm to my breasts.

I tell him Plato says lovers are like one half of an egg, looking for their other halves. Then I repeat David's question. "If Plato is right," I ask him, "and you and I are lovers, can the other half of my egg be a different color?"

He thinks for a minute, kissing my breasts. "If it's an Easter egg."

Garrin Holds the Elevator

Bob Garrin, the producer of HELLO, holds the elevator so I can step in. He doesn't know me, doesn't know I want to write for the show and have been trying to get an appointment with him for months. I take his politeness as a good omen. I'm sure both Milstein and Ahearne would have zapped the door in my face.

Reminding myself of Callista's generous take on my talent and intelligence, I introduce myself, telling him I want to write for HELLO.

"Oh, yes, Sunny mentioned you. She said you're good."

Another good omen.

"Aren't you a friend of Don Clyde's?"

Yes, I tell him. I tell him I know he's busy. Maybe I could come and see him at seven a.m., when the show starts. I don't mention my appointment for May.

"Hell, I'm not here at seven unless I sleep here," Garrin says. "Come at nine. It's fine with me if you have breakfast with your kids. You don't even have to fuck me for the favor. Talk to my secretary. Make an appointment."

You're a Boy Cunt

Tomorrow might be spring. The temperature is up to fifty, but the radio says it may drop this afternoon and snow. I can't decide how many sweaters the children should wear, whether to insist on coats and boots.

"You 're getting to be too much like a mother." Rebecca is putting on her blue winter coat and boots before sitting down to breakfast. David decides to eat in his underwear. I decide not to notice either.

Rebecca wants to know who are those Montagnard children that are dying from American herbicides. David asks what herbicides are and takes two bananas.

"Herbicides are poison for trees. Don't they teach you anything at school and one of those bananas is mine," Rebecca says.

"Why do we want to kill trees?" David asks and in one and a half minutes eats both bananas.

Rebecca stands up in her coat, hands on her hips, and yells, "I wish you would go live with Dad."

David stands up and hollers back, "Women are cunts."

Before I can ask him where he heard that and demand he never say it again, Rebecca yells, "You're a cunt."

"Where did you get that, David, and never use that word again."

"What word? 'Cunt?' Isn't it a great word? I got it from Herb." He exits to get dressed.

"Well give it back to him," I say.

What the hell is this all about? They spent the weekend with Martin. Maybe he has a new girlfriend. I do not believe in "dirty" words. I am not prepared to deal with this.

"What if there's still Vietnam when I'm grown up?" David comes back in jeans and a sweater.

"Coat, please, David."

"What difference does it make if there's still going to be the war and I'm going to get killed? Do you think there will be, Mom?"

"You couldn't pass the physical. You're too stupid," Rebecca says.

"Enough of this, Rebecca," I tell her.

"He ate my banana and he is stupid."

"I'm going to medical school," David announces, picking up his school books and giving Rebecca the finger.

This is news to me. "I didn't know you wanted to be a doctor."

"They don't draft doctors," he says. "I'm not going to be killed in some dumb war."

"All wars are dumb," Rebecca says, "and the guys who teach at New Trent got out of the draft by being teachers. Do you think that's fair, Mom?"

"Nothing's fair," I say. I am not prepared to answer any more philosophical questions. I take an oath on this. From now on I buy their clothes and serve breakfast and dinner.

"Is it fair that some guys get out and others get drafted and get killed? Do you know rich men used to pay poor men to fight for them? Three hundred dollars in the Civil War. Mrs. Harris told us," Rebecca says.

God bless Mrs. Harris, I think.

"I can't pay anybody but I'm getting out," David says. "And don't tell me it's not fair."

"It's silly to go to medical school. It's a lot of work," Rebecca points out. "Besides, I thought you didn't like the sight of blood."

"It's easy for you to say. You'll never be drafted."

"Maybe they'll be drafting women by the time I'm grown up. A lot of liberated women think women should be in the army."

"That's nonsense," I say. "What's liberating about being in the army?"

"Don't ask me," Rebecca answers. "I'm not going in any army."

"They don't take nutty radicals like you," David says. "Anyway, you'll probably be too busy blowing up buildings and killing policemen and doing things like kidnapping Patty Hearst."

"You're a boy cunt," Rebecca says.

On Her Own

Her mother told her to stick it out, wait until Stuart was making some money. Her father said Phillip was a very cute baby. He thought maybe Myra and the baby could live with them until she got back on her feet. Her mother didn't think that would work.

Myra found a cheap apartment on the lower East side and went on welfare. She was willing to take any kind of job, but it was hard to find baby-sitters in her building so she could go for interviews.

Phillip cried and fussed and wouldn't sleep. He ate and threw up his food. Myra stood in Barnes and Noble, holding Phillip, reading through Dr. Spock. She took Phillip to the clinic in Roosevelt Hospital and waited two hours till the pediatrician examined him, gave him some shots, and said he was healthy.

"I'm not healthy," Myra said. "I need to see a social worker. I need to talk to someone. I'm alone and I'm afraid of what I'm going to do."

"You look pretty healthy to me," the doctor said.

Myra tried to love Philip, and sometimes, she thought she did, but when he cried, she couldn't get him to stop. One day, after he cried for half an hour, she slapped him. He stopped and held his breath. She looked at the red mark on her son's cheek, hearing, through the walls, her neighbor practicing piano scales. It sounded so normal. Phillip was still holding his breath. She had slapped a baby.

"Oh, God, I shouldn't have done that. Phillip, I shouldn't have done that. Please, forgive me," she begged him, "Forgive me."

She was afraid to pick him up. When she told her parents that she was terrified she would hurt him, they agreed to take him till she felt she could deal with him.

Angie Wants a White Wedding Dress

Angie wants a white wedding dress. We've been to three stores and now, in the dressing room of the fourth, she tries on a two-piece outfit with leg of mutton sleeves and a full skirt. It's just right. A little Victorian, a little fifties.

She turns around twice in front of the mirror. "Do you think I should be worried?" she asks, She's anxious about her parents. She wants them to come to the wedding but how will they treat Kevin? Much as she loves them, she hates them for making it so hard for her to marry him. Sometimes she just plain hates them.

The saleswoman opens the door to tell us the dress comes with two skirts. Maybe Angie would like to try the straight model. "You have such a nice figure, dear," she says, leaving the skirt on a hanger.

"I won't have a great figure for long," Angie tells me as I'm unclipping the skirt. "No straight skirts, thanks. I don't want to show."

"Show?"

" I'm pregnant," she says.

I'm so astonished I drop down to a chair.

"I won't be the first pregnant bride," she says.

"Since when are you pregnant? Does Kevin know?"

"Sure, he knows."

"How do you feel?"

"I feel grateful," she says, taking off her wedding skirt, pulling her slip tight over her stomach to see if anything sticks out. "I feel lucky. I had a messed-up abortion two years ago and they said I'd never have children. When I found out I was pregnant again, we just thanked God. Well, I thanked God. Kevin said, 'That's it. We're getting married. Now.'"

"You had an abortion?"

"Yes, me. A good Catholic girl, and I had an abortion. Kevin wanted to get married right then, but I was afraid of my parents." She slips the blouse over her head. "I was more afraid of my parents than of burning in hell. And then when the doctor said I probably couldn't have children, she shakes her head. "Imagine being happy to be a pregnant bride."

"Pregnant brides are always beautiful," I say.

Genevieve Comes Through

"I have a problem," Shoshona says. I have an appointment at Sarah Lawrence in two weeks and I haven't figured out how to get there. I have to take at least two of my Bagatelles and some Kivas I could take the train and two buses. Or rent a car. But that costs a fortune."

"I could lend you my car," Genevieve says.

Shoshona is astonished. We all are.

"I have an expensive car that sits in my garage. I never drive anywhere. Where would I park it? When I go out, I take a taxi. The car needs exercise."

"What if something happens to it?" Shoshona asks.

"What could happen? I'll write down my address for you."

"That's what I should do," Myra says, "go back to school and get a Master's, like I planned to. Especially if I'm going to support Phillip. Maybe New Trent would help me do it. They encourage you to go to school."

"This is not about you," Genevieve says.

Anger

Myra is seeing a psychiatrist at the hospital clinic, twice a week. She goes to her parents to be with Phillip every Saturday. We can all see her changing. She credits the doctor for the difference, but it's clear she wants to change. She wants to be able to take Phillip back and really take care of him.

Instead of men, Myra now talks about discipline versus permissiveness. She eavesdrops on conversations about bedwetting, motor coordination. She queries the Roosevelt Hospital nurse about nutrition. Yesterday, she sat before Genevieve, legs crossed like an acolyte, and quizzed her. At what age did her children get measles? What are their bedtime rituals? What about security blankets?

Like most new mothers I know, she sounds confused and anxious. When Rebecca was born, I didn't even know how to diaper her. I didn't know how to hold her, bathe her, burp her. There were no prenatal classes to teach you how to breathe, to help your husband help you in the delivery room, to clue you in on what you could expect when you came home from the hospital.

I was afraid of nursing her. It wasn't the fashion, and no one encouraged it, certainly not the hospital nurses. There were no "lactation consultants." We were trained in modesty. Women did not sit in playgrounds or restaurants, opening their blouses, putting baby to breast. What was natural childbirth? Why experience it? The idea was to go into the hospital and be hit over the head.

We had no role models. I never saw my mother naked, though I did see her corsets in the bathroom we shared. My father claimed their bathroom. My mother didn't nurse me. No one I knew nursed her baby. It was another era. And the truth was, I was afraid of it, though I don't think I knew it. I was afraid of the sensuality. I went to see a psychiatrist about it, and he told me it was Ok, I wasn't a cow, that women who could afford it used to have wet nurses. That sounded good to me at the time, it was such a wonderful rationalization for not looking at my feelings.

I hear Shoshona saying to Myra, "All these questions are just a smokescreen," as though she's heard my thoughts. "It's your feelings that count. You're angry at everyone, but it's not fair to take it out on Phillip."

Did she say Phillip? Anger was another thing we didn't know about. That we could feel furious at people we loved, that it might even be natural, though it was not a good thing to ignore it. I knew that my mother was always angry at my father, but nothing about my own rage. It was hard to keep from screaming back at David when, at three, he sat down on Broadway at Ninetieth Street, kicking the cement, refusing to go home unless I took him for a Rocky Road cone. Or at four, when he couldn't sleep, and I sat on the floor in his room, willing him to sleep, angry at myself, angry at him, angry at Martin for not being there on the floor with me. Astonished that my pediatrician had told me to give him sleeping medication. To a four-year old? That sounded crazier than being angry. Something was wrong with the experts.

I was furious with Martin, furious that I had to divorce him; that I screamed at him on the telephone for a year; that I accused him of telling the children he would pay for something and go back on it. A year ago, I threw one of David's sports trophies on the floor when he told me his bedroom at his dad's was bigger and threatened to go live with him. "Rebecca's room is bigger than mine, and yours is twice as big."

"I'm the mother," I yelled back.

"That's why I hate you, I hate you, I hate you," he chanted, lying face down on his bed.

I hated him, too.

It seemed I was always alone, on my own, even before the divorce, alone and exhausted, with crying infants, with children who wouldn't sleep and later wanted bigger rooms, with the tiredness, the boredom, the frustrations that accompany the love of bringing up children. I understood Myra.

"I agree with Shoshona," I say. "All that anger, you have to get it out of your system."

Myra sticks out her tongue and crinkles her face in the Lion Pose, making loud gurgling noises at her image in the mirror. "You're right," she tells us. "Ah. Ugh. You're both right, I have to let it out. I'm always thinking about it. Stuart and I let it out on each other, like steam escaping. I want to see Phillip so badly. I know I'm changing. Is that crazy?" she asks me, giving up on the lion. "Listen to me," she says. "I need you to listen. Maybe he won't like me. Maybe I won't like him. And then I have to work. I need the money. I can't stay home all day."

"Let's take this conversation outside," Shoshona says. "Let's all go have dinner."

Garrin Wants to Do *Singles*

"Do you know there are forty-nine million single adults in America?" Garrin asks me on the phone. "I think we should do a program on them. A HELLO special. You're single, right?"

"Right," I say.

"The writers should all be single. We have an appointment next week, right?"

"Right."

"Come up with an angle. Think about forty-nine million singles." Garrin hangs up.

On my way to the gym, I try to think of an angle. I list the single women I know: me, Callista, Angie, for the moment, Myra, Sally, Shoshona, Rena, probably half the regulars at the gym, including the telephone operators. And the men: Larry, Martin, Sylvan Lesterberg, Angie's Kevin, and the sportswriter friend she wants me to go out with, all the guys I've gone out with the past two years. Pansy is more or less single. And Callista's housekeeper, Mrs. Reardon. How to think about them for TV? Interviews? Family portraits? Scenes from life? A woman dropping her children at a neighbor's day care on the way to work? A woman standing up as she eats dinner, like I do when the kids are at Martin's? A man in front of the TV with a row of empty beer bottles?

What's new about being single? There have always been poor single women, with or without children, involuntary dropouts. In the very old days, in Germany, for instance, if their children were illegitimate, single women might be stuck in a sack with a rat and dumped in the river. They never made the Lifestyle section. I'm the new kind of single, divorced, with kids, a type that's become mainstream. We're an end product of the sixties, when dropping out, finding yourself, doing your thing became fashionable.

Leaving the gym, I head for the bus stop and notice, among the bus stop crowd, two strange looking creatures with orange hair. Men or women? They seem nervous, almost frantic. One carries a small leather case. Rebecca would say it's probably a gun, so they must be men. Maybe that's why the SLA posed Patty Hearst with a gun.

The bus pulls up. One of the men pushes through the crowd and up the bus steps to ask the driver a question, then turns around and pushes back through the line waiting at the curb. He bumps his friend. His friend jostles a lady in a dark green coat. She drops a paper bag which holds her pocketbook. The friend grabs the bag. She grabs it back. What if someone pulls a knife? I want to get out of here.

"Hey, Lady, I think you've got my bag," one orange-haired guy says to her.

"That's mine," she says, fiercely.

"I don't think so, ma'am. It belongs to me."

"That's mine," she screams, shoving him, hugging the paper bag, pushing her way up the bus steps.

I think of the crazy lady on the Paris roof in *Devil in the Flesh*, right before the First World War breaks out. I imagine Nixon in a camouflage suit on a traffic bench and President in the White House. The orange-haired guy walks away, shrugging his shoulders.

I remember that Patty Hearst is single.

Shoshona and Paris

Shoshona looks for wood to knock on. She feels like a princess driving up to Sarah Lawrence in Genevieve's car and the thought scares her. She is not used to happy endings, she tells us later. Better to feel like an ordinary housewife, a "displaced homemaker," as the women's magazines call it, about to register for college. That way she can only go up in the world.

She's displaced, all right. But not from homemaking. She's displaced from finding out where she is, or where she should be. Come to think of it, everyone she knows is displaced in some way.

Her noon appointment is with somebody Paris, the head of the Art Department. Maybe he'll look like Kirk Douglas in the Van Gogh movie, young and bearded in a blue smock, standing at an easel. Not outside, of course. This campus doesn't look like anything Van Gogh would paint. The grounds are carefully beautiful, and the students look like fancy bohemians, the kind who buy their blue jeans at Bergdorf's and tear them in private. Myra would say they dress like *nouveau pauvre*. Whereas she, Shoshona Reitman, is poor the old-fashioned way.

She feels out of place in her high heels and short skirt. If it were Myra going for the interview, she would have told her, "Wear something else." And carrying her shopping bags of Bagatelles and Kivas! She feels like a bag lady.

There's no easel in Paris' office. He is sitting at a large desk with piles of manila folders neatly stacked, a man with thinning brown hair, both ears, and a friendly manner. No blue smock. He wears a black shirt, black tie, white jeans. "Shoshona Reitman? I'm Marvin Paris." He waves her to a chair.

"Paris, like the city?" What a jerk she is. She nearly said he didn't sound French. She must be very nervous.

He laughs and rescues her. "Paris like Paresky. One of those immigrant names that my father changed at Ellis Island."

At least he's no stuck up intellectual, she thinks. "I feel like an immigrant myself walking around this campus with my shopping bags, an old immigrant. Is anyone here over twenty?"

"I am, definitely," he says, opening one of the manila folders. "So besides being an over-twenty immigrant, how would you describe yourself?"

She hesitates. Which of the many definitions? She'd like to skip the housewife bit, the unhappily married part, the mother of two grown children. "I'm a part-time belly dancer," she says.

"Really?" He looks up from the folder. "That's different."

"I guess so," she says.

"Now don't take this the wrong way, because you know we've pretty much accepted you."

"Yes." Thank God.

"But what does being a part-time belly dancer have to do with your wanting to be an artist?"

She's relieved. "You're going to think it's pretty screwy, but it actually does. You know the Empress Theodora, the one with the mosaics?"

"The Empress with the mosaics? Is that a painting?"

"No, no. She's got that big church in Italy. Ravenna. Actually, she is in the mosaics. With her husband, naturally. Theodosius something."

"Ah, yes, of course, at Ravenna."

"Right," she says, delighted that he knows about it. "Well, she started as a belly dancer, that's what my belly dancing teacher told me."

"That's what they say. And you've been to Italy? To Ravenna?"

"The closest I've been to Italy is Mamma Leone's restaurant. But I've seen the pictures, and I started drawing because I loved the funny way all those mosaic figures looked. Especially the animals."

"I see. And how would you describe that funny way?"

"Stiff," she says. "Rigid. No shadows or anything. It's all perfect, like they believe it. But still, you know they're very passionate."

"Not bad," he says. "You were telling me about your drawings."

"I tried to draw them, but I couldn't get the colors right. I mean those colors are so brilliant and all. And I had no idea what to do but I knew I couldn't do it like that."

"I see."

"So, I started making my own kind of mosaics, little stories only in boxes."

"In boxes?"

"Yes. Like that Cornell guy."

"Joseph Cornell?"

"Yes."

"He doesn't exactly do mosaics."

"I know," she says impatiently. "But he does all those crazy weird things in boxes."

"Constructions," he says. "Assemblages."

"Whatever."

"You've seen them?"

"Of course," she says. "That's what I'm telling you. And then I started making these little sculptures and putting them in kivas."

"Kivas?"

"That's what I call them. Like the Indian holy places. It may not be such a good name. I do other stuff, too. Bags."

"I saw the slides. I hope you brought some."

"Oh yes. Your letter said to bring some things. I brought these." She goes into her shopping bags and places several kivas on his desk.

"Hmm," he says. "Interesting. What else do you have in there?"

She rolls out her Eve Bagatelle and holds it up.

"You haven't had any art lessons?"

"Not many. I guess it shows. I took a couple drawing classes."

"And who taught you how to do this?"

"Nobody. I made it up."

"I see," he says.

That's the fourth time he's said, "I see."Shoshona feels defeated. She picks up a kiva, puts it back in the bag.

"Could you leave one or two?" he asks. "And that, uh, Bag. I'd like some people here to see them."

"Really!" she says. "You mean you like them?"

"Don't you like them?"

" I made them. I love them. I think they're wonderful."

"They are wonderful," he says.

Where Is Sally?

Ceil bursts into the locker room, makeup case in hand, garment bag over her arm, unusually agitated. "Where is Sally?" she hollers. "Where is she? I have to give this to her." She drops her makeup case on the floor, hangs up the dress bag.

"Lorraine's in the steam room. I'm just about to go in," I say, pulling off my shirt and tights. "I'll ask her."

"I'll ask her. I've got to find Sally." Ceil, in jeans, striped sweater and leather cap pulls open the stream room door. I follow her in.

"Where is that roommate of yours? Where's Sally, I've got to find her."

"Hey, close that door," Lorraine says irritably. She's lying on her back, knees up. "You're worse than Genevieve's twins."

"Where is she," Ceil repeats.

"Don't you want to take your clothes off, Ceil? Lorraine asks. I duck under her arm as she stands, holding the door open.

"I'll take my clothes off later. I have something I have to give her."

"Right now, she's over the Atlantic, returning from Rome. Probably saying 'no' to some salesmen. She's meeting me here at eight thirty. Ceil," Lorraine says, "please, if you're going to stand there, would you close the door?"

Ceil pays no attention. "I've got to get rid of that too small green velvet dress Sally told me to get. I'm never going to fit into that dress. I don't want to fit into that dress. It's making me sick, the whole thing. It is awfully hot here."

Shoshona walks past Ceil into the steam room and sits down on the upper bench. "Ceil, what's wrong? You've got your clothes on."

"I know I've got my clothes on." Ceil is exasperated. "They're just blue jeans. I'd wash them anyway. It's the green dress I want to get rid of." Ceil shuts the door and sits down on the lower bench facing us. Wet spots appear on her jeans, her Tee shirt. "The diet is driving me crazy. I can't think about anything except what I'm not supposed to eat. I count calories all day. I write everything down on cards and carry them around with me. How I feel. What I ate when I felt that way. I have to weigh everything I eat. I have to weigh myself every day. Barry and I can't go to a restaurant because I can't figure out how many calories I'm eating. Or we go for lunch and I have cottage cheese while he's having a Reuben sandwich.

"I've lost my sense of humor. The worst thing is I don't want to sleep with him. We haven't made love for three weeks. This morning

I decided, why should I go to all this trouble to be thin? For my ex-husband? For my ex-husband's wife? It's stupid. Barry likes me better plump. The minute I start eating again, I'll feel better. But I've got to get rid of that green dress first. I think it will fit Sally if she takes it in a little."

"Leave it," Lorraine says. "I'll give it to her when she gets here."

After I dress, I hang around the locker room, reading the paper, killing time. Larry and I are going to see *The Battle of Algiers* at the Carnegie Cinema, five blocks away, at nine o'clock. When I leave, at eight forty-five, Sally has not arrived, and Lorraine is worried. "I've checked and her plane came in on time. I've known her for ten years and she's never late."

"I'm sure she's Ok. Maybe she got stuck in traffic," I say.

"She's never late, Lorraine repeats. "Do you think someone is really following her?"

Roto-Rooter

"Six weeks?" Ahearne asks.

"That's what my doctor says."

"Six weeks in the hospital?"

"At home. The doctor says for this kind of surgery, it's absolutely necessary." Try to get through this, I tell myself. It can't be as bad as the operation.

"Is this a rotor rooter job?"

I am sitting in Ahearne's office among stacks of newspaper and piles of releases, most of which Angie and I wrote. I fix my gaze on his raincoat, hanging on a coat tree near his desk. Maybe he's a flasher.

"A rotor rooter job. Hm."

I keep my face blank, so he continues. "You sure ask for a lot of privileges. I think you're just trying to get out of six weeks work."

"I'm asking for sick leave for an operation. I don't think that's a privilege. It's called a fringe benefit."

"I guess you waited till you came to work here so WCBC could pay." Ahearne is not listening. He is following his own logic. "Fringe benefit," he mutters. "Sick leave. You women are all alike. Babies and headaches. You're just like my wife."

I have a sudden glimpse of Ahearne's wife. "I'm sorry," I say, wondering if we're talking about the same thing.

"Rotor rooter," he says. "She had one of those too. Then she couldn't have any babies. Just sits around the house and complains. You'd think it's my fault." He glares at me. "God damn women," he says. He swears and I suddenly feel sorry for him.

For a moment I think he's going to cry. Or I am. Then he gets hold of himself. He's thinking how he's been pushed around all his life by the same bosses who made him hire me. When I say "operation," he thinks of his wife.

I need the operation. I need the insurance. I need the job. I couldn't have paid for the insurance. I stand up and walk out of the office.

Blonde Stewardess Stabbed

Sally never got to wear the dress Ceil bought. That Friday night, while Lorraine waited for her at the gym and I watched *The Battle of Algiers* with Larry, Sally was murdered. I learn about it on Saturday morning when I go out for the papers.

"Terrible what happened to this girl," Sanjay says, holding up *The Daily News,* a full tabloid size picture of Sally smiling at me with the headline, BLONDE STEWARDESS STABBED IN BLOODY MURDER.

I stare at the picture. Sally smiles back. I read it again. It can't be Sally. I see her in her orange bikini as she leaves the locker room for the pool. I see her wheeling cocktails down an airplane aisle. It can't be Sally. Maybe it's some other blonde stewardess who just looks like her. Sanjay can't believe I'm buying *The News*. I go home and lock all three locks on the door.

It feels like an act of voyeurism and disloyalty. I object to Sally's picture being right there on the front page with that titillating headline. The paper says that less than five hours after she returned on TWA's late Friday afternoon 707 flight from Rome, Sally's body was discovered by her super, who called the police. No murder weapon has been found and the police have no immediate suspects.

The meager details of Sally's biography, some of which I knew, were provided by her parents, who were informed by police, then besieged by newspapers, TV, and radio reporters. Sally Sanders was from Plainfield, New Jersey and went to Eugene B. Debs High School. She was shy, according to her mother, and a good student. There was a picture of Sally, age five, in a bathing suit, her small stomach sticking out, her high school graduation photo in cap and gown, and a picture of her parents and two sisters in their Plainfield living room.

They reported nothing about Sally that was really important: that she had been overweight and awkward in high school until she found Weight Watchers; that, pretty as she was, she always felt fat and inadequate; that her favorite movie was *Three Coins in the Fountain*. She wanted to go to Egypt. She never had a real boyfriend, but men often tried to pick her up on the plane. For weeks, she thought she was being followed.

Suppose that jogger hadn't come along with his little white dog when I was backed up against the fence in Central Park. My picture on the front page of *The Daily News* would be headlined "Divorcée Found Stabbed in Reservoir Bushes." There would be pictures of Rebecca,

David and Martin, with the captions, "Ex-Hubby Comforts Crying Children of Murdered Mom." Detectives would go through my address book, my appointment book. "Divorcée's Black Lover a Suspect," the papers would say.

Hazards of the Single Life

The Monday *Daily News* front page recaps the weekend's story with the headline, WHO KILLED SALLY SANDERS? *The New York Times* has a small story in the second section. I read them both at my desk, drinking my morning coffee. Sally's parents in Plainfield must be trying hard to swallow theirs. At eight-thirty, Janice, Garrin's secretary, calls. "Could you drop up?" she asks.

I drop up to Penthouse, and make my way into his office, stepping over and around piles of books. Garrin is at his desk. He points to a leather sofa covered with papers. "Just toss that stuff and have a seat."

He's a good-looking man in his late forties and knows it. He's wearing jeans. His shirt and tie are black. His hair is black, too. Does he dye it?

"Coffee?" There's a silver coffee pot on his desk among the Sunday papers. "Milk? Have you seen this?" He holds up the front page of *The Daily News.*

My stomach hurts."I know her. I mean, I knew her."

"You knew her? What luck! Oh, God, sorry. That's terrible. Terrible."

He pours me a cup of coffee. "But you've got to admit, this is a great story. It may even be the angle for that program on singles. Hazards of the single life. Could be the first in the series."

Poor Sally. Dead two days and first in a series.

We Speculate

No men, not even the two detectives who have come to ask about Sally, are allowed in the Women's Gym. Hal, the manager, invites them and eight of us into his office. The detectives, both in brown suits, have a list of the members. They'll be talking to us one by one. Anyone who knows anything about Sally's life, please come forward and help. Often the smallest piece of information is useful.

Except for Lorraine, most of what we know about Sally is what we've just read in the paper. Sally came to the gym, put on her bikini, went swimming, took a steam bath and went home. She talked to Ceil about Weight Watchers. She loved Egypt. She thought someone was following her. A couple women mention the man who bothered her in the pool.

On Wednesday night the detectives come to question him. We hear about it from Hal. Reggie, the man in question, says he spent the evening Sally was murdered with friends. He never saw Sally anywhere but in the pool. The police asked him several times if he was sure he never followed her. The third time, he told them, "Fuck Off," and one of the detectives punched him in the stomach. The other detective told him to chill.

Bridget, the locker room attendant, is sure the murderer is "some colored guy." She says "colored" as if it soils her lips, brushing imaginary specks off the skirt of her blue uniform, patting her upswept blonde hair.

We ignore her. We are waiting for Lorraine to come and tell us what really happened.

Ceil buries the dress in her back yard.

We try to exercise but have trouble concentrating. Sally's ghost has taken over. We dream about her. We talk about her, trying to keep her alive, hold on to the little we knew about her. Then we make a place for her death and memorialize her the only way we know how. We retell Sally's stories, of the men who tried to pick her up on the plane, of the mothers who asked her to hold their babies while they took a fast nap. Of her sightseeing in Rome, and how she learned Italian on tapes. Shoshona remembers the way Sally handled her swimming pool admirer. She had been annoyed, not frightened. But the feeling of being followed bothered her.

She is every one of us, afraid to take the subway at night, fearful, walking home, alone in the hall, opening the door to our apartment.

What If I Don't Come Home?

Rebecca and David are doing homework. I am sitting with *The Street*, in the living room, trying to adapt it for the stage, but I keep thinking, who will take care of Rebecca and David when I'm in the hospital? When I come home, who will take care of me?

What if I don't come home? Suppose it's malignant. What if I die? It won't help to think about it. Maybe I should make plans.

Rebecca comes into the living room. "Mom," she says, "David woke me up last night to tell me the Stabber was in his room. I told him the Stabber wasn't a real person so he really couldn't be there."

"And?" I ask, thinking of Sally's stabber.

"David said the Stabber was in his room, real or not."

"Mom," David is hollering from his room. "It's on the radio. Nixon still has those tapes and he lied on his taxes."

"David," I holler back, "set the table."

"He's going to get impeached."

"Not for lying on his taxes," Rebecca says. "Everybody does that. Dad says it's just stretching the truth."

"Everybody does not cheat on their taxes," I say sternly. "You must have misunderstood your father."

"I hate it when you and Dad fight," Rebecca says.

"I'm sorry if it makes you feel bad, but even divorced people have a right to disagree. I don't cheat on my taxes. It's just too cynical to say that everybody bends the truth. I'm sure that's not really what your father means."

"Maybe it's just New Yorkers," Rebecca says, trying to find a way out.

"Nixon isn't from New York," David says, walking into the living room. "They just showed that Getty boy's whole ear on television." David pulls at his ear and pauses for emphasis. "His whole ear. I think I'm going to be a vegetarian like Rebecca was for two days."

"It was two weeks," Rebecca says. "You can't be a purist about everything."

"Why are we divorced?" David asks.

"I know you're upset about the divorce, but we should talk about it."

"I'm not upset. And I don't want to talk about it." David gets up and leaves the room.

"It's hard to have a conversation around here," Rebecca says.

I tell her David is trying to figure out how to be a man. "It's hard. They're not supposed to feel. And if they do, they're not supposed to show it. We have to help him."

"Men!" she says. "Women are oppressed and all that, but really, I think we have it easier. Hey, MVP," she says to David, "why don't we take some dinner outside to Captain and President later."

"David could be a radical yet," she reassures me.

David asks about it frequently but will not discuss the divorce. Not with me, not with Martin. We try a therapist who specializes in children. David tells us he won't discuss his feelings with some jerk he doesn't even know. He will play chess with him if I get him a Rocky Road ice cream cone afterwards. He says we can talk about the divorce when he's grown up. He sometimes agrees to talk about the Stabber, but not before bed."Let's do it tomorrow," he always says.

"But what if you get scared tonight?" I ask him.

"I'll wake you up," he promises.

As Freud recognized, it's impossible to be a parent. He didn't have any useful theories about it and neither do I. What kind of help did we give Myra on this subject? My advice is to be a good parent, have a wonderful marriage, a nimble mind, and enough money for child-care. Otherwise, get friends to baby sit and make the best of it. You don't know what's involved till you've got the position and the only training is on-the-job. Just love your child, totally. I think Freud does suggest that. A child with its mother's love goes through life with a full bucket. I think that's how he puts it. Sure, why not.

Tonight, David will dream about mutilated ears. Since Sally's murder, I go to bed and the scene jumps out at me like a pop-up book. Someone screams. A faceless man with a knife stabs Sally. Sometimes he takes off a leather jacket and ties her up. Or I see Sally, head thrown back, toes up, blood spouting from her mouth like a whale. That's what flashes by now.

I get up and check the children. I check the locks and slide the floor bolt back and forth. I think about turning on the TV but doubt I'll find anything soothing. Maybe Larry's right, we should leave New York. Everybody should leave and the whole city will be a deserted canyon. Eventually some Columbus will resettle it.

Where would we go? Back to the fourteenth century? The nineteenth? Did anyone get murdered in *Middlemarch*? Actually, someone did. It just wasn't the heroine. Bringing up children was not a major problem in fiction. Not till the modern novel, really. *Little Women*? Maybe, instead of leaving the city we should just go back in time. How about a knight on a pick-up-truck? What about Scarlett

O'Hara with Melanie and newborn, Charleston burning. Scarlett didn't wait for any knight. She got a horse and wagon and got the hell out of there.

Lorraine Thinks They Have Him

Five days after the murder, Lorraine comes back to the gym. We crowd around her. Everyone gives her a hug, a pat, as though touching her will give her some of our strength and remind all of us that we are still alive.

"I think they have him." Lorraine sits in the middle of us as though we're sitting at a campfire, telling horror tales. No marshmallows, just fear. "I think it's this guy who worked in the building, the porter. I think he was following Sally, but the police can't prove it."

"Colored?" Bridget asks.

"He's white."

"White trash. Same thing," Bridget says.

"I stopped at the supermarket to get something for dinner on the way home," Lorraine says, "When I got to the apartment, I asked the doorman if he had seen Sally, if she'd come home. 'Oh, yes,' he told me. 'About an hour ago, maybe more. She stopped and picked up her mail. I sent up her suitcases later with the porter.'

"I thought she must have come home and gone out, because I'd called from the gym several times before I left, and no one answered. But the doorman said he hadn't seen her again. I was scared.

"The apartment door was open. Sally never left the door open and unlocked if she was in the apartment. I looked in and saw cushions, books on the floor, the coffee table knocked over. I closed the door and got the next-door neighbor to ring down for the super.

"I knew Sally was in there. I sat down on the floor in the hall and waited. When the super came, he brought two policemen. They both pulled out their guns and held them straight out in front, like in the movies. One of them kicked the door in and hollered, 'Anyone in there, come out with your hands up.' He yelled it again, and then they walked in, whipping themselves around.

"With the door all the way open, I could see there was water on the rug, and on Sally's book, *Let's Go to Egypt*. There was a broken coke bottle next to the flowers on the floor.

"The policemen made me stay outside while they went into the bedroom. I heard one of them say, 'Oh, my God!' He said it a couple times. He called someone, told them he was Officer Hendricks, to get over fast and bring a photographer. 'We have a murder.'

"I walked into the bedroom while he was calling. 'You stay there and don't touch anything,' he said to me. The other guy left the room and put one of those yellow tapes across the front door.

"There was Sally on the bed with blood all over her, on her face, her stomach, her arms, all over everything, all over her mother's double-ring quilt. She was lying there with a gag in her mouth." Lorraine stopped for a minute and swallowed hard. "Her eyes were open. Her feet were tied, stiff. I went to get the blanket under her feet to cover her.

"Hendricks yelled at me not to touch her. I told him I just wanted to put a blanket on her. I couldn't leave her lying there like that.

"He said I'd have to wait so they could take pictures. I said, 'Not with her like that.' It wasn't fair. Naked with all that blood on her. Hendricks grabbed my arm and pulled me back from the bed. He said I could cover her up as soon as they got the pictures.

"That's when I punched him. I screamed at him. 'How dare you take pictures?' He sat me down next to the bed in her rocking chair and sort of squatted next to me, squeezing my hand. 'It's Ok,' he said. He was sweet. He kept repeating that, 'It's Ok.' I asked if he could leave me with her for a couple minutes. He told me he could if I promised not to touch anything. When he went in the other room, I got up and closed Sally's eyes. Then I sat down again and cried and wondered how I could sleep in that apartment."

Later the police reconstructed the murder. Sally let the murderer in. They had a fierce struggle. He hit her on the head with the coke bottle, which stunned her. Then he dragged her into the bedroom, took off her clothes, gagged her, raped her and killed her. She was killed with a knife from the kitchen, stabbed many times.

The doorman remembered when Sally came home. He had looked at his watch so he could tell her how long it would be until the porter came on for the night shift and brought up her suitcases. He found the porter in the basement, and he came right away to take up her bags.

The porter was an obvious suspect.

La Guerre Est Fini

We're having a late dinner at Larry's apartment after his tryout for the lead in the road company of *Carousel*. He's dejected. He says he's like the guy in the movie *La Guerre Est Fini* who doesn't understand the revolution is over. He keeps on playing at it. Maybe his career is finished, and he doesn't know it.

His apartment depresses me. The furniture needs dusting, the plants need water.

Larry is sure he won't get the role. He tried to persuade the producer it could be played by a black, but the casting director worries that would change the feeling of the play. The character's a no-good guy. He drinks, he leaves his family. If he casts Larry, he's afraid he'll be picketed by the NAACP.

Larry thinks that's just an excuse. "It could be interesting to have a black man in the role. The director's just a bigot."

"I think in this case the director may have a point."

"So, there's just Othello! And that's it for black actors?"

"Othello's not exactly a good guy," I say.

"Maybe he should be played by a white man so no one will think Shakespeare was a bigot."

"Don't jump down my throat," I say. "Some people do think Shakespeare was a bigot. Maybe you're right, maybe it would be interesting to have the lead played by a black man."

"Are you being snide?" he asks me.

"Oh, God, no. I certainly don't think I'm being snide. Am I?"

"I've got to get out of New York," he says. "Go out West. They're ten years behind New York in violence. We'd have some breathing space."

"We?" I ask

"Just a figure of speech," he says.

My Operation

Until the last minute, I hope Larry will call and offer to take me to the hospital. I could call him, but I figure rejection would be fatal before surgery. Callista is rehearsing. Angie is working. Pansy is staying with Rebecca and David. I take a taxi.

There are red roses in my hospital room when I arrive. Elated, I think Larry hasn't forgotten after all. The card reads

Love,

Kevin and Angie

I barely have time to be frightened when the anesthetist visits and then, before I know it, it's all over. The operation itself is a benign haze. I wake up in Recovery. His face floating above me, Dr. Vest tells me the cyst was benign and is gone. He boasts about my beautiful scar, "You'll be able to wear a bikini."

I thank him profusely through my doped-up haze. I never wear a bikini, but I'm thrilled with the prospect of a longer life. Now it's all over but the big scar on my abdomen which I finger just before sleep and think of Sally.

Everyone comes to visit. That is, everyone but Larry. Kevin and Angie visit with a bottle of Jack Daniels. Kevin tells me that Morrie, who will be best man at his wedding, is going to call me for a date. Can I deal with the idea of dates with anybody?

Callista brings me huge tortoise shell sunglasses and a sexy nightgown for when I go home. The word is out that Callista Dee is visiting and suddenly the floor is full of people walking down the hall to stop at my door and look in.

Children aren't allowed on the OB floor, so the next day I'm wheel-chaired to a downstairs room where Rebecca and David are waiting.

"It's from both of us," David says as he puts a bouquet of orange tulips on my lap. "What's wrong with your legs?" he asks. "I thought it was your stomach or something."

I tell him my legs are fine.

"I wish you'd hurry up and come home. Rebecca thinks she's the boss of me. Can't you walk?"

"She's recuperating," Rebecca says. "Mom, David is worried about the Stabber and he's sleeping on my floor."

"When I get home, we have to have a long talk about the Stabber," I tell David.

" I thought you said there isn't any."

"There isn't. That's why we have to talk about it."

"You're always trying to make me talk. You can't make people talk in a democracy."

"You can make people talk if you torture them," Rebecca says.

"Not in a democracy."

"You're so naïve. What about the police. What about the SLA? What about the army? We took those Vietnamese up in helicopters, and when they wouldn't talk, we threw them out."

"Mom, tell her to stop."

"Stop," I say. "I 'm changing the house rules. When I get home, I'm going to be a dictator. You talk only when I say so."

"You can't change the rules without an election. Can she?" David asks.

"I guess she can if she's a dictator.," Rebecca says.

As the nurse comes to wheel me out, Rebecca puts her arm around him "It's Ok," she assures him in a stage whisper. "Mom will be all right when she gets home. She's just having an aberration now. She's on drugs."

"Are you?" David asks.

"They're called pain killers," I say. I could get used to them.

"Hey, I didn't know the big day was this week." It's Larry on the phone the next morning. "I called you at home and Rebecca said you were in the hospital."

"You missed seeing me in my glamorous hospital Johnny," I tell him.

"How do you feel?" he asks.

"I'm angry I didn't even hear from you."

"Don't you remember? I'm in California. You can tell me next week. If you still remember you're angry."

I had forgotten he was in California."I'll remember," I say.

The Old Girlfriend

I cried when the children left, when Angie and Kevin left, when Callista left and Larry hung up. I cried when I got home, and the children were at Martin's. It wasn't just post-op depression. It was loneliness. And being alone. I won't argue whether they're the same thing. I felt them both.

Adrift. Can you be adrift on land? Afloat then. Treading water. How deep is it and how do I get out of here? My metaphors are confused.

Everything feels transitory, temporary, truncated. No children during the week to allow me complete rest, the silence on the weekend. No Larry. The idea of dating. At my age?

I try to console myself. Suppose, I couldn't afford Pansy, who comes on Wednesdays and now cooks enough food for a week. Suppose, Martin's insurance didn't help pay for this operation. Suppose I didn't have a job when I've recovered. Would Social Services take my children away? What kind of health insurance do single women have? A note for *Singles*. What if I wanted to just go to the laundromat, and had no baby-sitter? No ex-husband to share some part of the burdens and expenses? I wind up telling myself I'm lucky.

I recuperate, hobbling around the apartment. It's sick to feel so pleased with being skinny and embarrassing to ask the doctor when my pubic hair will grow in. Larry, back from California, comes over and orders take-out Chinese for the four of us, pours wine, makes tea, describes the California seals, the redwoods, the flowers on the streets.

"Did you see the bank Patty Hearst held up?" David asks while Larry shows him how to roll his pancakes.

"She wouldn't have done it if she hadn't been brainwashed," Rebecca says.

"How do you get brainwashed?" David wants to know.

"Think of your head as a blackboard," Larry tells them. "They erase what's on it and write something else."

"I guess they wiped her head out when they put her in a closet," Rebecca says. "They're terrible. Even if they do want to feed people."

David says he'd rob a bank if they locked him in a closet.

I'm wondering if we'll have another night of the Stabber.

After dinner, we throw out the paper plates and Rebecca and David go off to do their homework. Larry and I sit down on the sofa. "More wine?" he asks. There's a long silence. Finally, he says, "I'm embarrassed," walking the seven or so steps to the dining room to get the wine. "You know how much I like you."

"How much?" I ask, deciding not to make it easy for him, whatever he's about to say.

"I just saw my old girlfriend in California."

"Your old girlfriend?" I say, "How old a girlfriend is she?"

"We were together for a while. Here. Then she left. She's coming back this summer."

"Really."

He puts down the wine. "I'm sorry."

I'm still on the sofa, trying to get him to look at me. "What are you sorry about? That she's coming back? That she went away? Is she black?"

"What difference does that make?"

"I'm just curious. Is she black?"

"She's black."

"Really. She's black. Is that why you didn't take me to the Tony's? You were afraid she'd be watching on TV?"

"That's ridiculous," he says. "I would have told you about her, but I thought it was over."

"How over is it," I ask.

"It isn't over."

In His Shoes

I was hurt. I was angry. I was glad Rebecca and David were in bed. I poured myself a very large glass of wine and sat down to figure out what I thought. I was having trouble thinking. I tried to remember my conversation with Callista about Larry. What exactly had she said?

She said when he wasn't "in" anymore he didn't try hard enough. I went to a lot of his out of town concerts, so I thought she was wrong. He knew he wasn't "in" and he worked hard.

Whatever she'd said, I was feeling like a damn fool. I had taken him too seriously. I had taken us too seriously and never asked myself why. Was I hurt because I was in love with him, or just insulted? I had wanted to be in love, and there he was, so to speak, right in front of me.

Was I having too much wine to think straight? I was trying to think an even line.

I remembered the roses he had sent me shortly after we met that I thought were being delivered by my attacker from the park. I remembered how he never came over without bringing wine or flowers and always something for Rebecca and David. How he talked to them or joked with them. He was always just right.

I pushed myself into a corner. Suppose I had been in his situation. What if I had had a previous lover who had gone away? It was hard to imagine, but I made myself imagine it. I made up an ex-lover. Would I have started a relationship with Larry? Why not? Would I have told Larry about the previous lover if I thought it was over? Why should I? I would have acted the way he did.

I was still hurt and angry, but I told myself that I would have to understand. I was sure it would take a while, but maybe I would have to forgive him.

Watergate Cards

David's class project is Watergate. For his special report, he decides to make Watergate Cards. Like baseball cards. It's all his idea, though Rebecca and I are research assistants.

On the front of every six by eight file-card, David pastes a newspaper picture of each Watergate principal: John Mitchell, the Attorney General; Leon Jaworski, the special prosecutor; Rosemary Woods, Nixon's secretary. On the back, he pastes statistics.

There are several cards for Nixon. One is his Watergate Back Tax Card, with a list in numbers of what he owes in back taxes: Federal, four hundred thousand dollars; California, four thousand three hundred two. On the Nixon Expense Card, there are pictures of the president's houses at Key Biscayne and San Clemente and on the back, an accounting of the seventeen million dollars to fix them up. My favorite is the Milk Lobby Card with a cow on the front. On the flip side, there are milk bottles made of dollar signs for money the milk producers gave the Nixon campaign to raise price supports.

David says they're art, not politics.

"Even as art," Rebecca says, "they're better than baseball cards. And art is politics."

"You think everything is politics," David says.

"Everything is," she answers.

Our Pot Luck *Seder*

Since I'm recuperating, Rebecca suggests we have a potluck *Seder* for Passover and ask all our guests to bring something. She wants to invite Annette and Susie and maybe Jay Lieberman from her class.

"You're in love with him," David says. "Rebecca's in love, Rebecca's in love" He makes kissing noises against his palm.

She ignores him.

We decide to invite Myra and Phillip, Callista and Annette, Angie and Kevin. David wants to invite Herb and Larry. I agree to Larry. "I guess Dad wouldn't want to come, would he?" David asks.

Every year I tell the children why Passover is my favorite holiday, even if I don't think most of it ever happened. But it celebrates freedom and reminds me of my Polish grandparents. I think of white tablecloths and white candles, *Babba*, my grandmother, who apprenticed me in cooking and politics, *Zadi*, my grandfather, and my uncles in black silk yarmulkes, chanting and singing in Hebrew, red wine, too sweet to drink. We drank it, and spilled a little, making plum colored spots on the tablecloth.

On Passover, itself a metaphor, every morsel of food becomes metaphor, too: *matzoth*, baked on the backs of the fleeing Israelites is "The Bread of Affliction," the flat bread which our ancestors ate on the escape from Egypt, because they didn't have time to let the dough rise. We make *charoseth*, a rich concoction of apples, nuts and honey, to remind us of the sweetness of existence, even in exile; *marror*, from "bitter" in Hebrew, grated white horseradish for the mortar the Jews slathered on Pharaoh's bricks; hard-boiled eggs for life, dipped in salt water tears.

For me the *Seder* is for everyone to celebrate. Wasn't the Last Supper a *Seder*.

Babba , my grandmother, and I scrubbed the wooden kitchen table, making it worthy to receive the pike and whitefish for *gefilte* fish. We mixed, chopped, shaped and flattened it into rounds, held together with glistening black and silver fish skin strips, cooked it for hours. We rolled meal with egg for matzoth balls, dropped into boiling water, simmered for exactly thirty minutes, to go into *Babba*'s chicken soup, a savory of old hen, onions, celery and scary looking gnarled chicken feet. We stirred pot cheese into noodles for *kugel*, sprinkled with brown sugar and scraped our hands grating carrots for *zimmes*, cooked with honey. While we worked, *Babba*, her black hair pinned in fat braids around her head, told me how she used to round up anyone who would give half an hour to march outside the local bakery or butcher with homemade placards: Look for the Union Label. She loved to imitate the men, shaking their fists as they hollered, "Go home, Missus, take care of your children." She'd answer, "I'm taking care they should grow up union."

I loved *Babba*. I loved her black black hair, her warmth, the strength and purpose she gave off like heat, scraping the whitefish off her hands to tuck in the stray hair that escaped from her braids, or later, the bun at the back of her neck. I loved the fistful of clear, hard yellow candies she gave me when I came to visit; the shelves, whatnots, they were called, filled with small, cheap, painted dime-store dogs and miniature copper *shabbath* candlesticks on a tiny tray, which now belong to Rebecca and David.

If I loved *Babba*, I adored *Zadi*, with his bald head and steel-rimmed glasses. He read everything. My earliest memories are of sitting on his lap, looking down at his cheap, black shoes while he read me poetry in Hebrew, English, Russian, German, and for all I know, Sanskrit. With my mother, he talked literature and Jewish philosophy and what kind of state Israel should be. He said it had to be bi-national, everyone included. He talked domestic politics with my father. The *Seder* was always an occasion for passionate disagreement on all those subjects.

A dock worker when he came to America, *Zadi* made his living teaching Hebrew to aspiring *Bar Mitzvah* boys and often took me to his *shul* on those frequent Jewish holidays which rival Catholic Holy Days in number and obscurity. I felt total happiness standing next to him in the domed synagogue, dim light filtering in through stained glass windows, the cantor wrapped in a white *tallis*, singing some mysterious, holy abracadabra, the congregation swaying, chanting, and crowds of children, whom I joined marching around the aisles, singing in Hebrew, waving white flags with a blue, five pointed star on some holiday I can't remember.

Zadi's synagogue was conservative, but he was modern, even feminist when it came to ritual. He cut our *Pesach Seder* service from the traditional six hours to two, and he appointed me, the eldest grandchild, to ask the four questions, a role traditionally assigned to the youngest male. It's not just the *Seder*, but Judaism, which to me means my grandparents, means cooking and eating and marching, and more than anything else, means politics. That's what I always tell David and Rebecca before the *Seder*.

Changing Directions

Like Myra and Shoshona, Larry is changing directions. He's leaving New York. He tells me on the phone when I call him to invite him to our *Seder*. "It's not a good place for a black man. At least not this one. There's not enough work and there's too much hassle. I walk down the street and some white lady looks at me and I know she's worrying. Will I rob her? Will I rape her? Will I kill her? I want to say, 'Hey Lady, you got me wrong. I'm a good nigger.' But it makes me feel bad. I want to be somewhere I don't feel bad knowing what people think when they look at me."

It's easier out West, people are more relaxed. There are more opportunities for him. Maybe he'll teach at the university, do a course on black work songs, and he's going to build his own house. Paul Robeson went to Russia, but Larry can't believe in that, can't believe in China. "The only place to go is inside," he says.

He lectures me. "You've got to figure out who you are and what you want and find the landscape to do it in." He tells me I am still involved in the physical journey. The only place I go is the gym.

I'm too distracted to label it, but I realize that changing is exactly what I'm doing. Divorcing, moving, earning a living, taking care of children are all a detour from the inner journey. How can you go inside when there is so much noise in the living room and on the street?

I'm hoping *Singles* will be a new start and I'll move from HELLO to the theater. That's where I want to be, behind the scenes, making things happen on stage, putting the spotlight on what I think is played wrong in America. Larry is right when he says the landscape determines what you are, and your actions help define it. As long as you're in prison, you're a prisoner, no matter who you think you are. Since I'm a moralist, I'd add that there are many prisons. Sometimes it's your body. Sometimes it's your marriage, your job. You can't break out till you've completed the revolution inside. It takes study. It takes exercise. I'm working up to it the way I'm working at the gym. That's what I tell him.

We agree we'll still be friends because we still value the things we cared for in each other. He'll come to our *Seder*. After that, we'll be friends long distance.

Callista said I was intrigued with the idea of black and being in love with a black man, but I picked the wrong man. She always insists that I was in love with his voice before I met him.

Happy Easter

"I'm going to do it for Easter," I hear Myra say as I open the door to the sauna.

"Welcome back," Shoshona greets me and warns me not to strain myself. Myra admires my scar and tells me she's looking forward to the *Seder*. I settle down on a towel and close my eyes. The faucet sputters, the steam erupts, and I relax. It's good to be here again, taking care of myself.

"I called my parents yesterday and told them," Myra says. "I'm just dying to see Phillip. I've thought about it a lot and I've made a big decision. I'm going home for Easter and I'm bringing him back to the city with me."

"Good for you," Shoshona says.

"My mother didn't think so. She got very quiet. Then her voice got very tense. Strained. She said, 'I was planning to color Easter eggs with Phillip.' I told her she could do that anyway. She said they were going to have an Easter egg hunt and invite some friends. She asked me to spend Easter there. What do you think?"

Shoshona pours water over her shoulders and offers me the dipper. "I think that's an option," she says carefully.

I pour water on my wrists and ankles and pass the dipper to the Swedish sisters.

Myra looks at me. "What do you think?"

"If you can," I say, "I think you should try to work it out with your mother. Maybe you should talk to a therapist. There's one at New Trent. I could check out how good she is."

Shoshona likes that idea.

"I'm seeing a therapist already. I guess you two don't think I'd be a good mother," Myra says. "My mother doesn't either. I told her, 'Mother, Phillip is my child. I'd like to try and be a mother to him.' And you know what she said? She said, 'Well so far, you've made a mess of it.' Is that what you two think?"

"It's easy to mess up," Shoshona says. "I sure did."

"But do you think I did?"

"You know you messed up."

"Whatever you did, you're trying to change it," I say. "What's wrong with asking for help? We all need it."

"I just wanted to avoid a fight. I said, 'Mother, you and dad have been very good. More than good. You helped me when I really needed it, when I was down and couldn't handle it. I couldn't handle anything. But that was five years ago. I think I've grown up.'"

"You have," Shoshona says. "You really have."

"Not according to my mother. She is not going to let go." Myra's face is glistening from the steam. "She says, 'I'm glad to hear you've grown up, Myra.' I tell her again. 'Now I really want to be his mother.'"

"Good for you," Shoshona says.

"My mother doesn't feel that way. She sighs, and says, 'You know, Myra, there are some things you can never make up for. Neglect. Abandonment.' My own mother. I feel terrible, like I'm caught in some kind of vise. It's her anger."

"What about your anger?" I ask.

"Ok, my anger, too."

"Think about her," Shoshona says. "Maybe she's afraid of losing him."

"Maybe," I say, "you should go easy on her."

"She's never been easy with me," Myra says. "You know I didn't actually abandon him."

"I know," we answer.

"I told her, 'I didn't neglect him, mother. I didn't abandon him. I tried to do what was best for him. It wouldn't have been good for him to be with me then. I could have hurt him.' Was that wrong of me?" she asks us. "Should I have kept him and hurt him?"

"No," we say in chorus.

"I told her," Myra says, " 'You wanted to take him. It's not like I left him in a railway station or a garbage can.' There's another long silence and another big sigh. I say, 'Mother, are you there?' And she says, 'I knew as soon as I got really attached to him, you'd take him back. You just used me.'"

"Your mother sure lets it all hang out. Maybe that's good," Shoshona says. "Maybe you can all sit down and figure it out. Do it gradually."

"I keep flashing on that conversation. In class, when I'm teaching the kids some complicated step, I hear that angry voice of hers saying, 'I knew as soon as I got really attached to him, you'd take him back.' It's so awful because here I am doing the right thing, for once. Not just what I want to do, but the right thing. And my own mother is making me feel like a criminal. What do you think?" she asks me.

"You did the right thing before," I say. "You're doing the right thing now. But I'm sure she is attached to him. And she doesn't want to lose him. I think Shoshona's right. You should do it gradually."

"Aw honey, of course you're doing the right thing," Shoshona says. "Absolutely. For you and for Phillip. You should take him. Eventually.

But your mother probably does feel rotten. Maybe you should ask her to come and visit you for Easter. You know, arrange it ahead of time. Tell her you want her to be there. Don't push her away. Maybe you'll want her to baby-sit. You're going to want any help you can get."

"You sound like a social worker," Myra says.

"I'm taking that as a compliment. Who couldn't use a good social worker?"

"I don't want anyone taking him away from me. I know how I feel, and I feel I can handle it."

The Swedish sisters, both sitting up now, are going over their elbows and heels with a pumice stone.

"Myra, we're on your side," Shoshona tells her." You need some help negotiating this. And what you said doesn't make sense. No one can take him away from you because you don't have him yet."

Sunny Gets a Face Lift

When I go back to work, we are well into spring. Captain and President are sitting on their bench, playing Monopoly with a scruffy board retrieved from the trash. "How are you doing?" I ask Captain. He's clutching a stack of paper money in his grimy hands. I wonder when he last had a bath, if he was ever married. I wonder where his mother is.

"The bastard's winning," he says, pointing to the board. "He's got hotels. You put them hotels on the board or I'm going to impeach you," Captain threatens.

President puts his hotels on the board.

I enter the subway station at Eighty-sixth but there's trouble on the line and the platform crowd is four persons deep. I consider the odds of a real disaster, and a late edition headline: Sudden IRT Fire Takes 50 Lives.

I walk upstairs to the street and take the bus. The bus is crowded, too, but my paper is folded for stand-up reading. I can manage the front page. Nixon has five days to turn over forty-two presidential tapes for which he claims executive privilege. Former Treasury Secretary John Connally may have pocketed ten thousand dollars from the Associated Milk Producers. A tape-recorded message from Patty Hearst explains that she joined the Symbionese Liberation Army to fight for freedom for all oppressed peoples.

At work, Sunny Matthews calls me into her office and shuts the door. She has a new haircut, but something else is different. Is her blonde hair blonder? I tell her she looks great.

"It's my facelift. It's funny to think about getting a face lift to interview Patty Hearst."

"You're really going to do it?" I ask, ignoring the face lift.

"I think the SLA is going for it. They're all about publicity. We're negotiating with them to fly Patty Hearst to a secret rendezvous. Speaking of publicity, if it comes off, Garrin wants you to go to California with us. He wants to ease you into the writing."

"He told you that?" I ask.

"He's talking about some program on singles. He asked me what I thought. I thought it was a great idea using me for the anchor because I'm about to be single. That's why I got a face lift," Sunny says.

The Zoo

Myra's mother has finally agreed to let Myra take Phillip for a weekend. Myra describes the first day to Shoshona and me in great detail.

"Have you ever been to the zoo, Phillip?" I asked him. "We could go there this afternoon. Or the merry-go-round. Would you like that?" I took off his coat and cap and wondered why my mother dressed him in a spring overcoat with a velvet collar, as though he were going to Eton.

"Oh, sure." Phillip wanted to be agreeable.

"What would you like to do most?" I kissed the top of his curls.

Phillip ducked his head and looked up at me. He is brown-eyed like Stuart, with brown hair.

"You've got such nice curls. You've got my hair."

"I have?" he said, feeling his head. He looked scared.

"I mean it's curly, like mine used to be when I was your age."

"Oh," he said, relieved.

"Should we go to the zoo? Do you want to do that? Or would you rather go somewhere else?" I asked him.

"The zoo is nice. I mean, sure," he said, a bit uncertainly.

I knew I shouldn't confuse him with my nervousness. I could tell he was trying to figure out what I wanted. "Maybe we should have lunch first," I suggested.

"Ok."

"Then we can decide."

"Sure." He sat down on the edge of the sofa and looked around the room. "Is this your house?"

"It's my apartment,"

"Where do you sleep?" he asked

"Right here. On the sofa."

"Here? That's funny."

"At night, it turns into a bed," I told him.

"With pillows and everything?"

"Pillows. And blankets."

He thought that was a good idea.

"Would you like to sleep here tonight and try it?"

He thought about it. "Where would you sleep?"

"I'd sleep on the floor. In a sleeping bag."

"You'd sleep in a bag?"

"It's not really a bag. It's more like a big warm blanket. You lie down on it and zip up the sides."

"Oh." He paused picturing it. Then he laughed. "That sounds like fun. If I sleep here, could I sleep in the bag?"

"If you want to."

"I wouldn't tell grandma, though. I don't think she'd like it."

"Probably not," I said

"I like these pillows with the mirrors. And this." He pointed to a bright colored shawl draped over the sofa.

"It's called paisley."

"It's pretty. Could I touch it?"

"You can touch anything here".

He ran his hand along the shawl. "What's it for?"

"You can wear it like a scarf. But I put it here because it's beautiful to look at."

"Grandma has these plastic things on the sofa. To keep everything clean."

"Grandma does keep everything nice and clean," I told him. "Clean is Ok, but I prefer beautiful. I'll tell you a poem about it. Do you like poems?"

"I don't I know any," he apologized.

"What about 'Twinkle, twinkle, little star?'"

"Oh, I know that," he said, relieved. "I didn't know it was a poem. Do you want me to sing it?"

"Would you?"

He recited in a singsong, bouncing against the sofa:

Twinkle, twinkle little star,
How I wonder what you are,
Up above the clouds so high,
Like a diamond in the sky.
Twinkle, twinkle little star
How I wonder what you are.

"It's nice but it's not right," he told me.

"What's not right?"

"There aren't any stars when there are clouds."

"That's true," I answered. "It's true that you can't see them, although it does say that they are up above. But poems sometimes tell you how to think about things, not how to see them. Does that make sense?"

"I think so," he said. "You know what Grandma said when I told her about the clouds? She said, 'That's just what your mother would say.'"

"I guess you have more than my hair."

"What's your poem?" he asked

"My poem is about things like that shawl. And the diamonds in the sky. It goes, 'A thing of beauty is a joy forever.'"

"Is that a whole poem?"

"Part of a poem."

"It's harder than mine. Say it again."

"I repeated it. 'A thing of beauty is a joy forever. Its loveliness increases. It will never fade into nothingness.' It means that things that are beautiful stay beautiful no matter what bad things happen in the world. It says that beauty lasts forever."

"That's a good poem," he said. "Can we have lunch?"

"Gosh, I'm sorry. I forgot about lunch. What should we have?"

"Grandma makes macaroni and cheese."

"Do you like that?"

"Sometimes. Grandma says it's good for you. I like the cheese, not the mushy part."

"What else do you like?"

"Tuna fish. If there's lots of mayonnaise. Lots."

"More mayonnaise than tuna," I suggested.

He smiled.

My heart breaks. I had to stop and catch my breath. Nothing I might give him could equal that smile he gave me. "What would be your absolutely favorite lunch in the world?"

"What would yours be?" he asked.

"A hot dog with everything on it: relish, ketchup, mustard. What would yours be?"

"A cheeseburger with too much cheese. And no yucky pickles."

"What about dessert?"

"Chocolate ice cream."

"Well, let's go do it," I said, putting his coat on him.

"Could I have a coke, too?"

"If you keep it a secret."

"Are you really my mother?" he asked me.

"I am," I said.

"Were you there when I was born?" he asked.

Carlo

The bird lady is at the gym bar, practicing ballet in black tights and Tee, her gray hair braided with a pink ribbon and wound about her head. I nod to her. To my surprise, she nods back "You're never too old," she says softly.

Genevieve fills me in on the news while I try to stretch my feet into the lotus position without straining my abdomen. Myra has had several outings with Phillip. Shoshona is figuring out how to spend her stipend from Sarah Lawrence. Last Wednesday, ten black telephone operators staged a sit-down strike in front of the big lockers. The police have been working on Sally's murder. "I think it's that Puerto Rican porter," Genevieve says. I tell her Lorraine said he's white. "Half white," she says. "They're the worst." She plants her hands at the waist of her electric blue outfit and bends over.

Later, Lorraine tells us as much of Sally's story as she knows.

Carlo, the day porter, was just finishing his shift when Sally arrived from her European flight with three heavy suitcases. The doorman suggested she leave them downstairs and Carlo would bring them up. It was unusual for Sally to have so much luggage. Rome is just an overnight stop. But this time, she had stayed two days. Before she left, she told Lorraine she was going to change her life. There she was, zipping back and forth to Rome and Paris and all those terrific European places and she never got to see any of them. She was raised a good church-going Catholic, and she'd never been to the Vatican. Her sisters always teased her that she went to Rome and Paris and never bought herself any clothes. This time she'd decided she'd go to all the fancy stores and pretend it was Christmas. She was going to buy something for herself, for everyone in her family. And something special for Lorraine.

"After the murder," Lorraine said.... She had trouble telling us this part. She started to cry and had to start over. After the murder, when Sally's parents opened her suitcases, her mother found five pairs of Gucci shoes, a pair for everyone in the family. There were scarves, handbags, belts for her sisters and mother and two ties and a beautiful Italian sweater for her dad. There had been two sweaters, but Sally had stuffed one in her overnight bag, probably because the suitcases were too full. The Monday after the murder, Carlo came to work wearing it.

At first Carlo told the police he took the suitcases up to Sally's apartment but left them outside her door. When they asked him about his sweater, Carlo confessed. He told the police he thought Sally would make a great drug courier because she was so pretty, and the doorman told him she worked for an airline and went on overseas flights. Sometimes he just followed her because he liked looking at her and had nothing else to do. He followed her when she went to the cleaners, when she went to Gristede's, to the gym. He followed her everywhere. So, Sally wasn't paranoid. Someone had been following her.

Carlo knew everything Sally did. He was just waiting for his big chance. And when the doorman asked him to take her bags up, he knew that was it. That's what he told the police.

He said he knocked on her door and she told him to leave the bags in the hall. But he stayed there, waiting, and when she came to the door, he pushed the bags in and stepped inside. Sally was standing there in her white bathrobe.

Carlo shut the door behind him and told her he thought she was a nice, pretty lady. He asked her if she would like to make a lot of money smuggling heroin. She yelled at him. He said she swore and called him names. She told him to leave.

Lorraine said Sally must have been scared immediately. She had never heard Sally swear.

Carlo tried to convince her what a good deal he was offering her, but the more he talked, the angrier she got. "She said ugly, dirty words," he told the police repeatedly. "She was no lady."

He'd always thought she was beautiful, but it made him angry when she called him names. He told her women shouldn't talk that way. Only whores use such words. If she was a whore, he didn't need to leave. Sally threatened to call the police. That scared him. He was afraid the police would pick him up and with his record, if they heard anything about drugs, he'd be in worse trouble.

Sally had been drinking a coke when Carlo came in and the empty bottle was on the coffee table. He picked it up and hit her on the head. It stunned her. Then he pulled off her bathrobe, gagged her with the belt, pushed her down on the sofa and raped her.

She hit him and kicked him and even though she was gagged, she was making too much noise. She kicked the coffee table and the vase of yellow tulips fell over. He banged her head on the table. Sally reached out and knocked a lamp over, and he hit her head on the table again. She went limp. Then he went into the kitchen and got a knife. "It was just hanging there on the wall," he told the police "It was waiting for me."

He hit her head on the table several more times to make sure she'd stay quiet. Then he dragged her into the bedroom, onto the bed. "I stabbed her a lot of times to make sure she was dead. She got her blood all over me."

He took off his bloody clothes in Sally's bathroom, put them in a large garbage bag which he found under the bathroom sink, washed his hands, and wrapped himself in a dirty sheet from the bathroom hamper. Walking through the living room, he opened the overnight bag, the only one with no locks, saw a sweater and took it because it was blue and green and those were his favorite colors. Then he went back to the service elevator, which he had stopped less than an hour ago on Sally's floor. He took it down to the basement, put on the clothes he had come to work in, and left. On the way home, he dropped the garbage bag with his bloody clothes in a dumpster.

Scars

Today in the locker room, I inspect myself in the full-length mirror. I see a pretty lady in a brown, long-sleeved leotard, bulky white gym socks, track shoes striped in red suede. I don't see my scar .I'll find it when I take off my clothes, a purple seam, cutting across me, just above my pubic bones.

"Ladies, please bend and lock your knees." The new instructor's voice drifts in from the gym.

After Rebecca was born, after David, there were no visible scars. Flesh, muscle, everything that had stretched out, snapped back. The reward each time was a miraculous baby. My body returned to a semblance of its former self and the cords cut away at birth became invisible ties that link the children to me like extensions. Sometimes I feel like a many armed Indian goddess with Rebecca and David my extra limbs.

"Ladies, you are not locking your knees.," Anne, the new instructor, calls.

I bend and lock my knees, straighten up and twist my head so I can see my back in the mirror. My thighs have folds. I leave the mirror and go down to the jogging track.

As I run, I try to lift my legs higher and empty out my head. My legs obey, my head refuses. I see the white belt of Sally's robe. She ties it around her waist. Carlo pulls it off, stuffing it in her mouth.

Did Sally have scars? Did the blood from her knife wounds thicken in ridges after she died? Did the undertaker cover them with makeup?

Someone is breathing behind me. I stiffen, panic. A voice yells, "Fore," and a thin man in a blue sweat suit passes me, just another jogger.

Why did the man in the park choose me? Why did the SLA choose Patty Hearst? What metaphor can express the combination of accident and violence that was Sally's life? Was Carlo fated to be her executioner?

Genevieve worries that her children will be harassed, mugged, kidnapped, but politics, she thinks, is just silly talk, the Tupamaros are a bunch of crackpots. What does the SLA mean that we should feed the poor?

It's exhausting to live this way, your city a guerrilla zone, your children targets, your color a challenge, your sex a death threat.

Just how random is violence? Wasn't it Fritz Fanon, Larry's champion of violence, who argued it was a cleansing force, freeing the oppressed from their inferiority complexes, from despair and inaction, making them fearless, restoring self-respect? Isn't it my own daughter who says everything is politics? Doesn't my son, feeling left out by my friendship with Callista, and Rebecca's with Annette, turn to teasing, to revenge, by pulling Annette's braids, jumping out at her from behind the furniture, imitating the way Callista wiggles her hips when she walks.

Anne, the instructor, winds up her class. "Ladies, you are not listening to me. Am I not speaking good English?"

Oh, no, the class tells her. Her English is fine. They have not been concentrating. Maybe it's the vibrations. Maybe it's the weather.

I think it is Sally's spirit. How can we avenge her? How dare we identify without scaring ourselves to death? We are all potential victims, terrified that someday, when we open the door to our apartment, Carlo will get us.

Why are we in a gym, taking out our frustrations exercising. Didn't people used to walk? Wash the floor? Do something useful?

Garrin Comes for Dinner

Garrin and I are at what he calls the texture stage. He wants to know what it's like to be single with children, so I've invited him to come home with me after work and have dinner.

We are sitting in our abbreviated dining space eating Pansy's Jamaican meatloaf and David is quizzing us while Garrin listens. "How can she be single?" David asks. "She's got us."

"Single is Mom with us," Rebecca says. "In our case."

"What other cases are there?" David wants to know.

"Callista is single with Annette," Rebecca says.

"I mean different cases," David insists.

"My friend Angie is just plain single," I say. "At least right now. She's never been married. She doesn't have children."

"Aren't children people?" David asks. "How can you be single if you have children?"

"Forget about children," Rebecca tells him. "It just has to do with whether or not you're married."

"It's not a good word," he insists.

"Good point," Garrin says. "We should have that on the show."

"Me?" David asks. "Or Rebecca?"

"A child asking that question," Garrin says. "A child answering it."

"Could Rebecca and I do it?"

"You should interview kids," Rebecca says. "You could call it *Kids of Singles.*"

"Could I buy your idea?" Garrin asks her. "What's different for a single mother with kids?"

"Different from what?" she wants to know.

"From being married with kids."

"The apartment's smaller," Rebecca says. "This isn't a real dining room."

"Dad has a real dining room," David says. "And a bigger apartment."

"It's smaller than before we were divorced," Rebecca says.

"But it's bigger than Mom's," David answers.

"There it is," I say, "in a nutshell. Single women have smaller dining rooms. With exceptions. Like Callista. Hers is largest. And Myra doesn't have a dining room at all."

Garrin says it's a good starting point. By the time he leaves, we're farther along. We have decided on a series of interviews, a cross-section of men and women, some never married, some now separated or divorced. We'll ask the divorced how their life is different now: income, jobs, sex, hopefulness. We'll ask about their expectations, their sense of self-esteem. We'll do several with their children around and several interviews with only children: *Singles with Kids*. Maybe with a group of single friends.

Garrin is Producer. I'll be Assistant Producer and co-writer with someone from the HELLO staff. Garrin wants Callista and Sunny for the anchor people.

He'll talk to Milstein about me. I just want to know when I start. And I remind him again, that there have always been single. All the Greek heroines, Antigone, Iphigenia.

"Jane Austen," Rebecca says. "Charlotte Bronte."

"Patty Hearst," David adds.

We Are Gathered Together

Rebecca and David have placed yellow tulip plants around the living room and a vase of yellow freesia on a lace-covered table in front of the windows.

The judge stands to the left of the table, Kevin's parents to the right, holding hands, Angie and Kevin in front of the judge. Morrie, the best man, me, the maid of honor, and David, the ring bearer, stand behind Angie and Kevin. Rebecca is in front of the judge. Angie looks serene and beautiful in her white dress and white leghorn hat. She kisses Rebecca and hands her the wedding bouquet.

As the judge starts, "We are gathered together," there's a loud buzz from the kitchen. It's the intercom. "We are gathered," the judge repeats, and it buzzes again. David, who is closest to the kitchen, goes to answer. When he returns, he looks at me and says, "I guess we better wait. It's Angie's parents." He opens the front door and returns.

When she hears the elevator door open, Angie's eyes start to tear. Kevin raises her clenched hands to his mouth and kisses them.

Mr. Novella, a short, stout man with thinning gray hair, who looks as though he's spent a lifetime taking orders, appears embarrassed as he walks into the apartment. Mrs. Novella, in black silk and pearls, straightens her shoulders, her face, expressionless. David goes to close the door and takes his place next to Morrie.

"We are gathered together," the judge says for the third time, pausing a moment, as though he expects another bell. Then he reads through the short ceremony. David takes the rings from his jacket pocket and hands them to Morrie who hands one to Angie and one to Kevin. They exchange rings and kiss each other. Angie hugs me and whispers, "I don't think it shows. Do you?"

I whisper, "No."

Morrie kisses Angie. Kevin kisses me. Kevin's parents kiss Angie. Angie's father is crying. "You're a beautiful bride," he says. "You're a good daughter. She's a good daughter," he says to Kevin's parents.

"It's Ok, Poppa," Angie says.

"You'll come visit, won't you?" he asks.

"Of course," she says.

Her mother is explaining to Kevin's parents that the subway was late. "Oh, don't worry," Mrs. Donaldson insists. "We're so pleased to meet you. We've always been so fond of Angie. Wasn't it a lovely wedding?" she says.

The Donaldsons have arranged for dinner and dancing at the Tavern on the Green. Champagne is served and Morrie toasts the bride and groom. "I have a special wedding present for Kevin and Angie," he says, holding up a leather-bound volume of their high school yearbook. He holds up the book and reads, "On page one hundred thirty, under Kevin's picture it says: Ambition: To marry Angie Novella and become a newspaper reporter."

Everybody cheers.

"Now here's a guy who knows his mind and makes his dreams come true," Morrie continues. "To Kevin, who knew what he wanted, and to Angie, who was worth waiting for."

We all clap, cheer, and drink.

Mr. Novella stands up. He looks very teary. "To the best daughter a man ever had." He starts to cry. "Sit down, Bruno," Mrs. Novella says. "To the best." He's sobbing.

"To the best daughter-in-law," Mr. Donaldson says, rescuing him, while Angie's mother pulls at her husband's coat. Mr. Novella sits down and wipes his eyes with a napkin.

"To our families and our friends," Angie says, "may we always be together."

Then Angie and Kevin have a wedding dance.

At dinner, David and Morrie discuss the prowess of various baseball players and Morrie promises to take David to a Mets baseball game. Rebecca says she'd like to go, too. When David asks Morrie if he is married, Morrie says, "Not yet." Rebecca kicks David under the table, and David kicks her back.

"He always asks personal questions," Rebecca says. "He'll probably ask you how much money you make."

"I will not," David says indignantly.

"Not much," Morrie says.

"David wants Mom to get married again but he doesn't think anyone is good enough for her."

"Rebecca!" David is shocked.

"Well, it's true," Rebecca says.

"What do you think?" Morrie asks.

"I think Mom can probably tell who's good enough," she answers.

The band starts up again. David, Rebecca and I do the Twist. Morrie and I dance. I dance with Angie's father who cries and tells me they should have given her permission to marry years ago. "Her mother just wanted a good Catholic husband for her. We shouldn't have made her wait. By now, she'd have children," he says.

I assure him she will.

Shoshona tells us how she summoned the family around the kitchen table: Debbie in army fatigues, Bert in torn jeans, Harry, her Adam. She was surprised how tired he looked. It is hard to believe she was once crazy for him, that he came to court her at her mother's house with flowers.

She put a big pot of coffee on the table, four cups, two kinds of milk and cream, white sugar, brown sugar, saccharine.

"I have a plan," she announced. "You know I'm going to college."

"We know, mom. It's really great," Bert says.

"I was planning to move out."

"Move out?" Debbie is shocked.

"You're not going to live in a dorm?" Bert asks. "Aren't you a little old for that?"

"I told your father I was leaving."

"My name is Harry," he interrupts. "Let's give everybody credit here." He nods his head in the direction of Debbie and Bert, pours his coffee.

"You're leaving Dad? You never told us that."

"I don't believe this," Bert says.

Harry puts three sugars in his coffee and drinks the whole cup.

"Don't you have anything to say about this, Dad?"

"Your mother needs to be liberated. Haven't you noticed we've got her handcuffed here?"

"Your father and I have been talking about it," Shoshona says.

"Harry. Harry's my name." He pours another cup.

"Your father, I mean Harry, never liked the idea."

"That's the understatement of the year. At least you got my name right. Do we really need to have this conversation with the kids?" He puts in four sugars.

"Harry, you'll get diabetes," Shoshona says.

"We can leave," Debbie stands up. "I have plenty other things to do besides listen to this."

"You have a job? Either of you?" Shoshona asks.

"If you're going to college, take biology," Harry tells her. You don't get diabetes from sugar." To Debbie he says, "Your mother's talking. Sit down and show some respect."

"I don't need biology to know you eat too much sugar," Shoshona tells Harry.

"Mom," Bert says, "I'm taking a year out."

"Out of what? You're not in anything."

"Please," Harry smacks the table with his fist. The saucers rattle. "Let's not go through this again."

"It's Ok," Shoshona says. "We need to talk this through. Get off each other's backs."

"That would be a change," Debbie says. "How about getting off mine?"

"It's not your back that's a problem, it's your spine. You haven't any," Shoshona tells her.

"Really," Debbie says, standing up again, "I'm leaving. It's degrading to be listening to this."

"Young lady, I said sit down and I mean it," Harry yells, standing up. "How can we talk if everybody's always leaving?"

"Right. We should talk about this calmly. This family needs to get away from each other, but none of us can afford it. That's what we have to talk about. You have to help your father and me, Harry and me, work this out."

"Cut to the chase," Harry says.

"I'm cutting. Don't rush me. Some things need to be said. So, one, we need to get away from each other. Two, we can't afford to. Three, we don't hate each other, any of us."

"Ma," Bert says.

"You call this the chase?" Harry asks.

"Here's my idea. We'll live as a collective. We make a plan, divide up the living space, and share the duties and expenses."

"I'm not living in any collective, thank you. I had enough of that in Israel," Debbie says. "And anyway, how is that different from what we're doing now? Maybe we should all split."

"So split. Who's going to pay your rent?" her mother asks. "And your food?"

"I live here," Bert says. "Why should I split?"

"You take up space but you're not contributing anything. You have to give something back. We need a new contract."

"A what?" Harry asks.

"A contract. A legal document that tells everybody their obligations."

"I know what a legal document is. Remember, I'm the lawyer in this family."

"Really, mom, you sound like a Communist," Debbie says.

"I'm not signing anything," Bert adds.

"We need a contract to spell everything out," Shoshona repeats.

"We have one, Shoshona. It's called a marriage contract," Harry says.

"I mean the four of us. If we're all going to stay here, we need to spell it out. We're going to be a *menage à quatre*, and you have to draw up a legal contract."

"I don't think I believe this," Harry says. "*Menage à* what?"

"*Menage à quatre*," Shoshona says impatiently. "C'mon, you're all educated. *Menage* for household, *quatre* for four. You always hear about it for three, why not four? Here's the deal. We start from scratch. The three of you split the rent and the food money and everyone gets their own bedroom. Debbie and Bert pay one hundred fifteen dollars a month each toward rent. You kids have to earn it somehow. Harry pays the rest. You all three chip in seventy dollars each a month for food."

"Where am I going to get one hundred eighty-five dollars a month?" Debbie wails. "And what about you?"

"One eighty-five a month, and don't interrupt your mother." Harry pours more coffee, looks at the sugar, drinks it black.

"Right, don't interrupt. I should have taught you some respect when you were growing up." Shoshona says. "Where are you going to get a better deal? I pay nothing. I get the maid's room rent free and the maid's bathroom and my meals. My job is to do the food shopping and cook dinner five days a week and clean up after. That's it. Except for after dinner everybody helps. And does their own laundry, cleans their own room. Gets their own dinner weekends. I vacuum, dust, clean, whatever. Once a week. In the living room, dining room, big bathroom."

"Where am I going to get the money?" Debbie starts.

"It's either that or we all move out," Shoshona gambles.

"I'll do the contract tomorrow," Harry says. "No charge."

"You're kidding!" Bert says. "I'm not signing anything."

"Me neither," Debbie says.

"You've got a choice. You can leave," Harry tells them.

He looks a little like the old Harry. "Shake." Shoshona puts her hand out.

She and Harry shake.

Let's Celebrate

"We sign it tomorrow." Shoshona tells Myra and me. "We should celebrate."

"It's brilliant," I say. "Why didn't I think of that?" If I'd stayed on Riverside Drive, I could have had two maid's rooms, and maybe bargained in the butler's pantry, though I don't think Martin would have gone for it."

"You're not serious?" Myra says to Shoshona.

"Sure, I'm serious."

"You mean you're going to sleep in the maid's room and be the maid."

"I'm going to sleep in one of the small bedrooms off the kitchen, rent free, food free, in exchange for certain services. The other small bedroom is mine, too. That's what it says in the contract."

"I think you're crazy. I can't believe it will work."

"Why not? It's a bargain for everyone. Our personal relationships are our own business. We're all obliged to stay civilized and contribute our share."

"But you'll be their maid.," Myra says.

"You should understand, Myra. It's a great deal for me. If I left, how could I pay my rent? Or my heat, my electricity? Where would I get the money for the laundry? For maybe twenty hours of work a week, I have a place to live. Utilities. A washing machine and dryer. Twenty hours just teaching belly dancing wouldn't do it. And Sarah Lawrence gives me a studio and a rent and food stipend. I can use that for my art supplies."

"It's oppression," Myra says.

"It's a great deal. Think about it."

"Financially, I guess."

"You should be the last one to minimize financially. Where else could I get that kind of deal? Now I do all the shopping and cooking and the cleaning because no one else will and I fight with Harry every time he wants to screw. Which isn't very often, thank God. I even have my own room. And I still have another job."

"What about pride? And what if you want company or if you meet some guy?"

"Pride is too expensive. I'll see what happens when I get my Fellowship. I'll have a studio. They'll pay my rent. Right now, staying is the way I get out."

I'm Fired

Since Ahearne has insisted on two-weeks-notice, I start at HELLO two weeks from today. My salary is twenty thousand dollars to start. I'm elated. I'll take the kids to dinner and the movies and give Pansy a raise. A modest raise. I'll give Captain and President five dollars each. I wish I could give David a new room. If I didn't need the paycheck for next month's rent, I'd quit Ahearne right now. Divorce has taught me that satisfaction is too expensive when there are unpaid bills.

Ahearne fires me at the end of the day. He drops by my cubby to give me tomorrow's assignment. I'm to update a bio of Herb Shriner, a WCBC TV reporter who covered Vietnam for two years, now being rewarded with a cushy job as news show anchor. I hate doing those bios. They're so predictable. And Shriner's reporting from Vietnam was mealy mouthed.

"Great," I say. "He's such a patriot. I'll just ask him what he felt about the war."

"You think you're better than the rest of us, don't you just because you went to a fancy school and live in a fancy apartment."

The apartment is what does it. I lose it, totally. "My apartment is a dump. My life is anything but fancy. And Angie and I are the best writers here though I wouldn't call it writing. It's publicity. We'd probably do reruns if someone committed suicide on camera. Like that announcer in Florida, spattering herself all over TV."

"What announcer in Florida?" he asks.

"Chris somebody or other. The one who killed herself on TV a couple weeks ago. The one that said, 'In keeping with Channel 40's policy of bringing you the latest in blood and guts in living color, you're going to see another first, a suicide.' Then she pulled a gun out of a shopping bag and shot herself in the head."

Ahearne is staring at me intently. "Right on camera?"

"Right on camera."

"Did we carry it?" he asks.

"I don't know. I was in the hospital."

"Well find out if we carried it and if we did, find out what the ratings were."

"That's not my job," I say. "I'm a writer."

"You were a writer," he says. "Forget the two weeks. You're fired."

I should have quit, dammit. I'm mad because I need the money and I brought it on myself.

Did Dante ever get fired? He was exiled, it's true, but that has some drama. It means you're dangerous, important, challenging. Governments in exile are the real thing. Being fired is simply ignominious, even if it's some sexist anti-Semite that fired you. And two weeks isn't long enough to collect unemployment. Maybe I could get a magazine assignment. Maybe I could proofread. Maybe I could just explode.

It's not a disaster, like a drowning, I tell myself. It's more like keeping your head above water. It makes my neck stiff. The budget will be miserly.

I rehearse how I will break it to the children. I'll say,"I'm just going to take the next two weeks off, stay home and relax before I start at HELLO." David will look at me and ask,"What do you want to stay home for?"

"Well," I could say,"I really have to work on that play for Callista." That's a good ploy, I decide. I'll tell them about HELLO and focus on the positive.

On my bus ride home, I read a *New York Post* interview with the former governor of California, indicted for lying about some offer to pay for the '72 Republican convention. Maryland has disbarred former Vice-president Agnew for taking a bribe in his office and lying about it. A New York congressman has accused Nixon of lying to Congress for four years about the bombing of Cambodia. I decide it's up to ordinary citizens like me to be honorable and save the republic, so I walk into our apartment and come clean. I am so intent on self-criticism, on atoning for past sins, on being an honorable example to my children that I sacrifice subtlety, caution, and plain common sense.

"I've just been fired," I tell them, after several big hugs.

"Shit. Are we going to have to move again?" David asks, aware of the concreteness with which the mother's sins are visited on the child. About to cry, he runs into his room and slams the door.

I open it. He's lying face down on his bed. I sit on the edge, put my hand on his back. "Look, it's Ok."

"Do we have to move to a smaller apartment?" His voice is muffled. "Couldn't we could just not have a dining room?"

Rebecca comes to the door. " David and I could share a room, like at Dad's."

"Wait a minute," I say. "You share a room at you father's?"

"It's a very big room," David mutters to the pillow, "bigger than our living room."

"But he has to promise not to watch TV before he goes to bed."

David looks up at her, disgusted. "I don't watch, anyway."

"Wait a minute, here." I try breaking in. "We don't have to move."

"I'm not sharing anything with you," Rebecca says. I'd rather share a room with the Stabber."

David looks at her, appalled.

"Oh, I didn't mean it," Rebecca says. She gets down on her knees and puts her hands together, as if to pray. "I got carried away. Honestly. I'm sorry, David."

"That's Ok," he says offhandedly. "I'm going to grow up and not believe in him anymore."

I make a mental note and underline it that honesty may sometimes be the most selfish policy. "That was stupid of me to scare you like that We're not moving anywhere. It's no big deal. Just two weeks without pay. Then I go to work for HELLO."

"Yea, Mom." David unpacks mentally and shakes his hands over his head like a prizefighter. "Hey, guess what. I won for class project. My Watergate Cards."

"Yea, David. That's great," Rebecca says. "See, you don't have to be an MVP. You can be an artist."

"Like who?" David asks. "I don't know any men who are artists."

"Well, Picasso" Rebecca says.

"The guy without the ear?"

"Picasso had both ears," I say.

We're the *Singles* Team

The *Singles* team consists of me, Jeff Stein, a veteran HELLO writer, and Garrin, the producer. We have started interviewing and come to some tentative conclusions. This is not about a change in lifestyle, as the media puts it. It's a change in the way we look at marriage and families and how we choose to live in them. I'd like to start the show with Engels telling Marx how marriage is a miniature of capitalism: the husband is the boss, and the wife and children are the workers. Single is a euphemism.

Of the women we interviewed for *Singles*, there were two who summed up the changes. The first was a college student who answered our standard question, who pays for the date? "I pay my way," she said, "because I don't want to be rented for the evening."

The other woman, who divorced her husband for infidelity, said, "I had a traditional upbringing. I married a traditional man. I cooked dinner every night, and we ate it with my grandmother's silver. Now my husband is in another city, the silver is in the closet. I have a life to make and a child to raise."

"Do you think one person is less complex than two?" I ask Angie. We are in my office, talking about the definition tacked on my wall"

Single, SIMPLE. Alone, unaccompanied; pertaining to one person only; separate; uncomplicated, free of elaboration.

"I guess you don't think so," she says.

I tell her that when I married Martin, I got rid of so much of myself that being two was less complicated than being one. I gave up the work of defining myself. I let myself be bought. That was longer term than being rented. And as much my fault as Martin's. When I was writing stories at home and publishing a few, he said, "This marriage can't support two careers," I should have said I'd pay my own way. I should at least have put up a fight. There must have been some part of me that said, "Be a victim."

I'm going to ask the next group I interview: can you be successfully married if you've never been truly single? Before I got divorced, I never knew what it was to be separate and distinct. I'm going to ask: Do you think you can be two in one without first being one?

"It's different with me and Kevin." Angie says. "He won't let me get rid of myself. He takes me more seriously than I do." As for being rented, Angie says she was the worst kind of single. Living with her parents, she was less single and less independent than she is now that she's married Does that sound turned around?" she says. "You might ask how could I have been rented when I was paying my parents rent, but they controlled me, and that's the point, isn't it? They controlled me by their dependence."

When I tell her, she was single with parents the way I'm single with children, she says she's never been single if that means living alone. If it means being independent, whatever he pays for, she'll be more single, in the best sense, with Kevin.

I met Martin my last year in college, his last at Harvard Law School. He was Law Review. I was impressed. I remember how handsome he was, how courteous, how much I wanted to go to bed with him, how much I wanted to be married. On our first date, we went dancing at The Pike. We talked politics and disagreed about drugs, student radicals, preventive detention. I was for the first two, against the third. Martin said I'd better marry him since it was clear, with my ideas, I'd need a good lawyer. I thought that meant he'd take care of me. Why did I think I needed to be taken care of?

We married after graduation and Martin joined a prestigious New York law firm he'd worked for summers. I was writing for *The Village Voice* and wanted to live in Greenwich Village. Martin argued for the East Side. We compromised on Riverside Drive.

I was shocked that weeknights he came home after nine, sometimes after ten. He worked every weekend. When I complained, he told me,"If you want to make partner, weekends are just two days of the week." I was supposed to be loving, supportive, and have dinner hot when he came home. Dinner wasn't hot, and neither was I. What was the point of being married? I got pregnant immediately.

I tried to write after the children were in bed, but I was tired and had trouble taking my work seriously. I was a wife and mother. I don't think I took myself seriously at all until I was single.

Moonlight on the Moon

"I love this car," David says, bouncing up and down on the upholstered back seat of Callista's Mercedes. "Dad's getting a Rolls Royce."

David, Rebecca and I are heading out the Long Island Expressway to Fire Island, for a weekend in Callista's rented house. Her new boyfriend, Jack Laredo, who hopes to produce our play, is driving. David is in back with Rebecca and Annette. I'm upfront with Jack and Callista.

"Stop bouncing," Annette tells David. "You'll ruin the leather."

Callista half turns to the back of the car. "You should be gracious, Annette, you're the hostess."

"David we're outnumbered," Jack says. "We guys will just have to stick together."

Callista pats him on the leg and turns the radio on to a presidential sound bite: Nixon's gravelly voice telling us "It's time to put Watergate on the back burner and get on with the nation's business."

Callista switches to music.

"What does he mean, 'the back burner?'" David asks.

"It means something you're not paying a lot of attention to, so you put it on the back of the stove," Rebecca answers.

"I didn't ask you," he says.

"Jeez Louise. I was just trying to be nice. Can you divorce your brother?"

"I'll divorce him, too," Annette says.

"Don't worry, nobody's ever going to marry either of you," David says.

Callista says to me, "Did we do anything right?"

We're three twosomes on the ferry, Callista and Jack, Rebecca and Annette, David and me. David and I sit outside, watching the wake. David doesn't know anyone who likes their sister. Sisters are creeps. He feels left out, "Do you feel that way with Callista and Jack?" he asks, as though reading my mind.

"Maybe we'll find some boys your age at the beach," I answer.

"I don't think there's anybody my age in the Pines. Rebecca says everyone there is gay. So why is Callista's house there?"

"It's not her house. She's renting it."

"But why in the Pines if everyone there is gay?"

"There are lots of places on Fire Island that black people aren't welcome. It's Ok in the Pines."

David leans back on the bench and looks at the blue-gray sky. "What happened to Larry, that guy you went out with? Didn't Callista introduce you?"

"Nothing happened. We're friends."

"Mom, I'm not a baby."

"But that's true. We just liked each other. Nothing happened." This is what's wrong about divorce, children asking parents such questions.

"Why did you and Dad get divorced?"

"Oh, David, not now. Could we talk about this some other time? What about going inside and getting a hot dog?"

"I'm not hungry. Why can't we talk about it now? You always say we'll talk later."

"We changed. We were young. Sometimes people get married and they don't know who they are."

"What does that mean 'who they are?'" He's getting angry. "How can you not know who you are?"

"Think about it. Do you know who you are?"

David lets out a big sigh. "I'm never getting married. I'm never having children."

"People don't have to make the same mistakes their parents do," I tell him, hoping I'm right.

The sun is setting when the ferry docks. We stand a moment to watch the orange pink glow. "It's better than anything on Broadway," Callista says.

"And no neon."

We each take a small red wagon from the dock and set off for the house, pulling our groceries, our overnight bags, and Callista's two suitcases.

"Who's here to dress for?" Jack asks.

David, Annette and Rebecca take turns pulling each other in what I pray will be a two-day truce.

The light is so tender as we leave the dock even the children are quiet. We walk down the boardwalk, across the sand to the fading echo of the boats slapping against the water, the banging of screen doors, the muffled excitement of guests gearing up for a party. The house next to Callista's rental is lit up like a cake, with laughter echoing from the deck. I shiver in anticipation of nothing.

The children let out excited wows as Jack opens the door of Callista's house and turns on the lights. There are large leather poufs on the floor, butterfly chairs with yellow covers, a yellow flowered chintz sofa. Sliding glass doors open to the deck and a spot-lit cactus garden. Jack takes Callista's suitcases into the master bedroom.

"Are you two sleeping in the same room?" Annette demands.

Jack puts up his hands. "I can share a room with David," he says, as Callista suggests she and Annette go out on the deck to talk

Rebecca, David and I take flashlights and leave for a walk on the beach.

"Remember last time we were here? We watched that guy land on the moon," David says, as we make our way down a steep pair of wooden steps and turn onto the beach. "What do you think it's like up there?" Rebecca looks up at the sky.

"Probably all gray and silver, do you think? Do you think your food floats out of your hand?" David asks.

"I bet it's lonesome up there," Rebecca says. "You can't do anything with those big gloves on."

"Do you think you could sleep there?"

"Why couldn't you sleep?"

"There's all that light and everything. I guess that's silly," David says. "I was thinking of moonlight on the moon."

"Moonlight on the moon," Rebecca echoes. Then she sings it, "Moonlight on the moon."

"Moonlight in my room," David sings back

"Moonlight on a broom." Rebecca answers.

They take hands, singing together and run down to the water.

We return to a domestic scene. Annette and Callista cutting fruit, Jack on the deck lighting the charcoal grill. The children find a MONOPOLY game. Jack comes inside and opens champagne.

"Here's to our play." Callista lifts her glass.

"To our gang of three," Jack toasts. "Your *Singles* is a good show for Callista to co-host," he says to me. 'It's exceptional for TV. It makes some good points and it's just serious enough. But Callista needs a really big juicy role for Broadway. She says you have something in mind."

"It doesn't have to do with just being big." Callista spoons fruit into her drink, sits down on the yellow sofa. "I want to do something big about being black."

"Hey, wait a minute," Jack says from the kitchen counter, where he's gone to make marinade for the chicken. "I'm the producer, remember. I thought we had settled on a musical."

"It can be a musical as long as it's…" Callista hesitates, puts her glass on the floor.

"Dark," I say. "Like *Lost in the Stars*.'"

"Not just dark," Callista says. "Shocking. *Lost in the Stars* isn't shocking anymore. And it's about South Africa."

"Right,'" I say, glad she's forgotten black Joan of Arc. "We want to do something that's shocking about what's going on in America, don't we? That's what I want to do."

"Right," Callista says. "And about women. Black women. What happens to their strength. How they get ground down. What they do with their anger."

"Hey, hold the shocking." Jack says. "People are sick of protest. Vietnam. Watergate. Everyone's unsettled. They want something entertaining."

"Hold the entertaining," Callista answers. "Last week I tried to get a taxi on Fifty ninth street and three white cab drivers passed me by. Probably thought I wanted to go to Harlem. Niggers don't live anywhere else, do they? And they all carry machine guns. Probably thought I had one in my Saks shopping bag."

"I have to get this chicken on the grill," Jack says, opening the screen door and disappearing onto the deck.

"Very funny." Callista raises her voice so he can hear her. "I can imagine how they treat some poor black lady with ashy skin. What do you Cubans know about Harlem?"

"Now wait a minute," Jack says, as he bangs back in from the deck. "I had to leave Cuba, remember. Half an hour till dinner." He sits down next to Callista and puts his arm around her shoulder. "How about kissing the cook?"

"God, you're good natured. What did I do to deserve this?" she says and kisses him.

"Ok," he says, "so three white cab drivers are bigots. Lots of people are bigots. That's no reason to commit professional suicide."

"Well, I want to do black. And I have just the right book to do it. And the right lady."

Jack puts his hands together in mock prayer. "Tell me it's not about a prostitute. What's the book?"

"*The Street*. Larry gave it to me and Lilly. It's about Lutie Johnson, a young black woman in Harlem. A singer."

"Hooray, a singer." Jack smiles.

"She's got a child, a boy. She works as a maid to some nice clean white suburban family in Connecticut, but it breaks up her marriage. She comes back to Harlem and some rich black guy who owns a nightclub offers her a job as a singer."

"Good," Jack says.

"He really just wants to screw her. So does her super. The super gets her kid in trouble with the police to get even with her. The nightclub owner tries to rape her, and she kills him. She leaves town."

Jack says, "The chicken's ready."

"C'mon Jack, react," Callista says.

"I like the singer part. I like the nightclub owner till she kills him. Not a good message. I like the sleazy super. Nix on her leaving town."

"She's got no alternatives," Callista says. "That's the point."

"Too dark," he says.

"It's not just about being black," I say. "It's about being a woman and being poor and struggling to raise your children in a rich society that crushes poor people. It's a wonderful book."

"So is *Moby Dick*," Jack says.

"Moby Dick is white," Callista says. "And male. 'I couldn't do it."

The next day the children go to the beach. Jack goes off to read *The Street*. Callista and I go out on the deck to discuss the play.

"What do you think of Jack?" Callista asks me.

"I think he's great," I say. "What do you think of Jack?"

"I love him. But Annette doesn't. And he's not black."

"He's Cuban, isn't he? And Annette's father wasn't black."

"I need to work on my thighs. And my stomach."

"What's wrong with your stomach?"

"It's not flat enough."

"It looks pretty flat to me."

"You are not looking at me naked," she points out.

"I thought we were talking about Jack." I say.

"I can't stand being a sexy black saloon singer," she says.

"Nobody's perfect," I tell her.

"That's why I focus on my stomach," she answers.

Shoshona Has A Date with Harry

Shoshona is wearing the usual high heels and short skirt but the skirt is brown chiffon and looks new. So does the copper-colored sweater.

" You got a hot date? You look terrific. Doesn't she?" Myra says to me.

"She does," I agree.

"I don't know about hot. Warm, maybe," Shoshona says.

"No kidding, you got a date? Who is it?" Myra asks. "That Paris guy from Sarah Lawrence?"

Shoshona lipsticks her mouth and makes a face. "It's so surprising I have a date?"

"Who is it?"

Blushing under her freckles, Shoshona says, "I'll tell you tomorrow."

"No fair. Who is it?" Myra, getting into her leotards, is insistent.

"It's not exactly a date."

"What is it exactly?"

"It's lunch. I'm having lunch with Harry."

"Harry?"

"Yes."

"You mean your husband Harry?"

"Well, I said it's not exactly a date. And we're not exactly married. I mean legally we are, but we haven't slept in the same room for two months. We're just having dinner."

"Well I'll be damned," Myra says. "How did this happen?"

It happened this way. It was Saturday. Shoshona was going downtown to look at some galleries as soon as she finished mopping the kitchen floor. She'd been going for years, but lately she felt she almost belonged there. Someday, maybe, her kivas would be in those galleries and other people would come to look. It makes her dizzy to think of it. The past month, she's been sitting in on a sculpture course Dr. Paris teaches and last week he gave her a list of things she should see. She was wringing out the mop when Harry walked across the wet floor, leaving a trail of footprints, and asked, "What's for lunch?"

He saw his prints, took some paper towels, bent down to wipe them up. Shoshona wondered if he was seeing a marriage counselor.

"I only make dinner. During the week," she said, pointing to their family contract, held to the refrigerator with a small magnet that read, Women on Top. "Lunch isn't part of the deal."

"Sorry about the floor," he said, straightening up, rolling the towels in a ball and tossing it under his arm into the trash can. "Why don't I take you out to lunch?"

She was sure he was seeing a marriage counselor. "Thanks for the offer, but I have to go downtown to look at some sculpture. For this class I'm taking."

"They serve lunch downtown."

"Harry, I've got to look at this sculpture. It's an assignment. I've got to go. I'll be late."

"Wait," he said. "We could have lunch after the sculpture."

What was going through his mind?

"You look different," he said.

He hadn't looked at her in years. Maybe he thought she looked younger. Maybe he missed her in his bed, though God knows how long that had been.

"This whole cockamamie arrangement we have, you in the maid's room, the kids paying rent, who ever heard of anything like this?"

"Now Harry, we all agreed. We all signed it."

"You're certainly an original," he said, pulling out a kitchen chair and sitting down at the table.

She stood there.

"I've got to hand it to you, the kids are actually working. Sit down?" he asked.

"Harry, I've got to go." But she sat,

"You know, I'm a little on edge. Remember how I brought you flowers before we were married, when you lived with your mother?"

"Red roses."

"You liked red roses."

"I still do," she said.

"What happened to us after the flowers?" he asked. "There's such a big gap. And here we are, you going back to college, a woman of forty-four. And me, I'm stuck chasing ambulances. Maybe I should go back to school. Do something worthwhile." He stood up and walked to the sink for a glass of water. "I've got to hand it to you, taking art classes"

"I have an Art Fellowship," Shoshona says.

"Here's to art," he raised the glass and drank. "You know I always liked going to museums. They smell better than Family Court."

She thought of a fly in amber. "Let's go and have lunch," she said.

On the subway, Shoshona remembered the Dickens novels she read when her mother was sick, how Pip and Estella found each other after being separated for years. Maybe that really happens sometimes. What's going on with her and Harry? It seemed better not to ask.

"What did you think about the sculptures?" Shoshona asked Harry over lunch, surprised that he had picked such an expensive restaurant.

"I don't think women give men a chance," he said, pouring her a glass of wine. "And it makes me damned uncomfortable."

"I think it's the other way around," she said. "That's what makes me uncomfortable."

"It's interesting, though, I have to admit. I'd like to see what you're doing."

She told him about a day last week, walking across the park, picking up leaves and twigs and pieces of bark. When she got home, she glued them together, stretched some canvas across part of it. It looked a little like a kite, a little like a mask. When she showed it to Paris, he liked it.

She asked him, "What is it?" And he said. "Don't worry what it is, just keep doing it." She's never told Harry anything so private. They had a long way to go. "I guess right now I'm just adlibbing," she said.

"Me, too," he agreed. "Do you have any of your work at home?"

"Of course," she said.

"I'd like to see it."

The Caller

Garrin, Stein, four TV critics and I have just seen the last rushes on *Singles*. The invited critics are full of compliments.

"You've got what's going on," the Digest critic says. "It's the seventies." *Variety*'s reporter called it "break-through TV, oral history on video."

"It describes a real shift in social values," said *The New York Times* critic. "A new kind of social organization."

And I have my own office.

The next problem is when to air it. A recent poll shows that fifty-three percent of the public think there's too much Watergate on TV, but Garrin worries that forty-seven percent won't be interested in anything else. Jaworski has just revealed that in March, the grand jury named Nixon an unindicted co-conspirator in the Watergate break-in and cover-up. The betting is that Nixon will resign, but if so, when? If he doesn't, and he goes to trial in the Senate, it could take all fall.

It's been a hard week for me, finishing *Singles* during the day, working on *The Street* at night, and worrying what to do with the kids this summer. Martin is taking them somewhere on his boat in August. I would like a vacation with them, but I can't take one till I've been at HELLO for three months. They can't sit around the apartment and it's probably too late to enroll them in a summer day camp. Maybe if I call the "Y" as soon as I get to my office. I have an attack of bad-parent guilt as I walk down the corridor. I should have thought of this sooner.

Janice, Garrin's secretary, stops me in the reception area. "That guy who's been calling all week, he's waiting for you in your office."

"What guy?"

"Someone from *The Daily News*."

"I don't remember him calling."

She pulls out her phone log. "I got three times right here. You must have thrown out all your messages."

I must have. Bad sign. I don't like forgetting to return phone calls. "What does he want?"

"He wants to interview you about that stewardess's murder. Says the trial is coming up soon."

"See if you can get rid of him," I tell Janice.

"He's cute."

"David is cute."

"Ok, Ok, he's not cute, he's handsome."

"Get rid of him, anyway. Tell him I'm out for the afternoon. I'm going to get some coffee."

"Lover boy's still there," she says, when I return with three containers, one coffee for Janice, two for me.

I tell her to buzz me in five minutes.

He is handsome, tall, with brown hair, and a determined chin. Of course, I remember him. He's the best man from Angie and Kevin's wedding. Who cares what he looks like? I'm not interested in men.

"Hi," he says. "Morris Delano. " He puts out his hand. "Remember, from Angie and Kevin's wedding."

How could I have forgotten? I danced with him. Deciding to be gracious if I can, I apologize for not calling back and offer him one of my coffees.

"Sorry to hang out in your office like this, but you're very elusive. I should have called you after the wedding. Nice office, though." He likes the Navaho rug, the cartoon of a man with golf clubs telling his wife: "Honey, I'm leaving. I want to thank you for all those years you took care of the kids." "Not the usual," he says, pointing to the Buddha on my desk with a peach in front of him.

"The peach is from my daughter. She's worried he'll get hungry. Listen, I know you've been waiting to see me about that murder, but I really have nothing helpful to tell you about Sally."

"You never know what's helpful," he says. "Do you mind if I sit down and ask a couple questions?" He pulls out his notebook. "What was she like?"

I sit down at my desk and open a coffee. "I hardly knew her. She was sweet, kind of diffident. She had a thing about Egypt. Men were always after her. She thought she was being followed and it turns out she was." I see her lying on the bed with blood coming out of her mouth and put the lid back on the coffee. "Look, honestly, it drives me crazy to go over this. I get nightmares. I start to think I'm being followed."

"I'm sorry. I don't blame you. Frankly, I don't like to write about it, I'm really a sports reporter."

"You're confusing this with sports?"

"I'll ignore that. I have an ambitious boss who thinks our readers need a rest from Watergate. The trial starts next week, and I'm supposed to do a think piece on it."

"You're kidding. A think-piece?"

"Right."

"I think it's what every woman in New York is afraid of. I'm afraid to go up in my elevator alone in my own apartment building. I'm afraid while I'm standing in the hall trying to open my three locks."

202

He's writing it down.

"Oh, please don't quote me. I don't want my name in the paper."

The phone rings. "It's himself," Janice says. She puts him through. "Hey," says Garrin,"we're going with *Singles* tomorrow. Could you get right up here?"

"Sorry," I tell Morrie, hanging up the phone. "That's my ambitious boss. He wants me upstairs A.S.A.P." I stand up and hold out my hand. I remember that I thought he was attractive at the wedding.

He closes his notebook. "I'd like to hear the rest of what you have to say. And I hate blind dates. How about dinner?"

"Dinner?"

"This seemed easier than trying to get you on the phone. I'm sorry," he says, seeing my confusion. "I thought you knew I was Kevin Donaldson's best man from their wedding."

"You pretended to be interviewing me? Should I be indignant?"

"No. I wasn't pretending anything. I'm assigned to the story and I've been interviewing women on the police list. When I saw your name, I realized you were the woman from the wedding. I was sorry I hadn't called you. I thought it might be easier to meet you again this way."

The phone rings again. It's Janice. "He's breathing fire," she says. "Get it up here."

"Look, I'm sorry, but I have to go."

"When can we have dinner?"

"I'm having trouble focusing. I'm so embarrassed at not remembering you. Why don't you call me?"

The phone rings again.

"I know your address," he says. "Saturday, at seven?"

They Love *Singles*

Spud Milstein is on the phone. "Great work," he says. "Smart to make it a two-hour special. Best thing? That interview with Callista Dee holding her champagne glass and toasting herself. Sums up being single. Damn glad I hired you. Way to go." He hangs up before I can answer.

Then Angie calls. "I loved that young mechanic with the kids. When he's fixing their dinner and the kitchen looks like a garage sale, and his daughter says, 'Mom should have taught you to cook before she left.' And he says, 'She did.'"

"Have you seen the reviews?" I ask her.

"Have I! I've read them maybe six or seven times."

When Angie hangs up, I read them again.

First, *The New York Times*: WE AREN'T WHAT WE USED TO BE:

"Most TV gives us what we feel comfortable with. *Singles* describes things we've tried not to recognize. The program emphasizes that living without a partner, with or without children, is an institution. Two of the divorced women, though not the two anchors, have less money and status than when they were married."

Variety says:

"Thank you WCBC-TV for giving us a special we can sink our minds into. *Singles* is simply the best documentary we've seen this or any season."

It's almost an anti-climax, though a stunning one, when Ahearne calls. "I guess you do have something in you after all. You should thank me for firing you."

I thank him.

Angie calls again. "I hear you have a date with Morrie. What do you think?"

I'm noncommittal.

As I'm hanging up, Janice walks in with a long white florist's box. "From the boss," she says. One dozen yellow roses and a card: "Not bad. Garrin."

Before I can call to thank him, Callista calls to report the *Singles* reviews are already helping Jack get backers for the play of *The Street*.

Then Garrin walks into my office. *Singles* just brought in two new sponsors. He's giving Jeff and me a raise.

I feel so rich going home, I decide to take Rebecca and David for dinner and the movies, their favorite treat. Captain and President greet me as I cross the traffic island. "What's new?" I ask.

"Haven't you heard I'm going to Egypt?" President says. "Get me one of them Giza-Giza girls. Play her my tapes."

"I'm going, too," Captain says.

I ask them if they need some money for the trip

"She is bribing us," President says. "I'll take her off my enemies list."

We Are in a Fifties Movie

He is a sportswriter like Spencer Tracy and wears a hat. I am a journalist like Katherine Hepburn, thin and sophisticated, and wear a suit with big shoulder pads. They make my waist look smaller. We go to a little restaurant with checkered tablecloths where everybody knows him and drinks red wine. There's a piano player like Sam in *Casablanca*.

I shouldn't get too dressed up. I'll wear a skirt and sweater, cotton. The purple one is good with my eyes. I put it on but it's too casual, even for Hepburn. Would I like it if he came in jeans? I wouldn't care, but I'm sure he won't. Maybe the dress I wore to Callista's party? I try it on. Too warm, too dressy. Oh, hell, I can't stand this. Who cares what I wear? I'll just wear the suit I had on the other day. He asked me to dinner so he must have thought I looked good.

Women always wore suits in those movies, Hepburn, Rosalind Russell. Even Ingrid Bergmann. That's ridiculous. I hate wearing suits on dates. I don't even like wearing them to work. I settle on a blue summer dress I've had for years. Plain, but the color is nice on me. And my old blue lapis earrings. Stupid, all this fuss.

Five minutes deciding not to use blue eye liner. Another five to get the mascara right. I try it on the lashes under my eyes and smudge my cheeks. You'd think I never had a date. In fact, it's been quite a while.

At five after seven, Morrie arrives in a tan suit and brown shirt. No resemblance to Spencer Tracy. No hat. He's carrying a bouquet of blue and purple snapdragons. We smile at each other and he hands me the flowers. "I hope they go with the decor," he says.

"There's not much decor here."

"They go with your eyes," he says gallantly.

I should offer him a drink while I go through all the kitchen cupboards looking for a vase, but, as usual, I don't have any liquor. I should have bought some wine instead of taking so much time getting dressed.

Morrie walks around the living room, inspects the books, sits down on the beat-up Danish sofa. "Beautiful photograph," he says, nodding his head at the Curtis photo of a Navajo reaper, a young woman with a scythe bending over a field of wheat.

"It's my daughter's," I sort of holler from the kitchen, where I've located a vase. I bring the flowers into the living room and set them down on the coffee table in front of the sofa. "I gave it to her two years ago for her birthday, but she lets us hang it here. Now that she's more grown up, she tells me Curtis, the photographer, really wasn't political. But we still like it. Thanks for the flowers. They're very pretty. The building is such a dump."

He looks at his watch.

A bad sign if he's doing that already.

"If you like, we can just make the game and have dinner later. I've got great seats," he says.

"Game?"

"Oh, sorry, I just assume everybody knows Jabbar is playing. It's kind of arrogant of me."

I tell him I know the name. "I know he's very tall and a great basketball player."

"I didn't know if you like basketball. I'm not covering it, I don't have to go," he says. "I just thought you might like it."

"Listen," I say, "I'll try anything once. An unexplored life is not worth living. I know there's a difference between football and basketball because in football the guys are all knocking each other over."

He promises we'll leave if I don't like it.

But I do. I like Madison Square Garden and I like watching the game. I like the maleness of it, the smell, the cries of the hawkers, the sense of carnival when we're standing in the back, before we start down the aisle to our seats.

I watch the audience as much as I watch the game. Everyone is so intense. Morrie leans out of his seat, as though he's left his body and he's out there on the floor. Every couple of minutes, he sits back and describes what's going on.

I forget about myself. Watching takes a lot of pressure off the ego. I understand why it's so heady and restful to be a spectator.

We go to an Italian restaurant for dinner and I tell him what I liked: the look of it, the public theater, the intensity, the letting go of self.

He offers me wine and says it's that letting go that sometimes makes him uneasy. "It's just a whiff of fascism. What I like," he says, between bread and wine, "is that it's on the merits. Whatever else is going on in the world, those guys are out there under the lights in their shirts and shorts being measured by their skill. And sometimes it's really elegant. It approaches art.

"Of course, there's a negative side, an occasional bribe, a scandal. But most of the time, it's pretty honest. It's hard to fake the results. I like writing about it. It's a challenge to keep the prose clean. And it doesn't keep me awake at night. I think that was a speech," he says. "We better order."

Over soup, he tells me, "I saw your show. Frankly, I was surprised TV could be so good. How are you going to top that?"

I tuck my napkin into the neck of my dress, to roll a forkful of spaghetti, and describe the plans for *The Street*. I am so wound up I eat my way through most of the pasta without tasting it.

"What about your love life?" he asks, as the waiter bustles about crumbing the table.

I wasn't expecting the question, but I tell him about Larry, that we liked each other, but something was missing. I mention my conversation with David on the ferry, about why love does and doesn't happen. And why it changes, when it does I have no idea," I say. Maybe it's all timing."

"What about now?" he asks.

"I guess the time is right for something, but I'm not in any rush."

"Once burned?"

"I like the heat. I just don't want any more ashes. And speaking of timing," I say, as the waiter removes the plates and I remove the napkin from the neck of my dress, "how do we happen to be here together? You haven't asked me anything about Sally."

"I've decided not to do the article. I wasn't happy about it from the beginning. What you said about not wanting to think or talk about it, about it being every woman's nightmare stuck in my mind. Then I spoke to her roommate."

"You spoke to Lorraine?"

"After I saw you. She couldn't stop talking about Sally's blood, about her nightmares, her dreams about knives. I felt disgusted with myself. And then I had two nights of nightmares about Vietnam."

"Vietnam?"

"I was there as a reporter. I saw enough blood and guts. It's why I like writing about sports. No murders in basketball. When my editor told me yesterday he wanted me to interview Sally's parents, I refused. I said I wouldn't put them through another interview. They still have the trial to get through, and I don't see the point of another story. You actually helped me decide not to write it."

"I'm glad. It makes me feel I finally found something I could do for Sally."

"You asked me how we happen to be here. I guess that means why did I go to so much trouble to meet you? Angie's talked a lot about you, and I liked what I heard. Ahearne sounds like such a bastard, I like the way you give it back to him. But when people try to fix me up with women, I get very resistant. My sisters are always trying to fix me up with their friends and it never works out. I don't like blind dates."

I think of Sylvan Lesterberg.

"But I did want to see you after the wedding. I liked your office. Quirky. And I like the way you look."

"First dates are really tough, aren't they," he says when we get to the door of my apartment. It's like auditioning."

"So how do you think this went?" I ask.

"Considering how nervous we both were, I'd say pretty well. I certainly want to see you again."

"Who was nervous?"

"I was. I thought the basketball game might break the ice."

"What makes you think I was nervous?" I say, fumbling with the keys.

He looks at me, then rings for the elevator. When I go in the bathroom to take off my make-up, I see what he was looking at: my earrings don't match.

Impeached

David wakes me on Wednesday, July 31, to tell me a Mexican Senator has been kidnapped by gorillas and Nixon is going to be impeached. It's too early for TV news, so I assume he's been listening to the radio while he gets ready for camp. "That girl is still kidnapped, isn't she," he says, as I get out of bed. "Do you think they'll ever find her? Do you think she'll be dead?"

"If you mean Patricia Hearst, I feel sorry for her. I bet she wishes she was dead," Rebecca says.

"I'd rather be alive," David insists. "What's the point of wishing you were dead?"

"We have to get dressed," I say.

"Mom, do you think she's still in the closet?"

"Of course not," I answer.

I'm in the kitchen making breakfast when Rebecca comes in and asks me. "How do you get impeached?"

I'm explaining that it's a long process when the phone rings in the living room and David goes to answer. After a brief conversation he comes back to tell us, "I got the gorillas wrong. Morrie says it's not animal gorillas. It's the soldier kind. He'll call you at work."

The phone rings again. It's Janice. The House Judiciary Committee voted impeachment last night. Peter Rodino, Chairman of the Judiciary Committee, will be interviewed on HELLO at eight a.m., followed by Jaworski, the Special Prosecutor. "Get down here A.S.A.P. We'd send a car but the subway's faster."

"Come see me in jail," President calls, as I pass him on the corner, rushing to the train. "Bring a file."

"Bring a bottle," Captain says.

The subway is late. I stand on the platform for fifteen, twenty minutes as new waves of would-be-riders surge down the steps, crowding in back, pushing me close to the platform's edge. "Where's the fucking train?" someone yells.

I'm sweating, getting warmer and increasingly anxious. I can't get out of here, I can't even push through the crowd to call the office. A burst of static is followed by "Testing, Testing," on a loudspeaker. "How about testing the fucking trains?" the same person hollers.

The loudspeaker erupts with a burst of garbled voices. Then, "Attention all passengers. The Seventh Avenue IRT has been delayed. Repeat. The Seventh Avenue IRT..." the voice crackles again. "Service on this line will be discontinued until further notice."

Now everyone pushes in the other direction. A chant starts, "Refund, Refund. " The crowd presses up the stairs. Outside, riders who have not heard the announcement, are trying to get down the steps. Afraid of being trampled, I decide to wait until the crowd thins out.

When I reach the street, it's after eight, there are lines at the bus stop, people spilling into the street, waving frantically for taxis. I wait for a pay phone, but all HELLO's lines are busy. I get in the back of the bus line and try to read my paper.

"See that, they finally got him," says the man in back of me, reading over my shoulder. "They ought to put him in jail next to that Commie Patty Hearst."

I reach the studio ten minutes before nine. Rodino and Jaworski have been interviewed and left. I feel like the soldier in *The Red Badge of Courage* who missed the battle.

Logging the Miles

It's Wednesday night, and the gym is crowded. Maybe fifteen or twenty telephone operators are here. Genevieve is in the pool with her twin girls. I am alone in the sauna, thinking about the way my life has turned around. I give myself credit for logging the miles. It feels like a million if I start with my attacker in the park.

It's more luck than brains that the jogger came along in Central Park and saved me, that Herb's father got me a job, that Sunny Matthews liked me and told Garrin. Maybe luck, like exercise, is what you make of it.I couldn't have written *Singles* until I'd lived it. Garrin is so pleased with Callista and the whole program, he wants to co-produce our play *The Street* with Jack Laredo.

I'm in a self-congratulatory mood when the door opens and Myra walks in with Shoshona, followed by Lorraine in a shower cap. Lorraine is describing her new apartment.

"I love it," she says, spreading out her towel. "It's got so much light. Even the bedroom. Sally would have ...." She sits down and cries. "It's not even five months."

Shoshona pats Lorraine's wet shoulder. "Maybe we could all come and see it, have a party or something, help you fix it up."

"I don't want to forget Sally. I just want to get rid of the murder," Lorraine says.

"Maybe you should talk to someone about it. See a therapist," I suggest.

"Why does everybody have to see a therapist?" Myra asks grumpily, handing Lorraine a towel to wipe her eyes.

"Some people die before they grow up. They go straight from adolescence to senility. Therapy's a shortcut," Shoshona says.

"I don't see you doing it," Myra answers. "Your husband in one room, you in another. You call that grown up?"

"I'll just ignore that," Shoshona says.

Genevieve opens the door and sticks her head in. "I have the girls here," she says. "Is there room?"

"Oh, shit, not now," Myra explodes.

"It's kind of crowded. Maybe later," Shoshona tells Genevieve.

"We're all going into therapy," Myra says when the door closes.

"Who is 'all?'" I ask.

"My parents and me. It wasn't easy to convince my parents. It was actually Phillip who did it."

"Phillip convinced your parents?"

"The shrink at the hospital saw him last week and asked him how he likes living with me. He said he doesn't live with me, he lives with his grandparents. She asked him if he'd like to live with me. He said yes. Then she asked him if he liked living with his grandparents. He said yes. She asked what he'd do if he had to choose and he refused to talk. She's going to try to work it out so he can live part-time with both of us."

"I'll be damned, another *menage à quatre*," Shoshona says.

"When Phillip told my mother the doctor said he could live with both of us, my mother called me and said, 'Who is this doctor? Absolutely not.' Phillip started to cry and then he went and locked himself in his room. He told my mother he wasn't coming out unless he could live with both of us. They agreed we would all go to the doctor. It wears me out just talking about it."

"Speaking of *menages*, how's yours?" I ask Shoshona.

"Harry wants me to go to Rome with him."

"Lucky dog," says Myra

"The lawyers have a convention there right before school starts. It's our anniversary and Harry thinks we should go to Rome to celebrate, but how can we celebrate our anniversary when we don't live as though we're married?"

"Don't be such a purist," Myra says. "Let him take you to Rome."

"I have to think about it."

"Who's going to Rome?" Ceil asks, walking in.

"Think of the art," Myra says.

"Think of the food." Ceil licks her lips.

"Things do seem better with us," Shoshona admits.

"You must have slept with him," Myra says

The bird lady opens the door "May I join you?" she asks.

"Of course," we answer, as she enters in a black skirted bathing suit and pearls.

"You slept with him. How was it?" Myra asks.

Shoshona blushes.

"What do you do, dear?" the bird lady asks Shoshona.

"She's an artist," Myra answers for Shoshona.

"And you?"

"I'm a dance teacher. And a mother, sort of."

"I'm an actress," Lorraine says.

Ceil adds, "Make-up."

"And you?" she asks me.

I think for a minute. "I'm in training."

"We're all in training, aren't we? I always wanted to be a dancer. It's wonderful what women do nowadays," she says.

August 10, 1974. Nixon Leaves

A hot, humid eighty-eight degrees seems just right for tonight's rebroadcast of Nixon leaving the White House. I have two fans blowing at each other and am tempted, like Marilyn Monroe in the movie, *The Seven Year Itch*, to put my underwear in the refrigerator. We have David's Watergate Cards framed and hung on one wall in the living room. "I wish he would have got impeached already," David says. "It would have made a better last card."

"He didn't even say he's guilty, he just resigned," Rebecca complains.

"At least he's resigning," I say. "Maybe that's better for the country."

Morrie arrives with wine and popcorn. "We have three things to celebrate," he says. "Nixon's going to California and I'm going to *The New York Times*. We're re all going to Angie and Kevin's to see Nixon leave."

When we get to Angie and Kevin's, the White House band is playing "Hail to the Chief" on TV. We all settle down as Mrs. Nixon in a white dress and pearls follows the President into the room. Then their children and son-in-law enter.

"She looks sad," Rebecca says.

"It's not her fault. She's not a criminal," David says. "Are those other people their children?"

"Imagine Nixon for your father," Rebecca says. "I guess you'd have to love him."

David sighs. "I guess you would."

Stepping up to the podium, Nixon thanks his Cabinet and staff for the spontaneous applause. He smiles and pushes hard against the podium. He wants to thank them all, his faithful servants.

"No man or woman left this Administration with more of this world's goods than when he came in."

His head wags from side to side as he pokes the air.

"What does that mean?" David asks.

"It means no one got rich working for him," I say.

"Do you believe him?" David asks.

"No one believes him. That's why he has to resign," Rebecca answers.

Nixon continues.

"My old man was a street-car motorman first. Then he had a lemon ranch, the poorest in California. He sold it before they found oil on it."

"He looks weird," Rebecca says. "I think he's crying."

"My mother was a saint, two boys dying of tuberculosis, nursing four others. Yes, she will have no books written about her. But she was a saint."

"Money, father, mother, death," Morrie says.

Nixon is shaking, perspiring, poking his finger at the air. "I had a little quote from Teddy Roosevelt." He puts on his glasses, his son-in-law hands him a book. Nixon reads, "And when my heart's dearest died, the light went from my life forever." He closes the book. People in the audience are crying.

"But he went on and became president and served his country. There are always those who hate you."

"Who's he talking about?" David asks. "Who died?"

"He's just mixed up," I say. "He's talking about Teddy Roosevelt's first wife. He's talking about loss."

"I don't get it," David says. "Who is Teddy Roosevelt? Isn't Pat Nixon his wife? Isn't she still alive right there?"

We all feel sad and relieved, embarrassed at this new revelation. The devil has a private face. He cries, he blows his nose.

"He is still a monster," Rebecca says, just as the Nixons board their waiting helicopter.

Rebecca is right, he is a monster, I think, as Nixon turns and gives the thumbs up sign. He's the larger public life that every private life is a part of. He's the nightmare that terrifies us, that we can't exorcise. The corruption of his administration is what makes Rebecca cynical about the fairness of our society, puts Captain and President on the street. He's the public terror.

He's the killer Carlo, he's the slasher in the park. He misses his mother, he is lonesome. He's our Stabber.

Confetti

Confetti, taped to the locker room ceiling, hangs down in streamers over the punch bowl and the sign, We Won't Have Nixon To Kick Around Anymore. Everyone is dressed up, lounging against lockers and counters as though they're waiting for a director and cameras. At first, Hall, the manager, refused to have a Nixon Leaves party on the grounds of patriotism, but WCBC TV's HELLO wants human interest stories on the resignation and Hal understands this is thousands of dollars of free advertising.

In the exercise room, a long table is covered with food disguised as flora and fauna, on the edge between food and art. There are blooms of cauliflower in ice and hollowed out cucumber boats filled with crabmeat. There are cherry tomatoes around a small hill of shrimp in a moat of sauce. Ann, the instructor, presides at an ornate cut-glass punch bowl, which she assures us is honest-to-goodness dietetic champagne punch, courtesy of Genevieve.

Myra, giving off light in a mirrored Indian skirt, is talking to Shoshona, who's wearing tights, sandals, and a long loose blouse. "Harry thought I needed some new clothes for Rome. He thinks this makes me look more like an artist," she tells us.

A group of women from the telephone company arrive and join the party. "We should celebrate together," Shoshona says, lifting her glass. Ann pours the punch, we clink glasses, and all drink together. It's only punch, and it's only a gesture, I think, but it is a start.

"I'm going to take a swim," Myra says. "What about you?" she asks me.

"I'm going to run. I'll watch you from the balcony," I say, finishing my punch. Back in the locker room, I part the white coils of confetti with my hands and see the bird lady in a black dress, black stockings, smoking a cigarette. I wonder what mix of circumstance and history kept her from becoming the dancer she's told us she wanted to be. She reminds me of so many of our mothers who hungered for roles they were untrained to play. Still with her very presence at the gym and her vigilance at the bar, she's an emblem of a history the younger women have escaped and a model of the elderly flexibility and persistence we all aspire to.

I change into my jogging clothes and pass by the mirrored counter where, for almost a year, I have watched so many women examine their reflections, discuss their children, their jobs, their fate, girding up to go out, again and again, into a hostile world. Getting in shape, toughening themselves up. We are here in all shapes and sizes and in startling variety. We are here for each other.

I take a few deep yoga breaths and start to jog.

Naomi Feigelson Chase was a 2015/16 Fellow of the New York Fiction Society. Her fiction has been published in many magazines, nominated for a PUSHCART, and anthologized in Milkweed Editions, New Rivers Press, and A Wider Giving, among others. Her two non-fiction books are *The Underground Revolution: Hippies, Yippies, & Others* (Holt, Rinehart & Winston) and *A Child Is Being Beaten, Child Abuse in America* (Funk & Wagnalls). She has published eight books of poetry.

www.ingramcontent.com/pod-product-compliance
Lightning Source LLC
Chambersburg PA
CBHW030517020726
47494CB00004B/1137